R.m.

Winds of Change

By Anna Jacobs

THE PENNY LAKE SERIES

Changing Lara • Finding Cassie
Marrying Simone

THE PEPPERCORN SERIES

Peppercorn Street • Cinnamon Gardens
Saffron Lane • Bay Tree Cottage
Christmas in Peppercorn Street

THE HONEYFIELD SERIES

The Honeyfield Bequest • A Stranger in Honeyfield
Peace Comes to Honeyfield

THE HOPE TRILOGY

A Place of Hope • In Search of Hope
A Time for Hope

THE GREYLADIES SERIES

Heir to Greyladies • Mistress of Greyladies
Legacy of Greyladies

THE WILTSHIRE GIRLS SERIES

Cherry Tree Lane • Elm Tree Road
Yew Tree Gardens

THE WATERFRONT SERIES

Mara's Choice
Sarah's Gift

❧

Winds of Change • Moving On
The Cotton Lass and Other Stories • Change of Season
Tomorrow's Path • Chestnut Lane • In Focus
The Corrigan Legacy • A Very Special Christmas

Winds of Change

ANNA JACOBS

Allison & Busby Limited
11 Wardour Mews
London W1F 8AN
allisonandbusby.com

First published in 2012.

This paperback edition published by Allison & Busby in 2021.

A CIP catalogue record for this book is available from
the British Library.

10 9 8 7 6 5 4 3 2 1

ISBN 978-0-7490-2817-6

Typeset in 11/16 pt Sabon LT Pro by
Allison & Busby Ltd

The paper used for this Allison & Busby publication
has been produced from trees that have been legally sourced
from well-managed and credibly certified forests.
Printed and bound by
CPI Group (UK) Ltd, Croydon, CR0 4YY

Chapter One

Australia

Miranda Fox had the dream again that night. She dreamt of freedom to go where she wished, and strode off towards the horizon in the rosy light of dawn to meet the daughter she'd given away at birth. She held her close – a young woman now, not a baby. Where had all those years gone? As always her daughter's face was indistinct, but she too had wavy ash-brown hair and wasn't tall.

Joy and energy pulsed through Miranda and she laughed aloud for sheer happiness. Then her half-brother Sebastian intruded on her dream, blocking her way, looking at her scornfully – as usual. The feeling of joy faded and the shackles of duty gripped her so tightly that when her daughter slipped from her grasp and walked away into the mist, even in a dream she could only watch sadly.

Then Sebastian grabbed her arm, dragged her back in spite of her struggles and she became Minnie again, because her family insisted on shortening her name.

Only her mother had ever used her full name, but her mother had died forty-two years ago when she was five. Her father had found another wife within six months, making his third marriage and creating his third child – to his disappointment, another daughter.

But Regina's mother left him after five years, not daring to take her daughter with her because Judge James Fox was a powerful man.

From then on, he had eschewed women and had nothing good to say about them. He boasted that he'd brought up his three children on his own, with the help of a series of housekeepers, and had created a son and heir anyone would be proud of. He never expressed pride in his two daughters.

Miranda woke suddenly, staring round the bedroom for a moment, feeling as if she was in an alien place. She'd slept later than usual. What had woken her? She sighed as she realised it was her father calling for help in getting to the commode chair next to his bed. He'd turned ninety-four two days ago and was as cantankerous as they came. Someone had to take care of him and Sebastian had made sure it was her.

What kept her going was her father's promise that after he died she'd be looked after and would be a woman of 'independent means'. It wouldn't make up for all the tedious, lost years, but it'd help her enjoy the rest of her life. And he never broke his promises.

He hadn't always been this bad-tempered. She

remembered another father, intelligent and quite good company as long as things went his way. But she'd lost that man during the past year or two and a querulous stranger had taken his place, a stranger who didn't always remember things clearly.

'I'm ready to die,' he grumbled as she helped him. 'What's it coming to when my daughter has to pull my trousers up?'

'I'm happy to help you.'

'It's still not right.'

No, she thought. Her whole life wasn't right. What he and her brother had done to her wasn't right or fair. But you couldn't change the past.

Her days had now blurred into a round of small tasks, small thoughts and even smaller hopes. Besides, she knew her father would have gone mad in a nursing home – and driven everyone else mad, too. She'd been locked away once herself and wouldn't put anyone else in that terrible situation. So she waited to be released from this duty with as much patience as she could summon up.

Mid-morning she caught sight of herself in the hall mirror and grimaced. Her hair was scraped back into a tangled clump, the grey streaks at her temples showing all too clearly. Her expression was grim and she looked older than her years. She tried to smile and when she failed, turned away from that unflattering reflection.

Her father spent the morning in his sitting room, which had once been the spare bedroom. When she peeped in, he was staring into space, which wasn't like him. 'Are you all right, Father?'

'Of course I'm all right. Stop fussing. Can a man not have a peaceful think in his own home?'

Just before one o'clock, he moved slowly along the corridor, leaning on his Zimmer frame, his breath coming in gasps with the effort. But he refused to let her take him in a tray and would not use a wheelchair, let alone contemplate one of the little motorised vehicles that would allow him to go outside again.

Five minutes after he'd taken his place, Miranda brought in the quiche she'd made for lunch.

He was drumming his fingers impatiently. 'You're late. You know I like to eat at one sharp.'

She knew better than to argue that five minutes made little difference. He set a great store by what he called maintaining standards. 'The food's here now. Quiche. Your favourite.'

Before she could even set it down, he pressed one hand to his chest, tried to speak and leant sideways, falling slowly out of his chair.

She dumped the tray on the table, but before she could get round to catch him, he'd fallen to the floor.

He didn't cry out as he hit the carpet or move from the twisted, awkward position.

She stood stock still for a moment, her breath catching in her throat, then knelt to feel for the pulse in his neck. Was he . . . could he be . . . ?

No pulse. No life in his eyes.

For a moment she could only stare at him in shock.

Then she reached out to close the staring eyes.

It was time.

She didn't feel sad or weep. Her father had had a long life, dominating the whole family until a couple of years ago, when Sebastian, also a lawyer, had taken on that role.

No, her main emotion was relief, huge waves of it washing over her.

She was free at last!

Oh, she had so many plans, so much lost time to make up for. Her father had promised to leave her enough to buy a home of her own with sufficient left to invest and live on. She wasn't going to rush into anything but would take time to explore the possibilities for an interesting and fulfilling life.

She kept telling herself forty-seven was the new thirty-seven, but she didn't really believe that. She felt nearer to fifty-seven.

Then guilt crept in and her moment of euphoria vanished. How could she think like that? For all his faults, he was her father. 'Goodbye,' she said softly and went to phone her half-brother at his rooms. 'Sebastian? It's Father. He's just died, I'm afraid.'

'What? Are you sure?'

'Of course I am.'

'Don't touch anything. I'll come round at once. Oh, hell, I can't! I've got an important client coming in ten minutes, only time I could fit her in. Look, I'll be round in an hour, hour and a half max. Don't touch anything.'

'Shall I call the doctor?'

'No! Leave everything to me.'

She put the phone down and went to change her clothes. A rose-coloured top didn't feel right on such a day. Her father had hated to see her in bright colours anyway, muttering comments like 'Mutton dressed as lamb'.

When she was more sombrely clad, she hesitated in the doorway of her father's bedroom. She'd been itching to clear it out for years. The drawers and shelves were crammed with decades of rubbish and old clothes because he would never throw anything away from his magpie hoard.

The top drawer was slightly open. Her father usually kept that particular drawer locked. She went to shut it, but saw something beneath the papers: a box. She recognised it at once. Her mother's jewellery box. Why was it here? Her father had told her years ago that he'd put it in the bank for safety, because some of the pieces were quite valuable.

The jewellery was hers, left to her by her mother, and was nothing to do with her half-brother and sister. She clutched the box to her chest, happy to see it again.

Guilt kicked in once more. He wasn't even cold and she was going through his things.

But the box and its contents *were* hers. She'd have claimed them years ago if her father hadn't made such a fuss about looking after them for her. And anyway, what chance had she ever had to wear expensive jewellery?

None, that's what. She'd always been shy, had dated a few guys in her teens, had had that one disastrous relationship and never had the chance to go out with anyone else since.

Feeling like a thief, she took the box into her bedroom and went through it. Two of the most valuable pieces were missing. Where could they be? She went back to check her father's drawers, but the matching diamond brooch and necklace weren't there.

She hesitated, unable to face going through the whole room. If the jewellery was there, they'd find it when they cleared out her father's things. She'd better put the box away safely. Where? In the end, she put it into her suitcase on top of the wardrobe, locking the case carefully and putting the key in her purse. Once he found out two pieces were missing, Sebastian would want to whisk the rest of the jewellery away for safe keeping but she wouldn't let him. From now on, she intended to look after her own life and possessions.

She sighed, not looking forward to Sebastian arriving. He was so like their father, both of them chauvinists, and while there was some excuse for a ninety-four-year-old man having that attitude, there was no excuse for a man of fifty-two, who'd been born in an era of women's liberation and should know better. Perhaps being a lawyer had made him so conservative, or perhaps it was his elderly father's influence, or maybe he'd simply been born that way. How his wife put up with him, she didn't understand, because Dorothy was an intelligent woman.

She heard a car draw up outside and hurried to open the front door to let her brother in.

'Where's Father?'

'In here.' She led the way into the dining room.

Sebastian knelt beside the body. 'Must have been a heart attack. Leave everything to me.'

While he made the necessary phone calls, Miranda wandered along to her bedroom and stared out of the window. It was a relief when the undertaker removed the body. Sebastian said he'd arrange the funeral and she nodded as she saw him out. He stopped halfway down the path to call, 'Don't touch anything, Minnie! I'll be round this evening to start on Father's papers.'

Then she was on her own. How long since she'd had time to herself? Too long.

With a tired sigh, she went to sit in an armchair and spent a lazy couple of hours with the latest book by her favourite author. No interruptions. No sharp rapping of a walking stick on the floor.

Bliss.

In the afternoon she did some gardening, another favourite pastime.

The phone rang at six. Sebastian.

'I can't come round tonight, after all. Dorothy and I have a dinner engagement that's too important to cancel. Remember what I said. Don't touch anything.'

What did he think she'd do to her father's papers? She knew roughly how things had been left and that was all that mattered. Anyway, she didn't want to go into her father's bedroom again. Every time she passed the door, she kept expecting him to call out, wanting something.

She poured herself a glass of wine, found her library book and settled down for another quiet read. She didn't even want to switch on the TV. What she craved was peace and silence.

In England, Nikki Fox leant against the kitchen door frame, staring defiantly at her mother. 'All right, so I'm pregnant. I wasn't going to tell you yet.'

For a moment the silence seemed to hum with her anger, then Regina snapped, 'You stupid girl! Didn't I teach you better than that? Couldn't you at least have gone on the pill?'

'I *was* on the pill. But I forgot to take the tablets with me when I went for that weekend in Brighton. I didn't think a couple of days without would matter.'

Her mother sank on to the bed, groaning. 'We'll have to arrange the abortion quickly. You can't be more than six weeks gone, so it'll be a very minor procedure.'

Nikki stared down at her feet in the fluffy pink slippers. 'I'm not sure I want to get rid of the baby.'

Another heavy silence while her mother looked at her incredulously.

'Let's get one thing straight. I'm not having a baby here. I've done my share of child-raising with you. Without any help from your father I've built a career for myself – and got a life. I'm not going back to sleepless nights and a baby screaming its head off.'

Nikki swallowed hard. She'd guessed her mother would react like this, which was why she'd not said anything.

'Who's the baby's father? Tim Whatsamajig?'

Nikki shrugged. She did a lot of shrugging when her mother got a bee in her bonnet about something, because whatever she said was usually wrong. She wasn't sure about having an abortion, but she was very sure she didn't want to get married, not at eighteen.

'I can't believe you've got yourself into this.'

She tried to think of an answer to that but couldn't. She'd asked herself the same question again and again.

'We'll arrange for you to have an abortion. It's the only sensible thing to do. You're an intelligent girl, sure to get into university, with your whole life ahead of you. You did brilliantly in your AS grades, and you're right on course for top A levels. There'll be plenty of time to have children later when you meet someone who—'

'Mum, I just can't get my head around the idea of killing a baby.'

'It's not a baby yet; it's a tiny blob.'

'It's a baby. Its heart is beating already. I looked it up on the Internet.' She glanced at her watch in relief. 'I've got to go to work now. I need to earn as much money as I can.' Thank heavens for fast food outlets! She might not enjoy the job, but the money did give her some independence. At the moment she was saving as much of her wages as she could . . . just in case.

'I'll look into what we need to do,' her mother

promised. 'You'd better get off to work. You don't want to lose your job.'

Nikki left the house without another word. She knew she wouldn't change her mother's mind. She never had before, so why should she succeed now?

Would she change her own mind?

The phone rang and Regina hesitated before picking it up, not feeling like chatting to anyone. Then she looked at the caller ID. Her brother. What did he want? He never called just to chat. 'Hi, Sebastian.'

'It's Father. He died yesterday. I didn't ring you straight away because, given the time difference between Australia and England, you'd have been in bed.'

'Well, it's not unexpected at his age. How did it happen?'

'He dropped dead at lunchtime. His heart's been failing for a while. Luckily, he'd seen the doctor recently, so they don't need to do a post-mortem. I need to know if you're coming to the funeral.'

She hesitated, then sighed. She'd never forgive herself if she didn't attend. Bad enough that she hadn't seen her father for several years and had left his care to poor Minnie, who had definitely not had a good life. Unthinkable to miss the funeral.

'Yes, of course I'm coming.'

'You can stay with us, if you like.'

She hesitated. Sebastian wasn't a comfortable person to live with. He seemed to think that she was as meek as his wife and barked orders at her. 'I'll probably split my time between you and Minnie, though that rambling old house of Dad's gives me the creeps. Is it still full of rubbish?'

'Worse than ever. He was getting very strange; Alzheimer's starting, the doctor thought.'

'What about the will? How are things left?'

'I'll tell you when you get here.'

'What's the big secret?'

'Nothing you need to be upset about. You'll get your share.' She put the phone down, chewing her thumb. Not a good time to be nipping off to Australia. But still, if Nikki was only six weeks gone, there was still plenty of time to sort out an abortion after she got back. She'd make it a quick trip, just a week or so.

She went online and booked herself a seat to Perth, then began to pack.

The following day, which was a Saturday, Sebastian and his wife arrived while Miranda was having her breakfast and walked straight in without even knocking. She pushed her plate aside, losing her appetite completely at the sight of him.

'I rang Regina,' he said by way of a greeting. 'She's coming to the funeral.'

'Oh, good. I'll get a room ready for her.'

'No need. She's staying with us.'

'But—'

'Finish your breakfast. I'll start going through the

things in Father's bedroom and sitting room. Dorothy will do the living room. We'll leave the kitchen till later.'

Did he think there were papers or valuables in the kitchen? she wondered. 'I've nearly finished eating. I'll come and help you.'

'It's not your job. I'm the executor as well as the main beneficiary, so it's up to me to make all the decisions about what's thrown out.'

'What if I want to keep something?'

He looked round scornfully. 'Most of this stuff's rubbish, but you can go through the discard piles afterwards, if you must. Anything valuable will be considered part of the estate, however.'

Her appetite gone completely, Miranda scraped the rest of her scrambled eggs into the rubbish bin as she listened to the sound of his heavy footsteps. In the living room Dorothy was opening and shutting cupboards and drawers. She and Sebastian were avid collectors of antiques and had been dying to get their hands on this house and its more valuable contents for years.

A door squeaked. Miranda recognised that sound and hurried along to her bedroom. Inside she found Sebastian opening a drawer.

'What on earth are you doing in here? This is *my* room!'

'I'm just looking at this chest of drawers.' He made as if to pull the drawer right out and she prevented him.

'I don't appreciate having you go through my things.'

'I need to check that it's a genuine antique. We'll have to catalogue all the furniture. This is about 1820, I should think. The wood's in excellent condition, mahogany, and that bow front is very elegant. I reckon it'll go for a couple of thousand pounds.'

She shoved the drawer back into its slot. 'No, it won't. The furniture in here is mine, so are quite a few of the other good pieces in the house. You were working on that project over in Sydney at the time I got them and it was before you got interested in antiques.'

'I didn't think they were particularly valuable.' He sounded as if he disliked the thought.

'My mother's aunt said they were nice pieces, but I like them because they're attractive not because they're valuable.'

'Your great-aunt wasn't wealthy and, anyway, I'm pretty sure I remember *this* chest of drawers from a long time back. Can you prove that it's yours?'

She stared at him open-mouthed. Did he really think she'd lie about this? The days of him browbeating her into doing what he wanted were over, and he wasn't getting his hands on her things. 'I can easily prove it. I still have her will *and* her lawyer's letter to me *and* a list of what she left me.'

He scowled at her as he looked round. 'Does that include everything in this room?'

'All except my mattress. That was new last year. Father did pay for that, so if you want it . . .' She went and tugged at a corner of it as if to pull it off the bed.

'Don't be stupid, Minnie. I hope you're not getting silly again.'

He looked at her smugly and she felt herself shrivel at the implications of that. He wouldn't. Surely he wouldn't do that again! 'I'm telling you the simple truth.'

'Well, I shall want to see your aunt's lawyer's letter. We have to do things properly.'

She recovered enough to say, 'Good. You can start by using my proper name: Miranda. Now Father's gone, I'm going to use that. I never did like being called Minnie, just because I was a small baby.'

He let out a scornful grunt. 'I couldn't think of you as anything but Minnie now. The name suits you.' He walked to the door with a last regretful glance at the chest of drawers, but popped his head back inside to add, 'What about your mother's jewellery. That's too valuable to leave lying around. If you give it to me, I'll put it into the bank for you.'

'That's not part of the estate, either. Father left it lying around and you didn't worry then.'

'I'm just trying to help. I didn't agree with him on that. Keeping expensive jewellery at home in a rambling old house like this is asking for trouble.'

'I've put it somewhere safe, don't worry. Father had it in his drawer. But there are two items missing, the most valuable: a diamond brooch and matching necklace. If I don't find them, I'll have to call in the police.'

There was silence, then, 'Ah. Dorothy borrowed those to wear to a special function. I've got them at home in my safe. No need to worry about them.'

Miranda nearly gave in, because he was so hard to pin

down, and as he'd said, the most valuable jewellery was safe, which was the important thing. But she was angry at the casual way he'd dismissed the idea of using her proper name, angry that her sister-in-law was using the jewellery without even asking her and found the courage to say, 'I want them back. Straight away.'

'There's a ball coming up. They go really well with Dorothy's blue dress, which is why Father lent them to her.'

'Then you'd better buy her some diamonds of her own. I want mine back.'

'Don't be foolish. You never wear them.'

She was so angry, she forgot her usual fear of him. 'That's not the point. You shouldn't have borrowed them without my permission. I want them back tomorrow.'

'I'm busy all day. You'll have to wait till I have time to sort it all out.' He fixed her with that gloating gaze which always made her shiver. 'You *are* acting in a foolish way today. What's got into you?'

When he'd gone, she collapsed on the bed, blinking away the tears. She'd tried to be brave and face up to her bully of an older brother, but as usual, he'd ignored her wishes. He might not hurt her physically these days, but he still continued to put her down and trample all over her. And he still continued to threaten her with her greatest fear. He didn't need to put it into words, only hint and she caved in.

She got out some yellow stickers and went round the house, putting them on her own pieces of furniture. She and Dorothy had sharp words about this several times. It appeared her brother-in-law had coveted these particular pieces for some time and had intended to have them moved out.

After that Miranda stayed mainly in her bedroom until her brother and his wife left in the late afternoon. She made short forays to the bathroom or kitchen, glad that such an old-fashioned house still had locks on the bedroom doors.

They didn't call goodbye, so she knew Sebastian was seriously annoyed with her and she could expect some sort of retribution from him.

Well, she was angry too. Only, what good had that ever done her before?

When she bought her own house, she would look in a country town, as far away from her brother as possible. Or go to live in England, as Regina had. Her mother had been English and her father had made sure Miranda kept her British passport up to date, because he considered it a valuable thing to possess.

Miranda strolled along the street, intending to go to the corner deli for some bread and ham. But before she got there she gave into temptation and took a detour through the small park, which was looking parched with the summer heat. It'd start getting cooler soon. February was the hottest month of the year, usually.

She came here sometimes for a bit of peace, snatching a few minutes to sit in the cool shade of a huge Moreton Bay fig tree.

Lou watched the woman walking towards him, thinking how sad she looked. He'd seen her a few times before and she never looked happy. Harried, yes, upset, yes, but never, ever happy. That intrigued him. Since he'd come out of hospital he'd been confined to a damned wheelchair, with only the short range of an electric mobility scooter when he went out.

He was a lot better now, though, and was planning how to reorganise his life to cope with his new disability. In the meantime he came here most days just to get out of his flat. He could only sit and watch others, for lack of energy to do more, but that was better than watching the wall. You could only spend so much time on a computer, after all.

The woman sat down on an empty bench, and brushed back her fair hair impatiently as she stared across the murky water of the small lake and the two black swans sailing majestically past.

When she wiped away a tear, he could bear it no longer. She was such a tiny, slender creature, surely not more than five foot tall, and had a vulnerable air. He moved his chair forward, stopping beside her bench. 'Lovely, aren't they?'

She jumped in shock as he spoke, but no one was afraid of a man on a mobility scooter, and he watched her relax a little.

'I've seen you here before,' he offered, hoping for some conversation.

'I've seen you too. Just in the past few weeks. Have

you recently moved to the area?'

'Yes.' He held out one hand. 'I'm Lou Rayne.'

'Miranda Fox.'

'Great name.'

She looked at him in surprise. 'Do you really like it?'

'I wouldn't say so if I didn't.'

'My family call me Minnie. I hate that.'

'Tell 'em not to.'

'They refuse to change.'

Perhaps they were the ones who were putting the deep sadness into her face. 'I can't resist asking: do you come here often?'

She smiled. 'Yes. I love to watch the birds. And it's so peaceful.'

He moved his scooter slightly so that he was facing both her and the water. 'You live in that big house on the corner a couple of streets away, don't you? I've seen you go in. I love the wrap-around verandas. They built much prettier houses a hundred years ago.'

'It's not quite that old. It was built for my father and his first wife. He died yesterday, so I have to move out soon.'

'I'm sorry. Both about your father and you having to leave.'

'He was ninety-four and ready to go. I always knew I'd be leaving after he died. I've a half-sister and brother to share the inheritance with, you see.'

'Chucking you out to sell it, are they?'

'I wouldn't want to stay. The house is far too big for

one person and the past few years haven't been easy, so the place doesn't hold very good memories for me. I'm looking forward to buying my own home. Where do you live?'

'In that block of flats custom-built for people with disabilities. Ugly place. The architect should be shot, and the sooner the better, before he inflicts any other monstrosities on the world.'

'Why did you move there, then?'

'I was between houses when I fell ill. My niece bought the flat for me when I was in hospital. I wasn't in a state to protest at the time. It was touch and go whether I'd recover.'

'But fortunately you did.' She stood up. 'I'd better get back, I suppose.'

'I'll keep you company as you walk, if you don't mind. I haven't heard a human voice all day.'

'I don't mind at all. Would you like to come in for a coffee? We can sit on the veranda and—Oh! There are steps.'

'I can manage steps if I take them slowly. I just can't walk far. That's why I have my trusty steed.' He patted the scooter affectionately.

Miranda set off, matching her pace to his. Impossible to be nervous of being alone with this man, not because he had some sort of disability, but because he had a friendly, open face – cheeky even, for all his hair was silver and very thin on top.

There was a book in the basket at the front of the scooter and she studied the title. 'Dean Koontz. Do you like horror stories?'

He grinned, a surprisingly boyish grin for a man who must be at least ten years older than her. She couldn't help smiling back.

'I love 'em,' he said. 'Silly, I know.'

'I couldn't sleep if I'd read something that frightened me.'

'They don't frighten me. Most of them amuse me, though this chap writes better stories than most. I don't sleep much anyway, so it doesn't matter.'

He said that matter-of-factly, not in a self-pitying or angry tone. Her father had been very angry after his stroke and had let the whole world, which mainly meant her, know it.

She watched Lou climb painfully up the veranda steps, then settle in the big upright chair her father had used. She went inside to make the coffee, bringing out a home-made cake as well. It was gratifying that he ate two large pieces.

'I've not eaten anything as delicious for months!' he said, as he pushed his plate away.

'I can wrap you up a piece to take home.'

'Yes, please!'

They didn't talk much or if they did, she didn't remember what they'd said. But time passed pleasantly and she was sorry when he said he'd have to get back.

'I'm afraid I need a rest now.'

'It must be hard coping on your own.'

He shrugged. 'You get used to it. I have a carer come in every day to help me shower, and a cleaner three times a week. My niece brings me food, or I have it delivered.'

'I'll walk back with you. I need something for tea from the deli.' She'd thought she wasn't hungry but now realised she was.

They stopped outside his block of flats and he scowled at it. 'Ghastly, isn't it?'

'More like an egg box. Did you have a stroke?' Miranda felt herself flushing. 'Sorry. None of my business.'

'It's cancer of the spine that's put me in a wheelchair. I had a minor heart attack and while I was in hospital they found the cancer. They operated a couple of times and now they've given up on me. I've got about six months to live.'

'Oh, Lou, I'm so sorry! I shouldn't have asked.'

'I don't mind you asking. And I'm sorry too. I'd wanted to slay a few more dragons before I shuffled off this mortal coil. As soon as I've sorted a few things out, I'm moving into a house more to my taste, whatever my bossy niece says. These flats are designed for disabled people, with lifts, wooden floors and wide doorways, but they're pokey places and the building echoes like a damned cave. It drives me crazy.'

'Your niece is probably trying to do her best for you.'

'She doesn't listen to me, just tells me what I want.'

'I can relate to that. Family can be . . . difficult!'

'Tell me about it. Your brother sounds a real control freak.'

'He is. And he's always so sure he's right. I can't wait to get a place of my own, I must admit.'

When she got back, she found she'd left the front door unlocked and got angry with herself for being so careless. Picking up the weekend papers, she took the property pages into the kitchen and indulged in some research and daydreaming as she ate a simple meal.

Nikki listened to her mother's parting instructions and waved goodbye from the window as the taxi pulled away from their smart town house. Not that her mother bothered to look up at her, she never did, was always too busy rushing somewhere else.

Rain was beating against the windows as she went to sit down, feeling wobbly. She'd been sick that morning, but had managed to hide it from her mother.

Two hours afterwards she woke, so late for school that she didn't even bother getting ready. She was feeling better so she had something to eat then worked on revision for a coming test.

When the doorbell rang she peered through the little spy hole. Her heart sank at the sight of Tim standing there, hunched up in a hooded anorak. She made no attempt to open the door, willing him to go away. But he didn't.

He rang again, then called out, 'I know you're in there, Nikki, because there's nowhere else you could be in weather like this.'

The bell rang again and again, until in the end she

flung the front door open and yelled, 'Come in, why don't you? How lovely to see you. Not.'

She ran through into the living room, terrified of throwing herself into his arms, but he followed and pulled her close. She struggled half-heartedly for a minute or two, then gave into temptation and sagged against him, doing what she'd promised herself not to: bursting into tears.

He rocked her and made soothing sounds until the sobs stopped.

With her arms laced around his waist, she looked up at him. His face was bony and boyish still, but he'd be quite good-looking once he filled out a little. 'Sorry, Tim. I didn't mean to do that to you.'

'Doesn't matter. Come and sit down. You look terrible.'

She led him through to the kitchen. 'I'll have a cup of peppermint tea. Can't stand coffee just now.'

'So it's true.'

She closed her eyes, furious at herself for blurting that out, when she'd tried so hard to keep her news from him. She opened her eyes to find him gazing at her so seriously that for a moment he looked just like his father. Not that she minded that. Everyone should have a father like Mr Heyter. 'How did you find out?'

'I met your mother in town yesterday and she stopped me to say she thought it pretty bad of me to abandon you at a time like this, when we'd been an item for so long. When I said I didn't know what she meant, because *you* had dumped me, she looked surprised. She told me you're having a baby. Is that true?'

'Mmm.'

'It's got to be mine. You've not been with anyone else for over a year.'

She turned her back on him, not knowing what to say. His voice grew softer. 'Nikki, why didn't you tell me?'

'Because it was me who was careless, not you, so why should you be lumbered with a child? And because I don't know what I want to do. I need to work things out – only I can't seem to think straight.' She began to cry again and when he put his arm round her shoulders, she leant against him with a tired sigh, not even aware they were moving across the room till he spoke.

'Sit down, Nikki. Peppermint tea, you said?'

He made two cups and came to sit across the coffee table from her this time, not beside her like he usually did. 'It doesn't matter who was careless. If it's my child, it's my responsibility too. What does your mother think?'

'She wants me to have an abortion as soon as she gets back from Australia. Grandfather's just died and she's gone to the funeral.' She peeped at him over her cup and saw him go very still.

'Do you want to do that, have an abortion, I mean?'

She took a sip, then another. When she looked up, he was still waiting. 'I don't think so.'

Then he was the one who cried, silent tears that he tried to wipe away.

'I don't want you to kill our child, Nikki. Promise me

you won't do that. *Promise.*'

'If I have it, I won't be able to go to university. If you and I raise it together, neither of us will be able to get a degree, or not for years and years. That seems stupid.'

He was silent for a minute or two, then gave her a wry smile. 'I can't imagine you with a baby.'

She couldn't help smiling back. 'Like, you're an expert on them.'

'I've never even held one.'

'Neither have I.'

They looked at one another. 'It's scary.' Her voice wobbled.

'I know. But don't do anything without me, Nikki love, especially not something so irrevocable.'

He moved across to sit beside her and she cuddled up to him with a sigh of relief.

His breath was warm on her cheek. 'Are we back together?'

'I suppose.'

'Aren't you sure?'

'It's Mum. You know what she's like. She says she's not having a baby here and I've got to have an abortion or get out. And . . . well, when she sets her mind to something, when she gets *that look* on her face, she's like, Bulldozers R Us. I've never been able to stand up to her.'

'You've never been responsible for a baby's life before, either.'

She shivered.

'Besides, you won't be alone. I'll be facing her with you.'

She didn't say it, because she appreciated the offer, but as if that'd make a difference to her mother!

Chapter Two

The following morning Miranda felt at a loose end. Sebastian had instructed her to leave all the funeral arrangements to him and had already decreed whom they'd invite – just the family, a couple of long-term acquaintances and the lawyer, since all father's friends were long dead. They'd gather at Sebastian's house for refreshments and the reading of the will afterwards.

There were one or two other people she'd have liked to invite, such as the community nurse who'd visited often and always cheered both her father and her up, but when she raised the idea tentatively, her brother was so sharply scornful she backed off. Again. She told herself she was saving her energy for a struggle that mattered, but knew she was being cowardly.

She was ashamed of how she still gave into him and let him bully her, most ashamed of all that he still had the power to frighten her. 'I'll do what I want in my own home, at least,' she told the empty house and went to fetch some big rubbish bags. There were things she wanted to keep that were no business of the others, like photos of herself and her mother, so she'd make a start.

In the dining room she threw open the window to let in some of the fresh air her father had hated since he grew frail. When she took out the family photo albums, she couldn't resist leafing through them. Photos of her mother, who looked so young because she'd never had the chance to grow old, photos of herself as a child. These could be of no possible value *to the estate*.

Sebastian would have to use legal jargon all the time, wouldn't he?

There was a bundle of papers in the secret compartment at the back of the old, roll-top writing desk her father had often used, small as it was. She hesitated, wondering if she should leave these for Sebastian. Then rebellion surged up again and she began to read.

It was a copy of her father's will, dated . . . a year ago. She frowned and checked the date again. She hadn't known her father had made a new will. Why hadn't he mentioned it? Then she checked again and realised she'd been away on her annual week's holiday at the time, a week when her father, highly reluctantly, employed paid carers full-time, because he refused absolutely to go into respite care.

That date must have been chosen specially to keep the new will secret. Impossible not to read the papers after she realised that.

She went to sit at the kitchen table with a cup of tea,

praying Sebastian wouldn't arrive for a while. The tea grew cold and the paper began to tremble in her hand as the meaning of the words sank in, and when she'd finished reading it, she burst into tears.

Her father had cheated her, stolen all those years from her, promised so much and given so little.

He'd left fifty per cent of everything to Sebastian, *the son and heir*, with the rest divided equally between his two daughters. Regina's share was to go to her to use as she saw fit, but Miranda's was to go into a trust fund administered by Sebastian. There was a clause in the will asking her brother to make sure she was properly looked after.

She didn't want or need looking after. She wanted the freedom to look after herself – had more than earned it. She knew instinctively that Sebastian would try to keep her in check through the finances. He was the ultimate control freak.

What was she going to do now? She'd counted on that inheritance, had more than earned it. If she wanted any freedom she'd have to get a job. But she had no marketable skills, unless you counted looking after cantankerous old men – and she'd had more than enough of that, had only done it because after her breakdown she'd been fit for nothing else at first.

In times like these, well-qualified people were out of work. What chance would she have? None.

It took her a while to calm down, by which time she'd decided to say nothing till the real will was read. After all, this was only a draft. Surely her father hadn't signed such a will? Surely even he couldn't have been so cruel?

Regina arrived two days later. Dorothy met her at the airport and they popped in to say hello to Miranda, then went on to Sebastian's house.

'I'll come and stay with you for a day or two,' Regina whispered as they said goodbye.

The funeral took place the following day. Miranda put on black clothing, stared at herself in the mirror, then changed her mind and added a multicoloured scarf, a minute flag of defiance which brought a frown from her brother.

Afterwards, at Sebastian's house, she accepted a glass of white wine, took a dutiful sip, then edged her way to a corner, from where she watched the others. Her sister hadn't changed. Oozing self-confidence, ferociously smart, Regina was chatting animatedly with Jonathon Tressman, their lawyer, son of the man who'd been the family's lawyer for decades. Miranda kept away from them. His father had been one of the people who'd ruined her life all those years ago and she wasn't giving the son a chance to do more damage.

Sebastian was listening to his sister but keeping an eye on everyone in the room in that way he had. Occasionally he addressed a remark to his wife or to one of the other guests.

Dorothy was standing with that bland expression on her face that said nothing about what she was thinking.

Miranda didn't feel at all close to her. Well, how could she feel close to someone who might report what she said to her brother?

Caterers served substantial but elegant titbits. The few other people present ate a little, drank a little and behaved in a restrained way, as if the family really was grieving.

Miranda could feel her determination to stand up for herself shrivelling by the minute as the others continued to chat easily, smiling at one another, ignoring her.

When everyone had left except for the family and the lawyer, Sebastian looked across the room at her. 'Come and join us, Minnie. I don't know why you always have to retreat to a corner. We need to explain Father's will to you.'

This was the final straw. She got up and moved across, forgetting all the tactful phrases she'd planned, forgetting her usual fear of standing up to him. 'I do speak English, you know, so I daresay I'll understand the will. And anyway, I read the new will for myself. How did you persuade Father to treat me like that? I warn you, I shall contest the will. I want full control of my share like Regina has.'

He blinked in surprise at her blunt words, then she saw his face grow dark with anger, which he mastered with a visible effort after a quick sideways glance at the lawyer. 'I don't see how you can possibly have seen the will.'

'Father had left a copy of the draft in a drawer. I was

putting some things away and found it.'

'I see. Well, it's changed a little since then. Mr Tressman can explain the implications to you. You've been generously looked after, will never want for anything, so you'll have no cause to complain or contest the will.'

She didn't trust him. He had that smug, I-am-the-winner look on his face.

The lawyer stepped forward, his tone soothing. 'Your father was worried about you, Miss Fox. He knew you . . . were sometimes in need of support—'

She broke in angrily. 'I had a postnatal depression many years ago. I've not had any trouble since.'

His smile was fixed and glassy. 'Of course, of course. But you aren't used to handling money, so he's left your share of his estate in a trust, which your brother and I will manage for you.'

'What does that mean in practice?'

Sebastian's voice was patronising. 'It means we'll help you with the big stuff, like buying somewhere to live, and we'll make sure your money is invested carefully, so that you have a steady income for the rest of your life. You're too old to find a decent job, not to mention having no training, but Father did appreciate the way you'd looked after him, as did Regina and I.'

'How much money did he leave me?'

They all looked at her disapprovingly.

'How much?' she insisted.

'Twenty-five per cent. It's in a trust. It's not left *to* you.

It's left for you to use, then when you die, the money comes back to the next generation – my children and Regina's. If you'd had a child, he or she would also be a legatee.'

'I did have a child.'

'Who was adopted at birth, so is not now a member of the family, may even be dead for all we know.'

'Do you and Regina have a trust too?'

'No. Father knew we were both used to handling money.' He was smiling at her as if she should be pleased. Well, she wasn't. She felt about an inch tall and sick with humiliation.

'Sebastian, that's a bit unfair,' Regina said. 'I'm sure Minnie can manage her money as well as the next person.'

'And I'm sure she can't. So was Father. Don't interfere, Regina. It's a done deal.'

Under his scowling gaze, Miranda felt like weeping and running out of the room. But that would only make him more certain that she wasn't to be trusted. Would he never forget that one episode of depression? Pride alone kept her standing there, kept her eyes dry. Well, almost dry. At least she didn't let the tears fall.

She couldn't believe this. If Sebastian was involved and if this Mr Tressman was as clever as his father, she was sure the money would be tied up so tightly that no one could break the trust. But perhaps she could still have the kind of life she longed for? The sort of home she craved. 'Well, then, I want to buy a small colonial house with a garden, preferably in a country town.'

'Ah.' Sebastian and the lawyer exchanged glances.

'Ah, what?' She watched her brother take a deep breath.

'Well, the thing is, Minnie, we've already bought you somewhere to live. We did this a few months ago, with Father's approval. It's a flat in a very upmarket block, built only three years ago, excellent location, bound to rise in value. And don't worry, the block of flats has gardens and they're really well maintained so you'll look down on to flowers. We snapped it up at a bargain price when the housing market dropped. I gave the tenant notice as soon as Father died and you can move in next month.'

'I don't want to live in a flat. I hate flats.'

'You won't hate this one. It has city views and great potential, financially. Besides, the market's still not buoyant. It'd be foolish to sell it now.'

'*I do not – want to live – in a flat!*'

Regina came across and patted her arm. 'Minnie, living in the country is just an impractical dream. You won't want to be stuck there in the middle of winter, believe me, you'll want to be near theatres and restaurants, places where you can meet people.'

'How can you say that when you live in a small country town? You must enjoy it and I'm sure it'd suit me too.'

'Well, it's a bit late for that. Sebastian is very shrewd financially and you should take his advice. Maybe you can sell the flat when the market picks up.'

Miranda looked at Sebastian's face and knew the answer to that. She got up and walked out, unable to take any more. Her dreams were ruined. Her life was never going to be her own.

She found she was still clutching her handbag as she strode down the street, though she didn't remember picking it up. When a woman she passed stared at her, she realised tears were running down her cheeks, but she didn't even try to brush them away, just walked on.

No one followed her. Well, they didn't need to. They knew she had nowhere to go except the house where she'd been born and where she'd been virtually imprisoned for the past twenty-six years.

Sebastian would probably be amused by her outburst, would feel it justified the way the money had been left. *Poor Minnie, so impractical. She's never learnt how to handle money. But we'll look after her.*

She could hear them saying it.

She couldn't bear to go straight home, so made for her usual refuge.

Regina looked at Sebastian. 'It's not fair, you know. She should be treated the same as me.'

'She'd do something foolish, fritter away the money.'

She didn't try to argue with him, knowing he'd not change his mind. She preferred avoidance tactics to beating her head against a stone wall, which was why she'd moved to England. They couldn't interfere in her life there.

She made a play of looking at her watch. 'I'm going to phone Nikki. I should just catch her before she goes to school.'

'Use our phone,' Sebastian said, waving one hand, generous now he'd got his own way with poor Minnie.

'Thanks, but I'll ring from my bedroom. My mobile's got international dialling.'

She waited impatiently for her daughter to pick the phone up. 'Ah, there you are. How are you, Nikki?'

'All right.'

'Have you made an appointment with the doctor yet?'

'No.'

'I'm back next week. We'll go and see him together.'

'No. If I do it at all, I'll do it on my own.'

'You'll do it, believe me. And I'm definitely going with you to make sure of that.'

The connection was closed abruptly. Regina sighed. She'd spoken too abruptly. She wasn't a bully like her brother, after all. But she was really upset by her daughter's unwanted pregnancy.

She didn't go back to join the others, couldn't face them at the moment, kept seeing poor Minnie's face. She wished she could do more to help her sister, but couldn't think of anything.

It was a rotten thing to do to anyone.

Miranda kept walking through the heat of the afternoon. It was three miles from Sebastian's house to hers and she hadn't taken her car because of going to the funeral. He lived in a prestigious older suburb, one with most of its early colonial houses still standing in large gardens.

You rarely saw people on foot round here, except for an occasional jogger. A large car with tinted glass passed her, waited for one of those high metal gates to slide open for it and moved slowly inside. Who rode in cars like that? She didn't know.

She wished she need never go back to her brother's house again as long as she lived, wished she need never see him again. How could they have bought her a flat to live in without consulting her? Her money was tied up and she was being treated like a child – and a stupid one at that. It was too much.

As she got nearer home, the suburbs changed, with modest blocks of old-fashioned flats standing up like sore thumbs in between run-down older dwellings. The street she and her father had lived in was no longer such a desirable place to live and the house was fit for nothing but demolition, but the land would be valuable, because the house stood on a quarter-acre block and someone would build three or four dwellings on it and make a huge profit, no doubt.

She saw Sebastian's car in her drive and realised he must have followed her, so turned sharp right, praying he hadn't seen her. Hurrying along the next street, she took refuge in the park, sitting on her favourite bench. If she stayed here till dusk, surely he'd go home? She needed time before she faced them all again.

She'd been sitting there for ages when she heard the faint whine of an electric motor and looked up to see Lou stopping next to her.

'Something's very wrong,' he said softly.

She nodded.

'Tell me.'

It all tumbled out and by the time she'd finished, she was crying into his handkerchief and he'd moved off his scooter to sit next to her. His arm felt so comforting round her shoulders. It was as if she'd known him for years.

'Why don't you come back to my place and have a glass of wine?'

'Are you allowed—' She broke off, realising it wasn't her business.

He grinned. 'Who's to stop me having a drink? I do what I want these days and what I'd really like at this moment is to share a bottle with you and take that hunted look off your face.'

'I'd love to.'

She was so terrified of meeting Sebastian on the way back that she insisted on waiting behind the street trees till Lou said the way was clear over the next open stretch. The ridiculousness of this made him smile and before she knew it, she was smiling, too. But she still took care not to bump into her brother.

By the time they got back to Lou's place they were both breathless with laughter, exaggerating the need for caution and making passers-by stare at them. That foolish fun didn't look to have done him any harm. In fact, he had more colour in his cheeks now.

They took the lift up to his flat. As he'd said, the building echoed. Someone had got the acoustics very wrong.

He parked his scooter in an alcove in his private hall, plugging it in to recharge, and made his way slowly towards the kitchen, walking as if each step was an effort. 'White or red?'

'White, please.'

'Good. That's what I like too.' He poured two generous glasses of wine and held one out to her. 'Potato crisps?'

'Why not?'

'I've given up eating healthily. I love salt and vinegar crisps.'

'They're my favourite too.'

He tipped a huge packet into a bowl and let her carry it and the wine across to the low table, while he followed her slowly and jerkily. Sitting down, he leant forward to clink his glass against hers. 'To hell with bossy relatives!'

'To hell with them all!'

It wasn't till they'd broached their second bottle that he asked, 'What *are* you going to do, Miranda?'

The words came out slightly slurred, because she didn't usually go beyond one or two glasses. 'I haven't the faintest idea. I wish I had.'

He opened his mouth, hesitated, then said, 'I've got an idea. Only you might not like it.'

'Try me.'

'I know you've probably had your fill of playing Flo Nightingale, but how about helping me slay my current dragon, by which I mean my damned niece?'

'Why is she a dragon?'

'She's threatening all sorts of things for later, like putting me into a hospice. I won't do that, Miranda, not under any circumstances. I have my own plans in place for the end. She's keeping an eye on me, not because we get on well, but because she's my only close relative now and she wants to make sure she inherits.'

'And will she? Inherit, I mean.'

'I'll leave her something because she really has helped me, I'll grant her that. Only . . . I'd like to fly a bit before the wax melts and I drop down to earth again.'

'Icarus.' Only it came out 'Icarush', which made her giggle. 'Oh dear, I'm tiddly.'

'Do you good.'

She took another slurp of the crisp, expensive wine, then realised he'd not finished explaining. 'How can *I* help you slay your dragon?'

'Come and live with me. Help me find a house I can move into quickly – and move into it with me. I don't need you to care for me physically. As I said before, I have a carer come in daily and I'll get one full time when I have somewhere to put him.'

She frowned, trying to work this out. 'Why do you need me then?'

'Because . . . I can hire as much help as I like, but I

want some congenial company in my final months. And you're fun to be with, easy to talk to, well educated.'

She blinked at him, wondering if she'd heard correctly. 'Am I?'

'Yes. And don't let anyone tell you differently.'

'You want me to move in with you?'

'Yes. And then I want us to have as much fun as possible. You'll help me do that, won't you? My niece won't. She'd like to clear all the wine out of my fridge and fill it with medicines and bland, nourishing food.'

'But . . .' Only Miranda couldn't think of any reason not to do as he was suggesting, because she did like him. And surely anything would be better than staying under Sebastian's control? Anything.

Lou lifted his glass and winked at her. 'Go on. Take a risk. I'll pay you a decent wage. You can save it and then you'll have some money behind you that Sebastian won't be able to touch. And getting away from him will give you some thinking time about the rest of your life.'

'All right. I'll do it.' She couldn't believe she'd said that without thinking it over and opened her mouth to say it was a mistake. But the retraction wouldn't come out because she didn't want to reject such a good offer. Instead she found herself asking, 'What about my flat?'

'Take it, say thank you very much and rent it out. Save the money you get for that as well.'

'Good idea!' She reached forward to clink glasses

with him, realised hers was empty and when he went to fill it, she shook her head. 'Not till we've had something to eat.'

'We'll send out for a pizza.'

'Great. I've not had pizza for years. Father didn't like them, said they were vulgar and smelt horrible.'

'What do you want on it?'

'Everything.'

The pizza delivery guy arrived promptly. He obviously knew Lou, who gave him a generous tip and teased him about his girlfriend.

Miranda carried the box back to the sitting area and found two plates. 'Father never gave tips. He said it was un-Australian.' The word came out mangled, but Lou just laughed at her.

'I like to tip people. I can't take my money with me when I go, after all, can I?'

'As long as you've got enough left to see you out comfortably.'

'I have. I'm quite good with money.'

By the time they'd finished eating they were laughing again. She couldn't remember the last time she'd laughed so much.

Miranda woke with a thumping headache. It took her a few minutes to work out that she was in Lou's spare bedroom. Good heavens! She'd got so drunk she couldn't even remember going to bed.

Well, so what? It was worth a hangover because she'd

enjoyed every mouthful of wine and pizza, every moment of shared laughter.

She heard the sound of movement and got up, putting on the man's dressing gown she found draped over a chair.

Lou was in the kitchen waiting for the kettle to boil. He turned round and smiled. 'You look a bit pale.'

'My head's thumping. I'm not used to drinking so much.'

'I hope you're not regretting it.'

'Certainly not. I can't remember when I've enjoyed an evening so much.'

'Bacon and eggs for breakfast? They're good for hangovers.'

'Shall I cook them?' She'd noticed how stiffly he was moving this morning and wasn't surprised when he nodded. 'Do you want one egg or two?'

'Two please, sunny side up. Are you having some?'

She shuddered.

As she cleared away his plate afterwards, he asked in a more serious tone than usual, 'Did you mean it?'

She didn't pretend to misunderstand. 'About coming to live with you? Yes, I did. Unless you've changed your mind.'

'Oh, no.' He closed his eyes for a moment, relief on his face. When he opened his eyes again, he said, 'Then we need to plan things carefully, Miranda my pet. We both have to escape from marauding relatives.'

She'd thought she was good at planning till she sat

down with Lou and watched him make lists, thinking of details that wouldn't even have occurred to her at this stage.

After they'd finished, he said, 'These first lists will get us started. Now, there's a photocopier in my office. Would you mind making your own copies? I will confess that I'm a bit tired this morning and the pain medication hasn't kicked in fully yet.'

When she came back he was dozing, so she sat down and waited for him to wake up. It had occurred to her while she was using his photocopier that she didn't need to hurry home. There was only Sebastian and Regina to worry about her and she doubted they would even notice.

Lou jerked awake a quarter of an hour later, stared at her, then smiled slowly. 'I'm glad you're still here.'

'Are you all right?' she asked.

'Yes. I always did take power naps and wake up refreshed. You look so much happier this morning.'

'I am. Will you be all right if I leave now? I want to go home and change into some clean clothes, something less funereal.'

'I'll be fine. You have my phone number. Give me a ring and let me know how it goes.'

'I'd prefer to walk round and tell you myself.'

'I'd prefer that, too.'

She set off, feeling slightly more confident because she had a plan to follow, a plan that gave her freedom from her family.

Her confidence began to ebb as soon as she saw Regina's hire car in the drive, blocking in her own vehicle.

What was her sister doing there? She was supposed to be staying with Sebastian.

Chapter Three

Regina was pacing up and down the veranda, seriously worried now about her sister. Then she saw Minnie coming along the street and stood up, staring in shock. Her sister's clothes were crumpled, her hair was untidy, she looked . . . as if she'd had a hard night.

Anxiety made her demand, 'Where the hell have you been?'

Minnie flinched. 'Staying with a friend. I didn't want to come back here last night. I was too upset.'

Regina gave her a quick hug. 'I'm sorry. I didn't mean to sound like Sebastian, but I've been worried sick about you.'

'I'm a grown woman. I can look after myself. I just needed to get away from our dear brother.'

'I don't blame you. He's a bit heavy-handed, isn't he? Gets more like Father every time I see him. I don't know how Dorothy puts up with his autocratic ways. She gets very tense when she's serving a meal. He has to have everything just so. As for not wanting to come back here, I don't know why you and Father stayed here so long. It's not as if he couldn't have afforded a more modern house. This one feels as if it's about to collapse any minute from extreme old age. I've never been in a place that creaks so much. I had a terrible night, kept jerking awake thinking someone had broken in.'

'You spent the night here? Why?'

Regina rolled her eyes at the ceiling. 'Why do you think? We were worried about you. I thought you'd come back here so I waited for you.'

'Oh. Well, that was very kind, but there was no need.'

Sebastian had said the same thing. He was a callous sod but Minnie was too soft for her own good and Regina felt protective towards her.

'You could have let us know where you were. I was afraid you might do something silly or that you'd been hurt. I wanted to call in the police, only Sebastian got furious at the mere idea, said it'd be too embarrassing for a man in his position.'

'We can't have him embarrassed, can we? And I'd never kill myself, if that's what you mean.' She pushed past Regina and went towards her bedroom. 'I need a shower.'

'Doesn't your friend have a bathroom?'

'Of course he does, but I waited till I could get a change of clothes.'

'*He!*' Regina stared at her. Minnie with a boyfriend!

'How long has this been going on?'

The bedroom door shut in her face and she hesitated, then went to put the kettle on. You could hardly chase after an older sister as if she were a naughty child. Minnie was upset, that's what all this was about. Regina would have been upset about that will, too. She was younger than Minnie, yet had been left money to do with as she pleased. Why shouldn't Minnie have been treated the same?

When Regina had actually said that to Sebastian, he'd insisted Minnie was too impractical, but she'd guessed that he really wanted to keep the money in the trust for the next generation. Which meant his two grown-up children, who now lived in Sydney and New York. Nikki would get some money too – eventually. Thinking of her daughter upset Regina all over again. How stupid and *unnecessary* to get yourself pregnant in this day and age!

When Minnie came into the kitchen, Regina waved one hand at the kettle. 'It's just boiled.'

'Thank you.' The words were stiff. Keeping her back turned, Minnie began to make a cup of tea.

'For what it's worth, I don't think it's fair.'

'What isn't?'

'How your money was left.'

She saw tears well in Minnie's eyes, but her sister brushed them away quickly, so she didn't comment.

'Are you hungry?'

Regina stood up and joined her. 'How about I do us an omelette and salad?'

Minnie shrugged.

'Sit down and let me wait on you. It's about time. You were wonderful with Father and he wasn't always kind to you. I've always been grateful you were there and I didn't have to get involved, though I could never have lived with him.' She shuddered at the mere thought of what that must have been like. 'I'd have wound up killing him.'

Her sister looked so surprised at this. Regina said gently, 'Sebastian and I could have helped more, though, given you more time off. I'm sorry about that.'

'You had a daughter to raise. That was much more worthwhile than looking after a selfish old man. And Sebastian isn't the sort to look after anyone. Dorothy waits on him hand and foot. He never had much to do with his own children, except to send them to expensive private schools and boast about it.' She began to stir her tea, keeping her eyes down.

Regina sighed. 'And even though he didn't do much to help, Sebastian got half of what's left because he's the *son and heir*, while you and I have only got a quarter each. I'm a bit peeved about that, in this day and age.'

Miranda shrugged. 'It was Father's money, to dispose of as he wished. Let's not talk about it any more. I haven't got my head around it all yet. If I get a steady income from the trust, maybe things won't be too bad. How's Nikki going on at school? She's going to university next year, isn't she? What's she going to study?'

She hadn't said a word to her brother, but found

herself confiding in Minnie.

'So I told her to get an abortion. It'll ruin her whole life if she has a baby now; stop her getting qualifications. She can always have children later.'

'I read somewhere that having an abortion can make it harder to get pregnant again. What does *she* want to do about it?'

'She doesn't know what she wants.'

'Who's the father?'

'A guy she's been going out with for a year: Tim. He's the same age as she is. Nice lad – well, I thought he was nice, now I'm not so sure. I saw him in town and told him what I thought of him for deserting her, only it turned out he didn't know about the baby and *she* had dumped him.'

'She'll be in shock still, not sure what to do. It takes time to get used to the idea that you're having a baby everyone will disapprove of.'

Regina stared at her in dismay. 'I'm sorry. I'd completely forgotten.'

'What?'

'That you'd had a baby.'

'*I* hadn't forgotten. I wonder every day what my daughter's doing and if she's happy.'

Regina could have kicked herself for bringing that desperately sad look to her sister's face. 'Couldn't you try to trace her?'

'Maybe one day, when I've sorted out my life.' Minnie looked at her uncertainly. 'Don't push Nikki into doing something she doesn't want to. I've always regretted my baby being adopted.'

'Why did you agree to it, then?'

'I don't remember agreeing. They kept me heavily sedated after the birth. Father could have afforded to help me a bit, just till I got my degree, but he wouldn't. And then he . . . sent me into that place.'

'Because you needed professional help.'

'Did I? Or was it a convenient way to get rid of me while he dealt with the baby?'

Regina stared at her in horror. 'You can't mean that!'

'Can't I? I wasn't mad, though you'd think I was from the way I was treated. Postnatal depression, they call it today, and treat it as a temporary illness. I'd not have brought this up, only . . .' She laid one hand on her sister's arm. 'Don't force Nikki to get rid of her baby if she doesn't want to. She'll regret it every minute of her life if you do.'

There was silence for a few moments, then Regina said, 'Well, I still think she should have an abortion. It's very quick and easy now, and she's only six weeks along. But I can't actually force her, can I?'

'I hope not.'

'And I wouldn't do anything to hurt her.'

Miranda smiled. 'I can see that.'

When her sister went to her bedroom to tidy her hair, Regina began to clear up the kitchen. But she kept stopping to wipe her eyes. She hadn't realised exactly what her father had done – and she couldn't have stopped him even if she had known.

Surely her sister was mistaken? Surely it had been necessary to have her committed to a mental hospital?

Lou spent the morning thinking hard. He'd really enjoyed the evening spent with Miranda and now he was wondering if he'd done right by her in suggesting she live with him. She'd just spent years nursing her father, after all.

He grimaced. She wouldn't have years looking after him, only a few months, the cancer specialist said. The heart specialist said you could never tell, and he could live for years without doing anything about his condition, so the cancer would probably kill him first. But what would Minnie get for looking after him? Temporary asylum from her family then out on the streets again? Not good enough. He had to make it truly worth her while.

He was disgusted at how she'd been treated by her family. Like a child, that's what, and a stupid child at that. She wasn't stupid at all, rather the contrary. From her conversation last night, she'd read widely, was up to date on current affairs and even though she'd been trapped with her manipulative father, she'd used her computer to explore the world. No, she wasn't stupid, but she was amazingly timid where her family was concerned. The word 'cowed' kept creeping into his mind. What the hell had they done to her when she was younger?

He went across to get himself a glass of orange juice

– half a glass. If he poured out too much he would spill it as he moved jerkily across the room. His niece had bought him a plastic cup with a lid, a child's cup, dammit. He'd thrown it straight into the rubbish bin. Nothing tasted nice out of plastic and he wasn't going to be treated like a baby, not now nor at any stage in his final months.

Thuds from above his head had him wincing. He was sick of noise echoing into his home, wanted some peace and quiet and a better outlook than this. He could afford it. Why had he delayed making the changes?

He was selfish enough to hope Miranda would come and help him through his last few months. If he'd met her earlier in his life, he'd have been attracted to her, might even have ended up marrying her. Now, he had to guard against her getting too attached to him, for her own sake. It didn't matter how he felt. He could do nothing about it now except protect her.

He put the empty glass down as that thought sank in. He'd talked about Miranda helping him slay his current dragon, which was his niece with her plans to have him safely locked away for these final months, instead of allowing him to fly free while he still could.

But he wasn't the only one with dragons. Miranda had at least one, that damned brother of hers. Perhaps her half-sister too. No. Though they didn't seem close, she didn't speak nervously of Regina. If Miranda came to help him out, he might be able to help her slay her own dragon. She certainly needed help.

Tears came into his eyes as he suddenly realised that he could still be useful, even in his present condition. It'd be very satisfying to help a decent person like Miranda Fox rebuild her confidence and make a better life for herself.

He dashed away the tears, glad no one was there to see this weakness. It felt so good to be *useful* still. It'd been horrible for a man who'd always led a very active life to come out of hospital and feel he was just sitting around like a piece of rubbish, waiting to be disposed of.

Smiling, he went to switch on his computer and start a new folder, calling it 'Miranda's Dragons'. With many pauses for thought he began to make a list, this one for his eyes only.

The afternoon had nearly gone before he knew where he was. Air conditioning whispered quietly around him, keeping another hot day at bay, and the other tenants were mercifully quiet.

The doorbell roused him from his labours and he glanced at his watch. Damn! It'd be his niece. Hilary came round twice a week to bring him a supply of healthy meals, most of which he threw away after she'd gone.

He signed off. He not only had it password protected, he stored some files permanently on another site. She wasn't getting a chance to see what was on his computer, whatever happened. He rolled his wheelchair slowly along the corridor to the living room, making a mental note that somehow he must find a way to stop Hilary chasing Miranda away.

She had let herself in and dumped some shopping bags in the kitchen by the time he joined her.

'There you are, Uncle Louis. You look tired. You spend far too much time on that computer of yours, you know. Come and have a rest while I make your tea.'

He did as he was told because it was easier and, anyway, he was a bit tired.

'Have you thought any more about the care home I found, Uncle?'

'Of course not. I threw the brochures away. I've already told you I'm not ready for that sort of place.'

'You need to get everything sorted out before it's too late. You don't have to go into it immediately, though you might enjoy having company and activities. You spend far too much time on your own.'

He let her talk on because he knew he didn't have to do as she wanted. He'd better change the power of attorney he'd given her, though, to make sure she couldn't override his wishes towards the end. He'd do that tomorrow. He pulled out his little notebook and jotted it down. *See Sally Patel re power of attorney*. He had one of the smartest lawyers in town, and Sally was a friend as well.

Miranda was relieved when Regina decided to go round to visit Sebastian that afternoon. She needed to think about Lou's offer.

Having waved goodbye to her half-sister, Miranda

went to sit on the back veranda, staring out across the huge garden. The near part was immaculately cared for but too neat for her liking. She didn't like to see plants regimented like this and suspected they never did their best under such conditions. But her father had considered that to be the purpose of human intervention in the plant world: to tame nature and force order on it. Her own patch of garden was further towards the back, out of sight. There, plants flowered riotously and tomatoes grew so well in the warm summer sunshine she had to give some of them away to the neighbours.

She couldn't focus on her own problems, however, because she couldn't stop thinking of Nikki. Poor girl! She was even younger than Miranda had been when she'd made the same mistake. And though people said they understood, they didn't. It was terrifying as well as exciting to think that you'd created a new life, to know that your body now housed two people. She hoped Regina would bear in mind what she'd said, wished she could have a chat with Nikki, offer her support.

Why not? She did a quick calculation. They were seven hours ahead of England, so it was morning there and she might catch Nikki in. Going inside she picked up the phone and dialled her sister's number.

It was answered almost immediately. 'Hello?'

'Nikki? It's Miranda, your aunt.'

'Hi, Auntie Min. Is Mum with you?'

'No. I wanted to speak to you on my own. I'm

interfering, I know, but she told me about the baby.'

'Oh. Well, if you've rung to persuade me to get rid of it, I've not decided yet and it's up to me, don't you think?'

'I certainly do.'

'You do?'

'Yes. Did you know that I had a child when I was only a couple of years older than you?'

'*You* did?'

She sounded so incredulous, Miranda felt hurt. Did they think her too unattractive to attract a man? 'Yes, I did. They made me have it adopted and then acted as if she'd never existed.' She couldn't stop her voice wobbling.

'Oh, Auntie Min, I'm so sorry.'

'I am too. It was the wrong thing to do, for me anyway, but I always consoled myself with the thought that the baby would have a better life, because I knew my father would never accept her. He'd have made the child feel unwanted and unloved and no one should feel that. Anyway, what I rang for was to say, don't let them push you into anything you're not sure about. It's your decision, no one else's. And if you're short of money, I've got some tucked away and I'd be happy to help you.'

There was the sound of someone weeping. She waited a minute then said gently, 'Oh, Nikki. Have I upset you?'

'Only in a n–nice way. Auntie Min, I felt so alone in the world and suddenly you're there, on my side. You've no idea how much better that makes me feel.'

'I'm glad. I'm not very good at standing up to them, I'm afraid, so I think we'd better keep quiet about talking to one another. But if I can help, if you need something, well, I'm here.'

There was the sound of Nikki blowing her nose. 'I'll remember that.'

'What about the father?'

'He wants to keep it. But he's the same age as I am and we have no money, and we were both going to university. Is it fair to burden him with a child?'

'A child isn't a burden, it's a blessing.'

'To hear my mother talk, I've been nothing but a burden all my life.'

Miranda sighed. 'It's just her way. Regina does love you, I'm quite certain of that.'

'In her own way and on her own terms.'

'We can't help being ourselves.' Miranda waited a moment or two to see if there were any more confidences, then said gently, 'I'd better go now, Nikki dear. Your mother might come back at any minute. Shocking to be nervous of her at my age, isn't it? But she can be very intimidating when she gets angry!' Not in Sebastian's league, but then, Miranda had never seen anyone get into such rages as he did.

'Tell me about it.'

'I'll try to ring again, Nikki. Or you could email me.'

'Thanks. And look . . . I really do appreciate your support.'

She put the phone down, feeling it had been the right thing to do, at least it felt right to her. She remembered so clearly how alone she'd felt in the same situation.

The phone rang. Sebastian. Her heart jittered in her chest. 'Minnie! We're taking you to see the flat tonight. Be ready at seven.'

He rang off without waiting for a response.

She picked up the phone and rang Lou. 'Can I come round again tonight? I've had orders from my brother to go and see the flat with him. He put the phone down before I could say I was busy.'

He chuckled. 'Rebelling, eh? That's good. Yes, do come round. My niece has left me a healthy meal. We'll inspect it and if we don't fancy it, we'll get some Chinese food sent in.'

Miranda hummed as she got ready to leave. She particularly enjoyed writing a note to her brother. It was so much easier to face him in writing than to confront him in person.

Sorry I can't be here, Sebastian. I already had an engagement. You should have waited to find out if I was free before you put down the phone.
  Miranda

She wished she could see his face when he read the note, but on second thoughts was glad she'd not be there. She left it on the hall table, knowing he had a key to the house and would come in if he found the door locked. She'd had a new lock fitted to her bedroom door the year before and hadn't given him a key, so felt her personal possessions would be safe from his prying.

She should have taken her jewellery to the bank today. She had to pull herself together and do that, if nothing else, tomorrow. If the worst came to the worst and she needed money to tide her over, she could probably sell some of the pieces. Her father had always said it was quite good stuff.

Lou got out two of his best wine glasses, feeling happier than he had for a while. Having a friend made such a difference and he'd been travelling a lot till the heart attack, so his friends were mostly scattered round the world. Most of the people he knew in Perth were up to their eyeballs in deals and business, a world he could no longer keep up with.

He studied the contents of the casserole dish: chicken and some strips of vegetables. He tasted it and found it totally bland, like all Hilary's dishes. He'd told her there was nothing wrong with his digestive system, but she still kept providing food for invalids.

He smiled when he heard the doorbell and pressed the button that opened the outer door without checking who it was. Who else could it be but his new friend?

Miranda stopped in the doorway. 'You're sure you don't mind me inviting myself round?'

'I'm delighted. I get lonely on my own.'

'So do I.'

She was looking better, he decided, had some colour

in her cheeks. If she wore prettier clothes and had her hair restyled instead of tying it back in an untidy bunch, she'd be quite good-looking for a woman of her age. He'd always found fair-haired, blue-eyed women attractive. 'How old are you?'

'Forty-seven.'

'You're wearing well. You don't look more than forty, if that.'

'How old are you, Lou?'

'Sixty-eight physically, and it varies between ten and twenty-five mentally. Now, before you sit down and try this lovely wine, come and give me your opinion of this sad-looking casserole.'

They stared at the beige concoction together.

'It's not very attractive,' she said. 'Can I have a taste?'

'If you can face it.'

She took a small amount of the sauce and shook her head as she swallowed it. 'Your niece could easily have made this more interesting. If you have some herbs and spices, I could tiddle with it. It's a shame to waste good food.'

'Go for your life. I usually dump her offerings in the rubbish bin and order a takeaway.'

'I like cooking, though Father only ever wanted plain, old-fashioned meat and two veggies. Can I look in your kitchen cupboards?'

'Be my guest. I'll pour the wine.'

Half an hour later they sat down to a much-enhanced casserole with a curry sauce, served with rice fried with onions and shreds of this and that.

'Politically incorrect, so much fried stuff,' he teased.

'I know. But I love spicy food and Father hated it, wouldn't have it in the house.'

'I love it, too.'

When they'd finished, he raised his glass. 'Here's to us. We're going to make an excellent team.'

'We are?'

'Definitely. Come and sit down. Leave the washing-up.'

'Why leave the washing-up when you have a dishwasher? It won't take me a minute to load it.'

When they were sitting down, she glanced at the clock and sighed happily. 'Sebastian will be getting to the house just about now.'

Lou raised his glass. 'May he be extremely irritated. He deserves it.'

She clinked her glass against his.

Lying on the sofa with her head on his lap, Nikki told Tim about the call from her aunt.

'She sounds lovely.'

'I've always thought her colourless. She hardly has a word to say for herself. Mind you, Uncle Sebastian tends to dominate the conversation and from what I remember, my grandfather was even worse. Fancy my little Aunt Minnie having had a child! But I don't want to ask for her help unless I have to, because they'll create a fuss and she's so soft she lets them boss her around.'

Tim began fiddling with her hair absent-mindedly. 'I'm going to tell my family about the baby tomorrow. Father's away on a training programme till then. I don't know whether they'll help us, but if not, maybe we could borrow some money from your aunt, just to get us into rented accommodation till we can sort out jobs.'

'I want to finish school first and get my A levels, at least. I'm pretty sure Mum will let me stay here to do that, even if I don't agree to an abortion. But it won't be pleasant, so I may have to move out.'

He began fiddling with the neckline of her T-shirt. 'You've decided then? About the baby?'

'I'm pretty sure I'm going to keep it.'

He let out a deep sigh. 'I'm so glad. I hated the thought of you killing our child.'

She heard him swallow hard and when he said nothing for a few moments, she stole a glance up and saw tears trickling down his cheeks. He was such a softie. That was one of the many things she loved about him. 'I'm glad we're together again, Tim.'

'Me, too. I really love you, Nikki. Look, I think we should get married, and the sooner the better.'

It was her turn to fall silent. Did she want to get married? She wasn't sure. Eighteen was a bit young to commit yourself for life. 'Let's . . . um, think about that sort of thing later. One step at a time. We'll see what your parents say first. And we don't have to get married to live together. These days it's the done thing to try before you buy.'

'Having a baby makes me feel rather old-fashioned,' Tim said thoughtfully.

Out of politeness Sebastian rang the doorbell at what he still thought of as his father's house. There was no answer and the front door was locked, so he used his key and led the way inside.

It was Regina who saw the piece of paper on the hall table. 'There's a note from Minnie!' She read it then held it out to him.

He stared down at it, outrage on his face. 'What does she think she's playing at? I told her to be ready at seven.'

'She says she had a prior engagement. Did you even ask her if she was free?'

'Of course not. Why should I? She's never had engagements before. She was with Father most of the time.'

'There's no reason she can't have friends.'

'I'd prefer to know about them.'

Regina looked at him in surprise. 'Why? It's none of your business.'

'I promised Father I'd keep an eye on her.'

'You mean you want to control what she does.'

'Well, why not? She's as naïve as they come, as well as being unstable. She'd get cheated out of that money in no time flat if I let go of the purse strings.'

Regina went to the kitchen with her brother trailing behind her, still radiating annoyance. 'You're out of order, you know, Sebastian. That will is totally unfair.

You've got your money and I've got mine. Why should hers be tied up?'

'I've told you.'

'No. You've told me the cover story. What you really mean is you want the money for your children.'

He shrugged and didn't deny it. 'Yours too. And let's face it, Minnie isn't going to do much with it, is she? She's a homebody, doesn't travel, isn't likely to marry.'

'Why not?'

'Have you looked at her? She dresses like a cleaning woman, has no style. And what if she left the money to some loony charity or other? That'd be wrong, that's what upset Father.'

She kept the thought to herself that Sebastian had probably used that as a selling point for setting up the trust. 'What's the flat like?'

'Compact but very nice. It's in a good area.'

'She hasn't even seen it. She may hate it.'

'Even Minnie isn't that stupid.'

She picked up a bottle. 'Want a glass of wine?'

'I'm driving.'

'I'll drink your share, then. Father certainly didn't stint himself on wine, did he?'

'He liked a drop in the evening. I must take this lot over to my house.'

'What about Minnie? She likes the odd drink, too.'

He went to inspect the rows of bottles in the little room attached to the kitchen and whistled. 'There's some really good stuff here. It'd be wasted on her. She has no palate for good wines or she'd not be drinking that wooded Chardonnay that bludgeons the taste buds.'

Miranda sipped her second glass with appreciation. 'I really like this wine. It's light on the palate yet with a full-bodied taste.'

'You know about wine?'

'A little. Father considered himself a connoisseur and insisted I share a special bottle with him sometimes. He could be good company until recently, when there were just the two of us.'

'I just buy what my wine merchant recommends. He's not let me down. I've more bottles where that came from and you can help me get through them.'

She looked at him ruefully. 'You're leading me astray.'

'I hope so. It's about time you stepped off the narrow, stony path and ran through a meadow full of buttercups at dawn.'

'What a lovely image!'

'It's a real memory not an image. I've done it. Have you?' He leant forward and took her glass gently from her hand. 'Miranda, I really meant what I said. I'd like you to come and live with me, help me enjoy these last few months and, in return, I'll leave you some of my money.'

She looked at him in shock. 'I don't need you to leave me money to persuade me to help you.'

'I have to leave it to someone. I can't leave it all to my niece. There's far more than she needs.'

'Oh.' She didn't know what to say.

'The main thing is to get you installed here, so you're safe from his bullying. Hilary was on at me again yesterday to go into a hospice – she's careful not to say the "H" word aloud, calls it a care home, but that's what it is. When you fled to me from your brother tonight, it all seemed so right. I'd love some company – but not in this dump. Is your new flat any better?'

'I don't know. I've not seen it.'

'Then go and do that tomorrow, just to be sure.'

'Will you come with me?'

'You're that frightened of your brother?'

She nodded. 'I always wind up doing what he wants because he makes it seem so reasonable and what I want sound stupid. I suppose that comes of him being a lawyer.'

Lou leant back. 'Yeah, lawyers can certainly twist your words. But the good ones can be enormously helpful.' He pulled a face. 'All right. I'll come. But tell him we'll meet him there. I'll drive you.'

'You'll find him . . . intimidating.'

He grinned. 'No, I won't. One thing about being in your last few months of life is you don't find people intimidating any more. Though I never did, actually, always was a cocky devil. Will Sebastian wait for you at your house tonight?'

'I doubt it.'

'Then you can go home safely and get a good night's sleep. We'll call you a taxi.'

'It's not far. I can walk.'

'Not at night, you can't, not these days. I'll give the taxi driver a big tip to see you safely inside and he'll be delighted to earn so much for a short trip.'

'Are you rich enough to throw money around?'

'I am pretty comfortable. Look . . . didn't your father leave you any money at all?'

'No. It's all in a trust, to be doled out by Sebastian and the lawyer. I don't even know how much.'

'We'll have to challenge the will, I think. Trouble is, I won't be here to see that through. It's a time-consuming business.'

'I wish you wouldn't keep talking about dying.'

He looked at her very steadily. 'I have to keep saying it because *you* need to understand that it's going to happen, and quite soon. I don't want you doing anything stupid like falling in love with me. And I shan't fall in love with you, either.' He held out his hand. 'Bargain?'

She took it reluctantly and shook it.

'Do you have Sebastian's home phone number with you?'

'I know it by heart.'

'Then ring him and say you'll meet him or a representative from the lawyer at the flat at eleven o'clock in the morning.'

'What if he refuses?'

'You just repeat the same thing and keep on saying it. It's called the broken-record trick and it's very useful when someone disagrees with you or you want to make a point. You have to stop running away from trouble, Miranda my dear. You're an intelligent woman and can rely on your own judgement. One day, if we play this game properly, we'll destroy your dragon of a brother's power over you and you'll be free to enjoy the rest of your life in your own way.'

'I can't imagine that. Even when he's not there, I seem to feel his presence.' She picked up Lou's hand and raised it to her cheek. 'I shan't promise not to get *fond* of you.'

He grinned. 'OK. It's a bargain. You can get fond of me, and I'll get fond of you, but don't fall in love with me. Now, make that call to the big, bad dragon.'

She picked up the phone. 'Sebastian?'

'Where the hell are you, Minnie?'

'With my friend. I'm just ringing to say I'll be available to see the flat at eleven o'clock in the morning.'

'Not convenient for me.'

'Then send someone to let me in. I can perfectly well walk round the flat on my own. I'll meet whoever it is there.'

There was a silence, then, 'Oh, very well.' He gave her the address.

She clicked off the phone and let out her breath in a whoosh. 'I did it.'

'Good. And I don't let my phone number register on caller ID, so he won't be able to ring back. Pick up that glass of wine and let's talk about something more pleasant. What sort of house shall we look for?'

'One that's available immediately.'

'That's my girl! You've got a good brain. Availability is the necessary first criterion.' He pulled out his notebook.

A little later she could see he was tired, so said she was and took the taxi home. No one was there but she was glad of that, and since she knew what all the creaks sounded like, she didn't let them worry her, but slept soundly, pretty certain that with Lou by her side, she'd manage to hold her own.

Surely she would?

Chapter Four

When the doorbell went at nine o'clock the next morning, Miranda thought it was Sebastian and her heart began to thud with apprehension as she went to open it. She found Lou on the doorstep and saw his wheelchair sitting on the path at the foot of the veranda steps. Knowing how hard it'd been for him to get up the stairs, she asked immediately, 'Is something wrong?'

'Nothing wrong, but I wanted to talk to you before we go to see the flat. I'm on my way back from a physio session – that guy's a sadist but he keeps me moving. Am I allowed to come inside?'

'Oh, sorry. Do come in.' She let him lead the way at his own pace. 'Kitchen or sitting room?'

'Kitchen.' He sat at the table with a sigh of relief. 'Steps are getting harder to manage.' He looked round and wrinkled his nose in displeasure. 'Couldn't your father afford to modernise this place?'

'He liked it this way.'

'I bet he didn't have to do the cooking.'

'No. He never cooked a meal in his life, except for making toast or sandwiches in emergencies. Coffee?'

'No time.' He looked at his watch. 'I've got an appointment set up for you with my lawyer in the city in half an hour – if that's all right with you? I thought you might like to have her for your lawyer too, you see. She's as shrewd as they come. I'd match her against your brother any time.'

'Is it worth all the hassle?'

'Wrong question.'

She looked at him in puzzlement. 'What's the right question?'

'The right question is: do you want to give Sebastian some grief over what he's done to you or do you want to play doormat and let him continue to walk all over you?'

She winced at that image. 'But will it do any good seeing a lawyer? He's a lawyer himself and is bound to have drawn up a watertight will.'

Lou grinned. 'Who knows? At the very least it'll upset him. I'd count that a success.'

She couldn't help smiling. 'Yes. It's a nice thought. But aren't lawyers expensive? I don't have a lot of money to spare.'

'I'm paying.' He held up one hand to forestall her protest. 'It's chicken feed to me, Miranda, and I'm really going to enjoy pushing your brother's buttons.'

'But you've never met him. You might . . . get on with him quite well. Most people do.'

'No, I shan't. I've met you and I like you very much, therefore I'm on your side, not his.' He waited and watched her blush at the compliment.

She spread her hands helplessly. 'All right. I'll give it a go. I'll contest the will. But I'm sure I won't be very good if it comes to court. He can out-argue me any time.'

'You don't have to argue with him. That's the whole point. Your lawyer and I will speak for you most of the time. Though I do think you should try to join in the mêlée now and then, just to show willing.'

'I can only promise to do my best.'

He didn't comment on the fact that her voice shook as she said that. 'Right, grab your handbag and whatever else you need and we'll be off for the first round.'

She started towards her bedroom, then turned to ask, 'Would you mind if I called at my bank on the way back?'

'Of course not. If you need some cash . . .'

'No, it's not that.' She explained about the jewellery. 'Good girl. You're showing a bit of sense there. And we'll get the other pieces back for you, too.'

Sally Patel held the door open for Lou Rayne and his wheelchair. He was one of her favourite clients. She studied the woman whose cause he was championing with great interest. She might have known Lou wouldn't fade away quietly.

He explained the situation, bringing Miranda into the conversation at intervals until gradually she was speaking freely and he was keeping quiet.

'I'd be delighted to help,' Sally said.

'You don't think . . . it's a waste of time?'

'It may or may not be, but I think you have a chance. And as Lou said, it'll waste your brother's time too. I hear Monsieur Fox has a heavy case load on at the moment. It's a great time to hit him with something else.' She grinned. 'Though I'd deny saying that.'

Sally wouldn't put into words to anyone what she really thought of Sebastian Fox, with whom she'd crossed swords several times in and out of court. The nicest thing she could say about him was that he was quite a good lawyer, even if he was a cold fish. The worst, that he was a covert racist and sexist.

'Can you come with us to see him today, Sally?'

'Sorry, Lou, I'm expecting a client I can't put off. Also, I want to check a few things before I confront him. When I'm ready, I'll make an appointment for us to see him together.' She could see Miranda's expression go apprehensive and felt sorry for the poor cowed creature. 'Don't worry. I won't let him eat you.'

She watched them leave and thought Lou was looking much better today, more alive in the head, however much his body was playing up. She was glad he had this to take his mind off things. Lou Rayne wasn't born to be idle.

Her new client didn't know much about Lou, that was clear, and he'd told Sally he didn't want Miranda to be enlightened as to how rich he was, because it might frighten her away. Pity, that. It'd have been a useful weapon against Sebastian Fox to reveal exactly who he was butting heads with.

To her horror, Miranda found Sebastian waiting for them at the flat not his clerk. She took an involuntary step backwards.

'I had a client cancel, so I came myself to show you how good this place is,' he said by way of greeting. He looked at Lou and then back at her questioningly.

'This is my . . . um, friend, Lou Rayne.' She hated the way her voice fluttered with nervousness.

The two men shook hands, Sebastian clearly dismissing Lou as a nonentity. He began to stride round the living area pointing out its features.

'Just a minute,' Lou said. 'I can't walk as fast as you.'

'It's Minnie who needs to see the flat.'

'I thought her name was Miranda.'

Sebastian made a scornful noise. 'She's never been called that in our family.'

''Bout time you started then if it's what she prefers.' Lou turned to her. 'There are steps up to the dining area. Bad choice, that, as you get older.'

Sebastian answered for her. 'There's nothing wrong with Minnie! And she's not exactly old yet.'

'There was nothing wrong with me two years ago.' Lou winked at her. 'Give me a hand, darling.'

She blinked at the endearment, but somehow his wink and the warmth of his arm linked into hers gave her the courage to ignore Sebastian's frown and help

Lou slowly and painfully up the stairs. She'd never seen him show so much difficulty in moving and it suddenly occurred to her that he was exaggerating. Oh, he was a darling, clever man!

'Not a big dining area,' Lou said. 'What shall we do when we have friends round?'

The sight of Sebastian's shock at this, on top of everything else, made her giggle and she hastily turned it into a cough. 'I don't know. And there's only just room for one small sofa and an armchair in the sitting area. Oh, didn't you say there was a balcony, Sebastian?'

They moved towards it and found it had barely enough room for the two small outdoor chairs and tiny table that were squashed there.

'Mean, I call that,' Lou said. 'Could you find nothing better than this place for your sister, Fox?'

'This flat is perfectly adequate for Minnie.'

'You can't know that till you ask her opinion, which I gather you didn't. Let's look at the bedrooms, then.'

Miranda grew angry as she went into a bedroom only just big enough for a double bed and a second room big enough to accommodate a single bed and not much else.

'Your father must have had less money than you thought, Miranda dear,' Lou said, 'or he'd have got you something better than this cat-box.'

'Look here, Rayne, I don't appreciate your snide comments and—'

Miranda surprised herself by interrupting. 'Lou's only saying what I'm thinking. We often think alike, don't we . . .' She summoned up her courage and added, 'dear' before turning to her brother. 'Is this really all Father could afford for me?'

'It's all you need.'

'No, it isn't.'

The look Sebastian threw at Lou would have soured milk. Then he looked at his watch. 'I can't stay much longer. When do you want to move in?'

'We'll take over here as soon as you hand us the keys,' Lou said. 'I'll help Miranda arrange the move.'

'*Minnie* can surely do that herself.'

'Miranda,' she corrected.

'I can never think of you as anything else, I'm afraid.'

'That's a pity, because you'll find I don't respond to anything but my real name from now on.' Suddenly words burst out. 'I'm going to do what *I* want from now on, which includes using my real name.'

She might just as well have kept that thought to herself.

'You'll soon forget this stupid whim, as you've forgotten others over the years.' Sebastian took a key off a labelled key ring he'd been jangling. 'You'll have to get another key cut if you need one for your . . . friend. I'll keep this one as a spare, just for safety, in case you lock yourself out. I'll come over to Father's tonight and discuss what furniture you can take from there. No need to buy new things when there's plenty of stuff going free.'

'I have my own furniture.'

He waved one hand dismissively. 'Antiques won't fit

in here. You need minimalist stuff. I'll take your antiques off your hands, save you the trouble of putting them up for auction. I'll get them valued, give you thirty percent less, to allow for the commission you'd pay at an auction and—'

'You are such a cheapskate,' Lou said in a cheerful, conversational tone.

Apart from a quick hiss of breath, there was no response as Sebastian glared at him, then turned to leave without waiting for his sister's answer.

Lou nudged her and whispered, 'Tell him about Sally.'

Miranda rushed to bar the doorway with one arm. 'Just one more thing. My lawyer will be in touch with you shortly, Sebastian. I'm not happy about how things have been left, so I'm taking legal advice.'

He spun round again, gaping at her and then scowling at Lou. 'I suppose I have *you* to thank for this.'

She was so angry at being ignored she raised her voice. 'No, you have *me* to thank. I'm the one who's hired a lawyer. I'm the one you're trying to cheat out of my inheritance.'

'If you ever say that again, I'll make you very sorry indeed!' he bellowed. 'And why on earth are you complaining? We've found you a home at a good address. What more do you need?'

She gestured around. 'This place could never feel like home. There's the money, too. You won't even tell me how much income I'm entitled to from the trust.' She took a deep breath and remembered what

Sally and Lou had dinned into her. 'My lawyer will be dealing with that. I've been instructed to say as little as possible.'

'Whoever you've hired, you're wasting your money. Believe me, I know how to write a will.'

'Sally Patel doesn't think so.' Miranda was delighted to see his mouth fall open in shock.

'I don't believe it! She'd not take on such a petty case.'

'She already has done.'

'Well, I'm very busy so your irresponsible lawsuit will have to damned well wait,' he said at once. 'I've got important cases and I can't possibly deal with such a minor matter now.'

'It's not minor to me,' she said quietly. 'I'm fighting for my happiness here.'

Again he looked at Lou instead of her. 'I resent your interference, Rayne.'

'All I did was introduce her to Sally. *You* set up the situation here by buying this cat-box without consulting her.'

Sebastian might have been sucking a lemon, so sour was his expression, but in the presence of another person he was at least holding back the anger he'd normally have unleashed on her, Miranda thought gratefully. It might be cowardly but she did so hate it when he shouted and shoved her against walls. He'd even shaken her hard once or twice until their father had stopped him.

'I'll see Sally when I have time and not before.'

After he'd gone, Lou went across to the wheelchair

and sank down in it with a groan of relief. 'Hurts to stand for too long. Come and sit on those steps for a minute.'

She sat beside him in the empty echoing room. 'I hate it here.'

'Who wouldn't? Congratulations on standing up to him.'

'He'll find a way to get what he wants, though. He always does.'

'We'll give him a run for his money, though. Now, let's get a locksmith in. We don't want him given access to this place day and night, do we?'

She looked at him in delight. 'Why didn't I think of that?'

'You've not had the practice I have at dealing with conniving rats. By the time I die, you'll be a much more cunning person, I promise you; a real she-devil.'

She got up and gave him a hug. 'Thank you.'

He patted her cheek as she started to move away and the smile they shared seemed to warm her right through.

Regina studied Minnie as they enjoyed cups of tea together that afternoon. 'Well, you certainly upset Seb today. He took Dorothy and me out to lunch and never smiled once. When I asked how you liked your flat, he said you were being influenced by some cheapskate businessman who was playing the sympathy card.'

'Lou's never asked for sympathy from me or anyone else.'

'Can I meet this friend of yours? I'm curious.'

'Lou's got a medical appointment this afternoon and will need to rest tonight.'

'Seb said he was in a wheelchair.'

'Yes.' She changed the subject. It was no business of Regina's what was wrong with Lou, especially as the information would inevitably get back to Sebastian. 'Have you rung Nikki today? Is she all right?'

'I'm not going to ring her. She put the phone down on me last time.'

'You must have upset her.'

'Well, she's upset me, too. When I think of all the time and effort I've invested in her – children can be very ungrateful.'

'She's legally an adult at eighteen, and these decisions affect her life, not yours.'

'Minnie, keep out of it. You don't understand.' The minute the words had left her mouth, Regina wished them unsaid because if anyone did understand it was her sister. She changed the subject. 'Look, Sebastian said we should go through the furniture and sort out what you want for the flat. Do you want to do that now? Apparently some of the furniture belongs to you already, but he's going to buy it off you.'

She smiled. 'He's really miffed about having to do that, because he's had his eye on that chest of drawers and some other pieces for a while.'

'Good. He deserves to be miffed. And look, I want you to call me by my proper name: Miranda.'

Regina looked at her in surprise. 'Does it mean that much to you?'

'Yes.'

'Well, I'll try then. I may make a few mistakes till I get used to it.'

'Thank you.'

After another silence, but not an awkward one, Regina said, 'You ought to know – Dorothy brought me here this morning while you were looking at the flat. She said she wanted to check the measurements of some of the furniture. Apparently you've had the lock on your bedroom door changed.'

Miranda could feel herself stiffening. 'She tried to go into my bedroom even now, after I'd told them all the things in there were mine?'

Regina nodded. 'I told her I thought it wrong, but she said Seb particularly wanted her to make a list of all the furniture there. She's always a very obedient little wifey, isn't she? Do you think she's afraid of him?'

'Could be. They used to argue at first, but then they settled down. You can never tell what she's thinking, though.'

She walked to and fro, too angry to sit down. 'Sebastian's gone too far this time. There are quite a few other pieces around the place that are mine, not just the ones in my bedroom. I suppose she checked those?' Miranda looked at her sister, who nodded. 'Why did you tell me what Dorothy did? You're usually on his side.'

'I'm not on his side. I just can't see the point of arguing

with him when I live ten thousand miles away. But this time, well, as I've told you, I think the will was unfair.'

'I've got a lawyer looking at whether I have any grounds for contesting it, a very good lawyer.'

Regina let out a long, low whistle. 'Sebastian didn't mention that when I told him he was being greedy.'

'That's a good word for him, greedy.' Miranda looked at a small bureau, a very pretty piece. Did she dare? Yes, she did. She began taking out the drawers and tipping their contents on to the floor.

'What on earth are you doing?'

'Taking the things that are mine, like this bureau, and moving out. You can phone Sebastian, if you want, but he won't be able to stop me. I can prove that everything I'm taking is mine.'

'I wouldn't do that to you.' Regina grinned. 'In fact, I'll help you move. Do you want to call your friend Lou, too?'

Miranda shook her head. 'No. I'm going to put them in that horrible little flat and I can do this on my own. Lou's a bit tired after today's excursions.' She picked up the phone directory. 'First I'd better arrange a removalist.'

The first company she rang could come round to do a small load if they started at six o'clock the following morning. It seemed like an omen.

Energised, she turned her attention to emptying the things out of her furniture.

Sebastian would be more angry than ever. But she wouldn't be here to see it.

Nikki started the day by throwing up, hardly managing to get to the bathroom on time. Afterwards she felt like death warmed up, but still better than she had for a while, so decided to risk going to school.

Tim hurried across as soon as he saw her come through the gates. 'You look dreadful. You should have stayed at home.'

'I have two important tests today. And I can't spend the next seven months in bed, can I?'

'What if you have to rush out to be sick?'

'I'm hoping not to. I feel a bit better this morning.'

But halfway through the first test nausea overcame her again.

Clapping one hand to her mouth, she ran.

Unfortunately the school nurse was passing and followed her into the girls' toilets, waiting till she came out of the cubicle to interrogate her.

'Have you got an upset stomach?'

Nikki hesitated then shook her head, sick of telling lies. 'No. I'm pregnant.'

'Oh. Does your mother know?'

'Yes. And I'll have left school by the time I get big, so I just want to continue studying till the exams are over. I might as well get some qualifications while I can.'

'That's very sensible.' The nurse's voice was more sympathetic than Nikki had expected. 'What are you going to do afterwards?'

She turned away, fighting tears. 'I don't know. Mum wants me to have an abortion. I'm not sure.'

'It's a big decision. Perhaps you could talk to the counsellor about it?'

How stupid could you get? The idea of seeing the counsellor hadn't even occurred to Nikki. 'Good idea.'

'What about the baby's father?'

'He's – um, my age, so we're seeing his parents tonight. Mum will be back from Australia next week and we'll both talk to her then. Granddad died and she had to go to the funeral.'

'Stay in the rest room. I'll fetch your test and you can finish it there.'

'Thank you.'

'I'm here to help, you know. Any time.'

Strange, Nikki thought. She'd not even considered seeking help at school. The nurse could be a terror with malingerers but today she'd been very supportive.

If only her mother would be the same.

The following morning Miranda waited for the removalists to pick up the furniture that belonged to her. She was taking every single piece she had because she didn't trust her brother. There was also a pile of rubbish bin liners stuffed full of her other possessions, and boxes of books. She'd take the computer herself.

Regina had gone back to Sebastian's at about eleven o'clock last night, but Miranda had worked until nearly one o'clock, getting up again at five to continue sorting and packing.

The house looked as if a cyclone had raged through

it, because she'd simply tipped the contents of each piece of furniture out on to the floor and left the piles there. Regina had giggled every time they did that and in the end they'd had fun together.

Miranda couldn't remember a time when they'd got on this well. Regina had left home at eighteen to study at Sydney University. Then her sister had gone to work in England, marrying an Englishman. The marriage had only lasted a year or so, and the family had never met him. Long enough for her sister to have a child, and keep it too. She'd never come back to live in Australia, though their father had tried to persuade her. Indeed, she'd only visited them two or three times, once bringing her daughter.

Regina arrived just before the removalists were due.

'I didn't expect to see you again today. Wasn't Sebastian suspicious about why you were coming back?'

'He wasn't up.' She peered into the sitting room, shuddering at the sight of piles of papers. 'You know, there might be important stuff among these.'

'If so, Sebastian can look for it. He made a point of me not touching any of Father's papers, so let him deal with them.'

'He's made you very angry, hasn't he? I've never seen you like this.'

'I've never been this angry in my whole life before.' Miranda paused in surprise. 'It feels good, actually.'

'Not even when they made you have your baby adopted?'

'I don't remember that time very clearly. They kept me drugged.' She fumbled in her pocket for a handkerchief and blew her nose firmly, determined not to cry. Then she remembered the list she'd made as it fluttered to the ground. 'Give this to Sebastian when you see him, will you? I was going to ask the removalists to sign it, but you'd be better.'

'What is it?'

'A list of what I've taken. I'd be grateful if you'd tick off the pieces of furniture as they're loaded into the van and tell him that nothing else was taken.'

'Surely that's not necessary?'

'I think it is. Sebastian's insisted on me proving that I've inherited these things from my Auntie Con, even though he knew perfectly well I had.'

Regina gaped at her. 'What's wrong with the man? Even I know you aren't the sort to tell lies. Can I come and see you at your new place before I leave?'

'I wasn't sure you'd want to. But it'll look more like a storage dump with my furniture in it.'

'I do want to. And by the way . . . I like this new Min – *Miranda* better than the old one.' Regina began fiddling with some papers. 'I hadn't realised, you know.'

'Realised what?'

'How badly Sebastian's been treating you. I'm surprised Father let him.'

'You know Father. He always sided with the men and he truly believed women's brains weren't as good as men's.'

'But he left *me* the money to do with as I please.'

'You're an accountant, and he always seemed to think you were an exception to the rule. I wasn't. And Sebastian must have thought you'd make a fuss if he didn't let you have your money. He knows I've always hated fusses. Well, it's been more than fusses. He can get into quite a rage.'

'I still find it hard to believe even Father would go so far.'

'In the last year or two, he was growing rather forgetful. Dementia starting, the doctor thought.'

'Oh, no! Why didn't you say?'

'Sebastian insisted we keep it to ourselves, said there was no need to worry you.'

'He knew?'

'Yes, of course.' Miranda was surprised when Regina came and gave her a big hug. 'You don't usually hug people.'

'Don't I? I used to think I had the keep-your-distance gene, like Sebastian and Dad. But once I got away, I found I didn't. I'm not a kissy-kissy sort of person to strangers, but for those I like, it's different.'

'That's a good way to describe it: *keep-your-distance gene*. I can't remember Father ever cuddling me. Can you?'

'No, never.'

'Do you cuddle Nikki?'

'I used to. Not now. Teenagers don't like being cuddled by their parents, at least she doesn't, so I have to keep my distance.'

'Lou's a very touchy-feely person. He hugs me quite often.' And she'd not hesitated to hug him. 'I think the keep-your-distance gene must have missed both you and me.'

Regina squeezed her hand, as if she could read her thoughts. 'I hope things go well for you with Lou. It's about time you met someone to love.'

Miranda nearly blurted out that she didn't dare fall in love with Lou, but held back. 'I'd better get going now.' She took a last look round and walked out to her car, carrying a bag of ripe tomatoes and a few other things from her garden. She'd miss her plants and flowers very much.

She was leaving her furniture at the flat for the moment. It was, after all, free storage space. The removal men dumped it where she told them to and the place soon filled up. They joked about needing a shoehorn to fit all those big pieces in, but she couldn't even smile at their joke.

When they'd gone, she put the kettle on. 'I hate it,' she said aloud. 'I'm not going to weep, though.'

She did but not for long. After she'd pulled herself together, she rang Lou and told him what she'd done.

He cheered down the phone. 'Well done, you! I'm coming round. Give me an hour. I'm expecting my niece any moment, but I'll get rid of Hilary quickly.'

'I'll go and get us something for tea. If you'd like to stay, that is.'

'That'd be wonderful. I'm too tired to go to a restaurant and celebrate as we ought to.'

'Celebrate what?'

'You, Miranda. You're starting to come out of your shell. I'd love to see your brother's face when he finds you've gone and sees the piles of stuff all over the floor.' He laughed again.

So did she. The smile still lingered as she put the phone down. Lou did that to her.

Why did she have to meet someone like him too late for anything to come of it? This inevitably made her think of Brody, the father of her child. He'd never got in touch. How hard had he tried? She still dreamt about him sometimes. She'd fallen hard for him. It had made her believe in soulmates and magic and happy ever after. For a short time.

Tim squeezed Nikki's hand. 'Cheer up! My mum and dad aren't going to shoot you at dawn.'

'No, but they can't be pleased about this.' She patted her stomach where the tiny creature who was causing her so much discomfort lay hidden, not even making a bump yet.

'We'll manage,' he said quietly. 'I'm not letting you face this on your own and I'll create a huge fuss if anyone tries to get rid of my baby.' He paused and added, 'You included.'

His expression was so serious she knew he meant it. Since she'd told him, Tim seemed much more mature, while she felt more vulnerable, more lacking in confidence than ever before. He parked his ratty old car in the street and came round to open her door. Normally she'd have got out already but today she was dreading facing his parents.

His mother came to the front door looking very solemn and Nikki reached for Tim's hand.

Mrs Heyter gave her a wry smile. 'You look terrified. Am I so fierce? Oh, Nikki, don't cry. Hush now.'

She was enfolded in a warm embrace. 'It's the hormones, Mrs H. I even cry at the news on TV if it's sad. I can't help it.'

'I was just the same with Tim. Come and sit down.'

Mr Heyter was hovering by the window looking uncomfortable. He nodded to her and took a seat next to his wife, but left her to do the speaking.

'Tim says you're not sure whether to keep the baby or not.'

Nikki hesitated. She'd seen another of those videos on the Internet that morning and, even at seven weeks, had been able to see a baby's heart beating and the outline of its little body. That had shaken her. 'I do want to keep it, but Mum wants me to have an abortion and she's due back from Australia soon.'

'We want you to keep it, too,' Mrs Heyter said, 'but it's not going to be easy. We've not told Tim yet, but Jim's firm is making a lot of people redundant. He's been offered another job, only it means us moving up to Newcastle upon Tyne. That was why he went on this course.' She looked at her husband, who nodded solemnly.

Nikki clutched Tim's hand even more tightly.

'We can give you a bit of money towards setting up together in a flat. Would your mother help too, Nikki?'

'I don't think so. She said if I kept the baby, I'd be on my own and I can't stay with her afterwards because *she* doesn't want to be involved in raising another child.'

Their soft murmurs of sympathy nearly had her in tears again. 'My aunt rang up from Australia and said she'd help, but I don't think she has much money and anyway, even if she wasn't living on the other side of the world, she's no good at standing up to Mum and Uncle Sebastian. She's, like, the family doormat, poor thing.'

'Well, there's no rush to do anything tomorrow, is there? We're not moving for a couple of months because Jim has to help close things down at this end. But with two other children to raise, we can't do as much as we'd like for you and there simply isn't room for you to come to us.'

As they drove home, Nikki thought how kind the Heyters had been and tears welled in her eyes again.

'What's the matter?'

'I'm thinking how kind your parents were, even though they've got their own problems. And my mother is . . .' She didn't try to finish the sentence, didn't need to. He'd met her mother. He knew what her mother was like. She wasn't unfair or anything, but she always felt she knew best.

The school nurse had been kind too, and, next week, Nikki was seeing a counsellor.

But though she tried to put on a brave face, she was terrified. She woke at night just about shivering with fear. She wasn't ready to become a mother, didn't know the first thing about babies, didn't want to give up her plans for university. She'd worked so hard to get on to an engineering course.

Her mother was right about one thing. She had been stupid. She shouldn't have risked anything once she realised she'd forgotten her birth control pills.

Chapter Five

Lou knocked on the door of Miranda's flat, grateful there was a lift. When she opened it, he said nothing about the fact that she'd obviously been crying, just reached up from his wheelchair and pulled her down for a quick hug. 'Clever woman! It can't have been easy.'

'No. I hardly got any sleep last night for worrying.'

He held out the bag. 'Wine. For our celebration.' He rolled inside, stopped and whistled softly. 'You'll have to clear me a path through the debris first.'

'I wouldn't have brought this much furniture with me, but Sebastian is still checking whether these really are my things and I thought if I left them behind, I might never see them again. It's a terrible thing not to trust your own brother.'

'I get the impression he's not one of Sally's favourite people, either.'

'What if he refuses to see her?'

He laughed heartily. 'No one refuses Sally Patel.

That woman will be a judge one day soon, mark my words.' He rolled his chair forward as far as he could, shaking his head as he stared round. 'You can't possibly sleep in this chaos. Why don't you move your personal possessions to my house today and just use this place for storage? I was going to offer to stay the night with you here, but there's not enough room for my hot rod.' He rolled his wheelchair to and fro, making vrooming noises, and managed to draw a feeble smile from her.

'You said you wanted to find somewhere else to live, Lou. I thought I'd move in with you then.'

'I want to do that quickly, so we'll get on to it first thing tomorrow. Come and stay for a few days, try me out as a house sharer. My spare bedroom's bigger than your main bedroom. Your things will be quite safe here. After all, we changed the lock and put in a security system, didn't we?'

She hesitated, the old Miranda still afraid to take this step, then what she thought of as her new self took over. 'I'd love to stay with you, Lou. I hate this place. It makes my soul shrivel.'

'It makes me want to sue the architects.'

She packed some things and followed him in her car, which, thank goodness, was registered in her own name; one of the few major presents her father had given her during a period when he was annoyed with Sebastian. Sighing in relief, she took first her suitcase then her computer up to the guest bedroom. She felt completely at ease here, at ease with him, too.

If only . . .

That evening Lou fell asleep as they watched TV and she studied him while keeping an eye on the antiques programme. He must have been good-looking as a young man, and still had quite a presence, but he'd been absolutely exhausted by the end of the day. He never complained but she'd seen him wincing a few times as if in pain. She'd try to make him rest regularly.

The next thing she knew he was waking her up, laughing at the way they'd both fallen asleep, and chivvying her along to bed.

As she snuggled down, she thought how easy it would have been to fall in love with a man like him. But he'd made it very plain that he didn't want that, and anyway, it'd be stupid when there was no future in a relationship. She wasn't stupid.

He couldn't stop her getting fond of him, though, as a dear friend. She already felt as if she'd known him for years.

Sebastian eyed Sally Patel across the desk. When she'd rung him personally, he'd not liked to refuse to see her because she was so well respected in the legal community. She'd said, 'just for a preliminary chat', so he hoped it wouldn't take long. He sighed. 'I don't understand why Minnie is making such a fuss.'

She smiled sweetly. 'To whom are you referring?'

'You know very well – my stepsister, your client.'

'My client is called Miranda.'

He felt anger rise but reined it in. 'The family have always called her Minnie.'

'She put up with that only because of her father. Now that he's dead, she's made it plain that she wishes to use her real name, and that's the only one we'll be using in court.'

He corrected himself grudgingly. '*Miranda*, then. She won't manage to overthrow the will, even with your help, Sally. I made very sure everything was done properly.'

She smiled, a gentle yet relentless smile that had put fear into the hearts of many a wrongdoer – and their legal representatives. Even he didn't like that smile.

'That remains to be seen. Apparently your father was starting to show signs of Alzheimer's and you knew it.'

'How did you find that out? Anyway, it hadn't progressed so far that he didn't understand what he was doing. I got that from the doctor in writing.'

Her smile didn't falter. If anything, she looked more confident.

'And even if you do manage to get a few things changed in the will, it'll cost Min – oh, very well, *Miranda*, what the estate's worth in legal fees. Where's the win for her in that?'

Glee danced in her eyes. 'As I shall be doing this job pro bono, your sister won't have to pay me any legal fees. It's only you who'll be out of pocket.'

'Why the hell would you do that, Sally? You don't know her from Adam.'

'I always enjoy a good tussle and I owe Lou Rayne

a lot. He cares about Miranda. I can't do much for him now, but he's happier knowing I'll be looking after her . . . when he no longer can.'

'You're bluffing.'

'Am I? We shall see. In the meantime, I'd like to agree on an income for Ms Fox, a *reasonable* income from her father's estate, as the will specified. I spoke to your fellow trustee and we agreed on a figure. Your initial offer was totally unacceptable.'

'Tressman and I had already decided what would be suitable, generous even – for a woman of Minnie's age living quietly.'

The look Sally gave him made him adjust his collar, which suddenly seemed too tight.

'Why should Ms Fox want to live quietly? I'm two years older than she is and I don't consider my life over yet. Not nearly over.' Sally's foot began tapping. 'So . . . are we agreed?'

'For the time being. As a temporary measure. We'll await the outcome of her legal challenge.'

'I hadn't realised how mean you were, Sebastian Fox.'

He blinked in shock at her frank insult. 'I prefer to call it prudent. I'm her trustee. I must be careful with her money.'

'Miserly would be a more accurate term. But we'll leave it at that for the moment. There's just one other thing to sort out. I believe your wife borrowed some of your stepsister's jewellery without her permission. If you'll send the pieces round to me by noon tomorrow, we can clear the slate about that.'

'Surely it can wait till after the ball?'

'I'm afraid not. My client is keen to get the jewels valued.'

'Oh, very well. I'll send the jewellery directly to Minnie.'

He caught her eye and amended it again to, '*Miranda*.'

'I'd prefer to check for myself that everything's in order. Things can so easily get . . . mislaid.'

When Sally had left, he rang his wife. 'Could you bring Minnie's jewellery into the office this afternoon, Dorothy? I'm afraid we have to give it back.'

'But you said I could borrow it for the ball. She never uses it, after all.'

'Yes. But she's being awkward. Do this for me.'

'I'll bring it round about two-thirty. Regina and I are going to lunch at the club first.'

'That'll be fine. Make sure you keep Regina on side. We don't want her supporting Minnie in any way.'

'Yes, of course.'

When he'd put the phone down, he began to doodle on his notepad, his favourite way of concentrating his thoughts on a problem. Minnie wasn't going to get away with this, Sally or no Sally.

He suddenly drew a triumphant flourish across the pad as a possible solution came to him. She'd been hospitalised for depression. With a little careful groundwork beforehand, he'd be able to suggest that this was why their father had wanted someone else to look after her money. He might even be able to go further.

Even Sally Patel couldn't win every single case.

He'd have to tread very carefully, though.

On his way home, Sebastian decided to stop briefly at Minnie's flat to check that the move had gone smoothly and make his ongoing presence felt.

He rapped on the door, then knocked again. She must be out. Good. He could check what she'd taken from the house. Pulling his key out, he tried to insert it in the lock, but it no longer fitted. When he studied it closely, he could see that it was a new lock.

The bitch! She didn't own this flat, the trust did. She had no reason whatsoever to refuse him access. He went downstairs and found the caretaker, a slovenly woman who lived in a small flat at the rear.

'I need to get into flat thirty.'

'The new tenant's just moved in. She's a female.' She consulted a list. 'A Ms Fox.'

'I'm her brother.' He handed her one of his cards. 'And her lawyer.'

'Ah.'

He waited while she studied him thoughtfully. 'Well?'

'You're Sebastian Fox, eh.'

'Yes. If that's any of your business.'

'Well, it is my business, sir, because I'm the caretaker here. I've been told by Ms Fox to let no one into the flat, whatever excuse they give. And you've been named as one who might try to claim he's an exception.'

'I am an exception. I'm Miss Fox's trustee. The trust owns the flat. She doesn't. So I have every right to inspect it.'

She shrugged. 'I wouldn't know about that. You'll have to arrange it with her. All I know is, she says not to let you in. Well, I'd not let any man into a woman's flat unless she told me herself it was all right. You can't be too careful these days.'

'Do I look like a damned criminal?'

Another shrug was his only answer and before he could stop her, she closed the door in his face.

He hesitated but the interview with Sally Patel still rankled. And he *was* the trustee. He took out his mobile phone and rang a locksmith he'd used before, then went up to wait outside the flat, pacing up and down the corridor impatiently.

A man arrived twenty minutes later. 'I've locked myself out. Can you let me in?'

Instead the man looked at the sign beside the door, saying the flat was under surveillance by the Andover Security Company. He pulled out his mobile phone.

After a brief chat, he asked, 'What did you say your name was, sir?'

'Sebastian Fox. I'm the owner's trustee and brother.'

'Well, you're listed as someone who might try to get in without her permission, so I'm not touching this lock. And if you persist in trying to gain entry, I'll have to call the police.'

'I have every right to inspect this flat.'

The man stepped back. 'You'll have to take that up with the owner, sir.'

'She is *not* the owner!'

The man shrugged.

Sebastian watched him walk away. Turning, he muttered, 'You'll be sorry for this, Minnie. Very sorry.'

Then he drove home, where he could let his temper out. His wife's attentiveness and obvious nervousness soothed him a little, but Regina's barely concealed amusement at his tale only poured salt on the wound to his self-esteem.

Miranda woke up feeling a sense of profound well-being. She lay studying the room, then heard sounds from the living area and got out of bed, pulling on her new dressing gown then going rather self-consciously into the kitchen barefoot, because she'd forgotten to bring her slippers.

Lou turned to smile at her. 'I hope I didn't wake you. I'm an inveterate early riser, I'm afraid.'

'I am too, usually, but I slept in a bit. What a comfy bed that is!'

'Or maybe you just feel more relaxed here?'

She nodded.

'I've been on the Internet looking at rentals. I think that'd be the best solution for you and me. Thank goodness Australia's not a land of two- and three-storey houses, like the UK! I've found one or two places for us to look at, which say they're wheelchair friendly.'

'You must have been up for hours.'

He shrugged. 'I've never needed much sleep, even less now.'

'Shall I make breakfast?'

'For yourself. I've had a bite of toast. It's all I want this morning. But I'd love to sit and chat to you while you eat, if that won't give you indigestion?'

By lunchtime they'd inspected two houses, both unsuitable, discussed their needs with the real estate salesman and arranged to see another place that afternoon.

When they got back, there was a light blinking on the answering machine.

'See if you recognise this number, Miranda,' Lou called.

She glanced at it and sighed. 'Sebastian.'

'It might be your sister.' He pressed the play button and put the phone on speaker.

Sebastian's voice boomed out. 'Call me back at once, Minnie.'

Lou grinned and she found herself growing less tense by the second. 'Erase it,' she said.

'Good idea.'

The phone rang and he checked it. 'Someone's mobile . . . Yes? Lou Rayne here.'

He listened for a moment, then held the phone out to Miranda. 'The caretaker at your block of flats.'

She took it reluctantly. 'Mrs Sarino . . . ? Yes . . . Yes,

you definitely did the right thing . . . He didn't! Well! Thank you so much for letting me know. I'm really grateful.'

She put the phone down. 'Sebastian went round and tried to get into the flat. When Mrs Sarino refused to let him in, he called a locksmith. Luckily the man rang our security firm and they not only refused to let my brother in, but threatened to call the police.'

Lou roared with laughter.

Her smile was fleeting. 'No wonder Sebastian sounded furious on the voicemail.'

'He can be as furious as he wants. And stop looking so worried.'

'I get worried too easily, don't I?'

'Yes, but by the time I'm finished with you, you'll cope better. I'm a good mentor, Miranda, and in case you start worrying about me, as well, I'm enjoying having something to do.'

'But you get so tired. I shouldn't be imposing on you.'

'Better to be tired and have plenty to think of than sit and worry about how fast my health is going downhill. Now, I'd be grateful if you'd make us some lunch, then I'll have a little rest before we go out again.'

The house they went to look at in the afternoon was huge and two storied, with a lift. It overlooked the Swan River and to one side, further down, were the pens of a yacht club, with luxury vessels berthed row upon row. Miranda dreaded to think how much the rent would be in this area. Tactfully, she moved out to the patio as Lou discussed terms with the agent.

When she went inside, he was beaming at her. 'We can move in tomorrow.'

'But what will a place like this cost? I can't afford—'

'You don't have to afford anything. I'm paying. Don't worry. I can easily afford it.'

Which made her worry that he might be spending everything he had on renting this huge house. If so, what if he lived longer than the doctors expected? She bit back further questions. He must have the freedom to choose what he did the rest of his life. She'd had enough people telling her what to do to ensure she wouldn't try to force her opinions on anyone else.

'The letting agent is bringing the paperwork round tonight.'

As they went into the flat, he added abruptly, 'Would you mind if we put the house rental in your name? That way you won't have to move straight out after I die.'

It made her want to weep that he was looking after her in all this, but she wasn't going to burden him with her feelings. 'I wouldn't mind at all.'

'They gave me four to six months to live, but I'll take the house for a year.' He grinned, an urchin's cheeky grin, in spite of the silver hair. 'I'm going to have a damned good try to prove them wrong.'

She signed the paperwork that evening with a steady hand. Lou had rung up a removal firm and arranged for them to do the packing and moving the following morning.

'If you'll take charge of overseeing them, it'll save me wasting my energy.'

'Don't you want to keep an eye on your possessions?'

'Nah. I'd trust you with my life, let alone my possessions. I've got some other things in storage, so I'll arrange to have them sent round, then when the movers come, I'll wait for them at the house. I can sit out on that patio in my wheelchair, so I'll be perfectly comfortable. When they get this stuff to the new house, you can tell them where it's to go. There are just a few pieces, artworks mainly, that I have views about.'

'All right. I'll be glad to help. Um . . . what about your niece?'

'I'll tell Hilary once the move is a fait accompli.'

Just after nine o'clock, Miranda's phone rang. She looked at it. 'Sebastian.'

'Shall I?' At her nod, Lou picked it up. He listened for a moment, then said curtly, 'She's busy.'

There was a wasp-like sound at the other end.

'She's still busy. Contact her lawyer. Miranda won't be available for the next few days.' He put the phone down. 'Your brother again. Does he always rap out orders and expect people to jump to attention.'

'Yes, he does. What did he want?'

'To talk to you. He said it was urgent.'

'Perhaps I'd better ring him back.'

'Nonsense. You can help me get ready for bed and then either watch TV or read for a while. I've had it for the day. If you don't answer the phone, you won't have anything to worry about.'

She remembered his words as she sat watching one of her favourite TV shows, because her mobile phone rang twice more. She looked at it the first time, saw Sebastian's number again, so didn't answer. The second time it was Regina's number. She hesitated then answered.

'Hi, Min – Miranda, it's me. I'm going back to England in a couple of days and we thought we'd all meet up for lunch.'

'Is Sebastian with you?'

'No. I'm ringing from my bedroom. Why? Do you want to speak to him?'

'On the contrary, I want to avoid him. Don't tell him you were speaking to me. And I'd rather not have lunch with him, thank you very much.'

Regina chuckled. 'All right. Can I come round to see you tomorrow afternoon after my final luncheon with our dear brother?'

Miranda couldn't decide what to answer, then took a risk. 'If you can keep a secret.'

'How intriguing! You mean, keep a secret from Sebastian, of course?'

'Yes.'

'I'd love to. He's been in a foul mood all evening. And Dorothy is the biggest wimp I've ever seen. She seems terrified of upsetting him. It's really weird. Have they always been like this? I'm not looking forward to spending the next two days with them, I can tell you.

So . . . what's the big secret?'

'Come to this address at four o'clock tomorrow and I'll tell you.' She spelt out the new address. 'And if you want to stay for a meal and a drink, that'll be fine. But don't, under any circumstances, give the address to Sebastian. It's Lou's new house, you see, and I'm staying with him there, not at that nasty little flat.'

'OK. Just let me find a pen. Right . . . got it.'

When she put the phone down, Regina glanced towards the door and saw a shadow darken the thin strip of light from the landing. Intrigued, she went to open the door just a crack and saw her brother going quietly down the stairs.

She shook her head. He'd always been sneaky and suspicious, but really, he was being ridiculous now. She hoped Minnie managed to stay out of his clutches, but she was doubtful. He usually got what he wanted in the long run.

She went to lie on the bed, trying to read her novel, but tonight even her favourite author failed to hold her attention because she was worrying about her daughter, who was not answering the phone.

What was Nikki doing? Had she come to her senses yet? Regina was hoping desperately that Nikki wouldn't opt to have that baby and ruin her whole life.

In England, Tim had found them a flat, or more accurately, a bedsitter. He and Nikki went to look at it.

'How can we fit into this?' she asked, hating the dingy place and the bathroom on the landing, shared with two other tenants.

'It's all we can afford. We'll get somewhere else before the baby comes, somewhere better. I'll have left school and be working by then.'

She went to bounce on the old-fashioned double bed, pulling a face as it sagged and creaked.

He came to sit beside her, taking her hand. 'We'll make it work, Nikki. We have to. And you won't be looking after the baby on your own. I intend to be a modern, hands-on father.'

'I think you want this baby more than I do.' She'd meant it to tease him, but it came out too sharply for that.

'Does that upset you?'

'I don't know. I don't know anything lately.'

Chapter Six

Miranda enjoyed overseeing the removal. She knew she was good at organising things – well, she'd had to be, living with a perfectionist like her father. The packers came at six o'clock in the morning, by which time she and Lou were both up and fed. He seemed to sleep very little at night and was always up earlier than her, though he did doze from time to time during the day.

She sent him off to the new house with a packed lunch and his laptop. At least with a wheelchair she didn't need to worry about him finding a seat. When she'd waved him goodbye, she turned her attention to the packing. Others might be doing the physical work, but she still wanted to keep an eye on everything.

It surprised her how quickly the flat's contents were put into boxes – but then, Lou didn't have many smaller personal possessions, not even a lot of clothes. Strange, that. Had his niece got rid of everything else he owned? Perhaps most of his stuff was in storage.

By nine o'clock they were ready to leave, so she called the house-cleaning service before taking a last walk round the flat with the man in charge of the removal, checking that cupboards were empty and every single possession removed.

If sounds had seemed to echo from other flats before, they were doubly noticeable now that the place was empty.

Fancy expecting Lou to live here! He wasn't a poor man and he'd need more space not less as he got increasingly confined to the home. And yet, even this was nicer than the place her brother had bought for her. She got angry every time she thought of that.

She hoped Lou was taking it easy this morning. She didn't like to see him fighting exhaustion. He got so upset when his energy wouldn't enable him to do what he wanted, though he tried to hide that from her and never spoke sharply or took his annoyance out on her, unlike her father and Sebastian.

Far from taking it easy, Lou was directing another set of removalists, who were bringing some large pieces of furniture, books, artwork, all the personal possessions and treasures that his niece had put into temporary storage when she moved him into that stark flat which he hoped never to see again. Hilary had urged him to get rid of these things, but hadn't dared sell them herself, because some of them were quite valuable.

If he hadn't been between houses when he fell ill, he'd

have made sure he had a proper home to come out of hospital to. He'd taken over management of the storage from Hilary as soon as he was himself again, just as he'd taken back every facet of his life that he could control.

He rolled his wheelchair into the main living room and took great pleasure in directing the men where to put the sofas, tables and paintings he'd chosen so carefully in happier times. At one point he realised he hadn't done anything about Miranda's financial situation. Frowning, he found a piece of paper and scrawled an impromptu codicil to his will, bequeathing the contents of this part of the house to Miranda. He called in the two removalists and had them witness it, then called a courier service and sent the paper off to Sally Patel. He'd do a proper will later.

Miranda would have a few surprises when he was gone, and she deserved them too. Already she'd made him feel happier, not just given him a purpose in life but a friend to share his final days.

He smiled at that thought, then frowned. If he made things too easy for her, she'd not continue to grow. He'd set his heart on her becoming independent and fulfilled, felt that it would be a worthy final achievement to give another human being what he'd been born with: the gift of confidence.

Not only had her family treated her appallingly and, even now, like a person with an ongoing disability, but from things she'd inadvertently let drop, friends had deserted her, too. Mental illness still had a stigma to it.

He took out his hand-held computer and made a note to ask Sally about making a better will. It'd be complex but it needed to be watertight. The temporary will was just insurance.

No, this had to be done properly and carefully. Miranda deserved that protection.

There were still packing cases full of smaller items to sort out, but he wanted to do that slowly. He'd enjoy having objects he considered old friends around him once more and was looking forward to sharing his treasures with Miranda. He hadn't collected them for their value or to show off, but out of love for them. He told the removalists to put all the boxes with red stickers in one of the empty rooms.

Then the men were gone and peace reigned for a time.

He smiled as he looked round the hall. This beautiful house had cheered him up greatly even in the short time he'd spent here. He'd not worked hard all his life to end his days in a poky flat, or in one room of a hospice, either.

How lucky that he'd met Miranda that day in the park! Fate's final gift in a life that had been highly satisfying and fulfilling until recently.

When Miranda arrived at the new house, the front door was open, so she went inside, stopping in the magnificent hall to gape at the living and dining areas, which had the basic furniture in them already. There was no sign of Lou, so she went out to the patio.

As she'd expected, he was there, looking tired but

at the same time happy, his fine silver hair ruffled, his cheeks flushed. She saw the empty flask of coffee and a used mug on the little wall beside his chair but no sign of the food she'd packed. 'Are you hungry? Shall I get you some lunch?'

'Good idea. I've been too busy to think of food.'

'You should have let me arrange the removal of your other things. Why didn't you?'

'I wanted to do that myself, to give you a surprise. Come and look at what I've got set out so far.'

The furniture was beautiful, though it needed smaller items like side tables to set it off.

'I've got artwork and ornaments in boxes in that room across the hall, but I want to unpack them gradually. Sit on that couch. Try it out. If you don't find it comfortable, we'll get you something else to sit on.'

'It looks far too elegant to use. *White leather!*'

'*Things* are made for people to enjoy, Miranda. Never forget that.'

So she sat down for a moment or two, sighing with delight at the comfort and watching the pleasure on his face as he looked round.

But she couldn't settle. 'The removalists will be here in a few minutes. Is it all right if I give them something to eat? We have enough to make sandwiches for them as well as us.'

He looked so angry she wondered what she'd done and her heart began to pound with anxiety. She watched him close his eyes, take a few deep breaths then open them again.

'Miranda, let that be the last time you ask me what you're *allowed* to do in your own home.'

To her relief his voice was gentle. It took a minute for his words to sink in and longer for her to realise what he meant. 'But it's you who's paying for all this.'

'As you very well know, the house is leased in your name. You could throw me out if you wanted to.'

She was shocked to the core. 'I'd never do that. You know I wouldn't.'

'Yes, I do know. But I want you to be safe after I die.'

'You're incredibly kind.'

'So are you.' He held her gaze for a minute then continued. 'I want us to *share* this house and I'm relying on you to manage it for me. I've never run a house, have always been too busy running my . . . um, company, and I'm not going to waste my final months on learning about domestic details.'

He held up one hand as she opened her mouth to apologise so she waited for him to finish.

'I don't mean I want you to cook and scrub for me, either. I'll hire people for that. But I do need you to manage them.'

'I've never had more than a cleaning lady, but I'll try.'

'I'm sure you'll succeed. If anyone gives you trouble, we'll sack them. But we can't sack your family, especially Sebastian, so you need to learn to stand up to him if you're to enjoy the rest of your life. I won't be here to help you for long.'

Tears came into her eyes and she tried to blink them away, but she could tell he'd noticed. He didn't miss a thing. 'I do wish you wouldn't keep saying that!'

'I have to.' His voice grew quieter, as he added, 'For myself as well as for you.'

After a few quiet breaths, he continued more robustly, 'Now, how about we bring your antiques here as well. There's plenty of room. Then we can sort out the horrible furniture Hilary bought me for that flat and put it into the servants' quarters.' He grinned at her expression. 'You hadn't even realised there were servants' quarters, had you?'

'No. We didn't go to see them. Goodness, what else is there here?'

'All sorts of outbuildings, including a six-car garage. We'll go and explore everything later, after I've had a rest. Once the removalists have gone, we'll have the rest of the day to ourselves.'

'Oh, dear. I've invited my sister over for a coffee this afternoon. She's leaving for the UK tomorrow, you see. I told her this was your house and asked her not to tell Sebastian where we are, and I'm pretty sure she won't betray us, but—' She saw his frown come back.

'You can tell Sebastian where we are yourself. Tomorrow would be a good time to do that.'

'Can't we wait a few days? He's bound to come stickybeaking.'

'The sooner you tell him the better. Practice makes perfect.' His grin returned. 'Now, what's for lunch? I dumped the food you gave me in the kitchen.'

'Come and choose. I'll need to go shopping soon, then I'll really show you how well I can cook.'

'Lay on, McDuff!'

'And damned be him that first cries, "Hold, enough!"' She continued the quotation from *Macbeth*, not at all surprised that Lou knew it correctly, though most people said, 'Lead on, McDuff.'

He showed a better appetite for his midday meal, she was pleased to see. By then the removalists were working with goodwill after clearing a plate of hearty corned beef sandwiches and drinking mugs of tea.

Oh, how she loved this house; the spacious rooms, the lack of clutter, the peace that settled when she and Lou were alone!

Regina thought at first that the taxi had brought her to the wrong place, but when she checked the address, it was correct. Was Miranda really living in this huge house now?

Her sister opened the door so Regina waved off the taxi and went inside, eyeing her surroundings curiously. 'Wow!'

'Isn't it lovely? Lou's having a rest. Come and sit on the terrace.'

'Can I look round first?'

'I'll show you the main living areas, but I don't want to disturb Lou.'

'How long have you two been together? And how

did you hide your relationship from Dad and Sebastian? He's hopping mad at you anyway, but he'll throw an absolute hissy fit when he sees where you're living.'

'It's none of his business, but I'll probably ring him tonight or tomorrow.' Miranda hesitated, then added, 'We only moved in today so I've not got the place straight yet. It's bigger than we need, really, but we had to find somewhere with a lift for Lou, you see.'

'What's wrong with him?'

'Problem with his spine.'

'Poor thing.'

Miranda glared at her so fiercely Regina was amazed. '*Poor thing?* I'd never think of Lou like that. Never! He copes with whatever life throws at him, and copes well.'

'Sorry. Didn't mean to upset you. He must have a pile of money. You've landed on your feet for once.'

'I'm not with him for the money!'

Regina didn't need telling that. 'No. You wouldn't be.'

'Let's not talk about that. Have you heard from Nikki?'

She let Miranda change the subject, wondering if she'd meet this Lou before she left. 'No. I rang her again very early this morning, which would be late yesterday evening in England, but she didn't answer. She was probably out with that idiot who got her up the duff!'

'Don't you want grandchildren?'

'Not particularly, and certainly not now.'

'I wish I had some. Well, I may have some already,

but I'll never know, will I?'

Regina patted her sister's shoulder, but couldn't help wondering whether Nikki would be upset all her life if she was forced, no *persuaded* into an abortion. She shook her head in bafflement. Surely not in this day and age? Things were different from when Minnie got pregnant, nearly thirty years ago.

'You could register your adoption and your willingness to make contact, you know,' she suggested.

Miranda nodded. 'I could, couldn't I? I mentioned it once to Father and he said he'd throw me out if I did that. But since he died, I've been thinking of it again. Sebastian won't be happy, though.'

'You're out of our dear brother's clutches now, surely?'

'Not really. He's still in charge of the trust.'

'Look, Miranda, don't let him stop you from doing what you want. You need to grab hold of life and do your own thing. It may be a cliché but it's important, because this isn't a rehearsal, this is *it*.'

She was pleased to see her sister nod and look thoughtful so didn't labour the point.

Upstairs, Lou was listening unashamedly to the two women's conversation, using the intercom system to eavesdrop. This house had had a few extra tricks like that added, accessed only from the master bedroom and upstairs office. The more he learnt about the house from the notes the agent had passed to him, the more he liked it.

He listened to the two women for a while longer, then picked up his phone and dialled an employment agency he knew. Paying well above the usual rate should get him all the help he wanted, and quickly.

Miranda came to join him half an hour later, running lightly up the stairs, a physical ability of which he was now deeply envious. He banished that thought firmly. It wasn't her fault he was a damned cripple.

'Do you want to join my sister and me for coffee, Lou, or shall I bring you one up?'

'I'll join you.' He gestured to the notes by the phone. 'Someone's coming round tomorrow morning from a domestic employment agency to suss out this place and advise us on what staff we need. The main thing for me is a full-time manservant.'

'Don't waste your money on other staff. If we don't use all the rooms, I can easily manage with a daily help.'

'No, you can't. You'll be too busy keeping me company. I'm not wasting my precious time waiting for you to mop floors.' He beamed at her as he rolled his wheelchair into the lift. 'We were lucky to find this place, weren't we? Life is so much easier with a private lift.'

His happiness banished her fears. 'The house is gorgeous. I can't believe I'm going to be living here. Regina is jealous.'

'Sebastian will be too.'

She sighed, losing the bright edge to her happiness at the thought of her half-brother.

'You have to face him soon.' He chuckled. 'And you should enjoy his jealousy. I shall.'

That evening, at Lou's prompting, Miranda gathered together her courage and contacted her brother, working on the principle that it was better to get it over with than have it looming and disturbing her sleep. She put the phone on loudspeaker so that Lou could listen in.

'It's taken you long enough to return my calls,' Sebastian grumbled by way of a greeting.

'We were busy.' She heard him start to say something and quickly spoke over him before she could weaken. 'I just wanted to tell you that I've moved in with Lou. This is my new phone number.'

'Just a minute. I need to write that down. What's the address?'

This was the moment she'd been dreading, but to her relief she managed to say it steadily.

There was dead silence from the other end, then, 'That street overlooks the river.'

He sounded indignant. How mean-spirited was that? 'Yes, it has great views.'

'What about your flat?'

'I'm going to let it.'

'I'm not sure you can do that. And if anyone's going to let it, it should be the trust.'

You might have known he'd be like that, she thought despairingly. Why did he always have to make difficulties? 'I'll add it to the things to ask Sally about, then.'

'I suppose you were intending to keep the rent money, too.'

'Of course. I thought the flat was mine to do with as I pleased.' She heard how faint her voice was and told herself to speak more firmly.

'Well, if you keep the rent money you won't need as much income from the trust.'

'Yes I will. I'm going to have a lot of expenses. Clothes for a start. Lou goes to some very smart places and Father was mean about such things. My clothes are old-fashioned and frumpy. You've been making fun of them for years. Did it never occur to you that I *wanted* better clothes?'

She waited but he made no comment on that, only sighed as if exasperated that she'd even mentioned it, so she said, 'I have to go now. Lou's getting tired.'

'Min—'

But she cut him off because she'd pushed herself to her limits. She set the phone gently in its cradle, then buried her face in her hands.

Lou's voice came from close by and she looked up to see that he'd moved across the room. When he held out his hand she took it.

'You did well, Miranda, far better than I'd expected. Has he always been so tight-fisted and grasping?'

'He was much worse as a boy.' He'd hit, pinched and even kicked her when she refused to do as he wished, but she wasn't going to tell Lou that. 'And Father always believed him, not me.'

'One day, you're going to tell me the whole tale,' he said quietly. 'But I think you've had enough for tonight. You did well.' He grimaced. 'Go and sort us out a bottle of wine. We deserve it. I'm going to ring Hilary and get that over with, too. I told her I was going in for some tests, but she'll be expecting to come round tomorrow, as usual.'

He picked up the phone. 'Ah, Hilary. Yes, I'm well, thank you . . . No, I wasn't in for tests, actually, I was moving house.' He held the phone away from his ear.

To Miranda, it sounded as if someone had speeded up a recording. She might not be able to distinguish one word from another, but the shrill anger came through loud and clear.

She listened as he gave his niece the address. That generated another burst of staccato noises.

He listened for a while, then cut his niece short. 'Look, come round tomorrow, by all means, but don't bring me any more food. I have a full-time housekeeper now.'

When he put the phone down he rolled his eyes. 'I'm sure you heard that. She gets very shrill when she's annoyed. And look, whatever she says don't let her upset you tomorrow.'

'Do you want me to meet her?'

'Of course I do. This is your home as well.' He gave her one of his mischievous looks. 'I've one more call to make.'

She listened again as Lou rang Sally at home to ask how Miranda stood legally about letting her flat.

He chuckled at her response and put the phone down.

'What did she say? Did she mind you ringing her at home?'

'Of course not. If she had a business query she'd ring me any time too.' He chuckled. 'Give me that glass of wine.'

But he spilt some as he shook with laughter, trying and failing to get the words out to explain what was amusing him.

She waited patiently.

'Sally says not to quote her, but it'd be really bad for your brother's reputation if it got known that he was being so stingy with his sister, and since the courts take ages to sort out these little matters, we should try that route first to save time.'

Miranda gaped at him. '*Threaten Sebastian?*'

'Yes.'

'I don't think I can.'

'Of course you can.'

But she knew she couldn't.

Chapter Seven

The following morning Regina rang Miranda early. 'Look, since I'm leaving tonight, how about coming out to lunch with Sebastian and me?'

'We've got Lou's niece coming around noon. Why don't you pop in here for a coffee after your lunch? Just you.'

'It's better to stand up to him, you know, Min—I mean Miranda. Sorry, that just slipped out.'

'Lou keeps telling me that I should stand up to him, but I've always preferred to avoid trouble. I'm doing my best to cope with the situation, truly I am.'

'Well, you upset him again last night, so I reckon you're lifting your game.' Regina smiled at the memory of how angry he'd been when he put the phone down. 'What did you say to him this time?'

'I told him I was living here and that when I rented out the flat, I intended to keep the rent money.'

'Good for you.' She paused, frowning. 'Why should

you not keep the rent money?'

'He says it should go back into the trust if I've found somewhere else to live.'

'He was always careful with his money, but I don't remember him being this bad before. I mean, that's *your* money.'

'I've always found him . . . difficult, but in recent years he's encouraged Dad to count every penny too.'

'I notice he doesn't stint himself.'

They chatted for a little while longer then Regina put the phone down with a grimace. Poor old Miranda! She'd always been a softie. You had to wonder what a man like Lou Rayne saw in her. His name seemed vaguely familiar and she frowned as she tried to remember where she'd seen it before. She went to her laptop, intending to check him out on one of the search engines, but before she could switch it on, Dorothy tapped on her bedroom door.

'Sebastian just rang to ask if we can go to lunch an hour earlier. There's something he wants to do this afternoon.'

'Fine with me.'

'Good. I thought it would be. We'll need to leave fairly soon though, because I have to drop some things off at the club on the way. I'm organising the next speaker for them.'

With a sigh Regina closed the lid of her laptop and went to get ready. She'd never met anyone as busy as Dorothy. Charity activities, a prestigious women's club, golf – one thing after another.

Was this to make Sebastian look good? Or to avoid thinking time?

'Do you enjoy being on these committees and leading a hectic social life?' she asked idly.

Dorothy shrugged. 'It's what women like me do. I make some good contacts for Sebastian.'

'Don't you have any hobbies of your own?'

'I used to do needlepoint, but he doesn't like me wasting my time on that sort of thing. It's not as if I was a needlepoint artist or anything. It was just . . . relaxing.'

It was on the tip of Regina's tongue to ask what was wrong with relaxing once in a while. She'd wondered more than once if her brother's marriage was happy, but she'd not probed. It really wasn't her business and she didn't see the pair of them very often, thank goodness. After a week in her brother's company, she'd decided this was an even better thing than she'd realised, though she'd not have let him boss her about as Dorothy and Miranda did, even if she lived here in Australia.

After their luncheon, which Sebastian let Regina pay for without even a token protest, he leant back and asked in that patronising tone she'd noticed him using towards women in recent years, 'What are you two doing this afternoon? More shopping?'

'I have a meeting,' Dorothy said at once.

'I'm going round to say goodbye to Miranda,' Regina said. He frowned at her for a moment or two then said grudgingly, 'I'm going to see Minnie too, so I'll drive you. My next appointment isn't till four.'

Regina guessed then that this was the reason for the earlier meal.

She went to the ladies, intending to phone Minnie and warn her, but Dorothy came too and waited for her, so she didn't like to.

Oh well, he couldn't kill their sister, after all. And if Lou was there, *he* would no doubt protect Miranda from being bullied.

Lou's niece wasn't at all what Miranda had expected. Hilary was slim, beautifully dressed and radiated good health. But there was a lack of genuine warmth in her, for all her loving words to her uncle.

After greeting his niece, Lou beckoned Miranda across. 'This is my partner, Miranda Fox.'

His niece gaped first at him, then at her. '*Partner!*'

'Yes.'

'But – how long has this been going on?'

'Miranda and I have known one another for a while. When we met again, we decided not to waste the time I've got left but move in together straight away.'

Hilary nodded but made no attempt to do the kissy-kissy routine with Miranda. 'Could I talk to you on your own, Uncle?'

'Nope. I've got nothing to hide.'

Miranda would have preferred to leave, but if he wanted her to stay, she'd stick it out.

'I was hoping you'd come to terms with your

condition, not try to deny it like this, Uncle Louis. I've been speaking to my priest about you and he'd be happy to have a chat with you.'

'I thought we'd agreed to disagree about religion. I shan't change my lifetime beliefs just because I'm dying.'

'You were born and raised a Catholic.'

'But I shan't die one. Leave it be, Hilary.'

Silence, then she scowled at Miranda. 'Would you mind leaving us some privacy?'

Lou made a growling noise in his throat. 'I'll meet you on the patio in a few minutes, Miranda.'

After she'd left, Hilary said, 'Your *partner* is just staying with you for the money.'

'No. She's definitely not. If there's one thing I'm sure of in this uncertain world, it's that Miranda isn't a scheming sort. Do you think, after what I've done with my life, that I can't judge character?'

For a moment the air between them fairly hummed, then she shrugged.

His voice softened. 'Look, Hilary, Miranda makes me happy. Do you begrudge me that?'

'If she does make you happy. I suppose you won't need my help now.'

'No. But I'm grateful that you stepped in when I wasn't able to manage my own life, and I shan't forget that, I promise you. I hope you'll still continue to visit us. Now, come and see round the house. I've got my paintings unpacked and we're going to choose where to have them hung.'

He rolled across to the French windows and beckoned to Miranda. 'Come and join us for the grand tour of the house.'

Upstairs the two women stood together on the landing while Lou answered the phone in his office. He was talking about his plans for the room and gesticulating wildly, as usual, insisting that someone come and fix things the very next day.

Hilary said in a low voice, 'If you hurt or upset him, I'll make sure you regret it.'

'I'd never do that,' Miranda protested.

'What's more, if you really do care about him, you'll persuade him to think of his immortal soul instead of objects and possessions like these.'

'I care about him. But I also believe he's more than capable of managing his own affairs. He's a very intelligent man.'

The look Hilary gave her was like an engraving etched in acid. She left soon afterwards.

Lou muttered, 'Thank goodness!' as the door shut behind his niece. 'She's even worse than her mother, dominated by two obsessions.'

'Oh?'

'The church and good health rules. She's such a food Nazi, she always makes me want to drink a bottle of brandy and gorge on doughnuts, and the latter are the sort of rubbish I'd never normally eat, though I do like a brandy.'

'I think she does care about you, though.'

'Does she? It's happened a bit late is all I can say.'

Sebastian slowed down when his sister said, 'There. It's that house.'

He stopped the car completely at the entrance to the drive, which had a huge gate across it, and stared at the riverside mansion in shock. 'Are you sure this is the right place?'

Regina tried to hide her amusement. 'It was when I visited Miranda yesterday.'

'I can't think what that man sees in her. She's stupid and colourless.'

'She's not stupid.'

'Why does she never open her mouth, then?'

'Because you and Father have never let her. If you were half as rude to me, I'd have tipped my wine glass over you.'

'Rubbish. It's exactly that sort of timidity that makes Minnie unable to cope with modern life. She's an anachronism, not fit to be let loose. They should have kept her in sheltered housing when she left the mental hospital.'

She stared at him in amazement. 'You're being grossly unfair. She had one depressive illness – postnatal depression – and has been all right ever since. Why will you not let it go? And if she could manage Father all those years, she's certainly fit to manage her own money and life – just as you and I do.'

He looked at her incredulously. 'You saw what happened when she went to university. Someone took advantage of her and she got pregnant.'

Regina laughed. '*Took advantage!* You're a dinosaur, Sebastian. She fell in love, as most young people do, and acted carelessly. And maybe if Dad hadn't forced her to have the baby adopted, she'd not have got so depressed. She's recovered completely now.'

'I don't think she has, and I know her better than you do. You can see what she's like in company, hiding in corners, hardly saying a word.'

'I've seen both you and Dad cut her short when she's tried to join in. I've heard you speak scornfully about her, not caring whether she can hear or not. I wouldn't put up with it. She backs off and you complain. You complain even more loudly when she refuses to do what you want. She can't win.'

'Why are you taking her side, Regina? You don't usually.'

'Aren't we all on the same side? She is our half-sister, after all.'

'And that's why I'm looking after her. Come on. Let's get this over with.' He drove slowly forward and pressed the button beside the gate, speaking into the intercom. 'Sebastian Fox here. I've brought Regina to say goodbye to Minnie.'

'Miranda is busy for the next few minutes. Come in and chat to me while you wait. The front door's open. Go straight across the hall and turn right at the far end. I'm out on the patio.'

There was a loud click and the huge gate began to roll slowly sideways.

As he got out of the car Sebastian stopped again to stare at the house, feeling more than a little annoyed. Minnie! Living here. Where was the justice in that? She hadn't lifted a finger to earn it, had been living off their father's money for years. Why, even he couldn't afford a place like this.

Regina led the way but he refused to be hurried. Once inside, he turned round slowly on the spot, taking in the spacious two-storey entrance hall with its magnificent chandelier.

'Hurry up!' She set off without him and reluctantly he followed.

Lou had parked his wheelchair next to a large swimming pool surrounded by beautifully landscaped gardens, which overlooked the River Swan where it widened out into Perth Water. Already this was his favourite spot to sit. He watched the two visitors walk across to him, noting Sebastian's sour expression with amusement.

'Take a seat on that wall. We've not got any outdoor furniture yet. I don't think Miranda will be long.' He waited till they were seated and turned to his female visitor, who seemed a lot friendlier than her sour-faced brother. 'So you're going back to England tonight, Regina. What time does your plane leave?'

'Ten o'clock.'

'Bad time, that.'

'I don't mind. I always sleep well on planes.'

They chatted politely for about ten minutes, then Lou

saw movement inside the house: Miranda. She stopped dead at the sight of the visitors, one hand going up to her mouth in what was now a familiar gesture whenever she was upset or nervous about something.

He didn't mention to the others that she was nearby but watched intently, pleased when she slid the door open and came out to join them, patting her hair self-consciously. He'd expected her to look better after over an hour with a hairstylist he'd called in, but he hadn't realised what a big difference it would make to cut her hair shorter and give her a feathery fringe. She had elegant bones in her face and neck, but that long hair had swamped them before.

'Regina's here to say goodbye and your brother's come to see where you live,' he called, grinning when Sebastian glared at him for this frankness.

As Miranda walked slowly across the patio, Lou's heart ached for her. Every step looked as if it was an effort. This was more than shyness. Something had definitely been done by her brother to cause this reaction when they were together.

Regina stood up, clapping her hands. 'Miranda, you look fabulous. Turn round. Oh, yes, beautifully cut. Who did it?'

'Janus sent someone,' Lou said.

Sebastian choked. 'Someone from Janus came to *you*?'

'Yes. The owner's an old friend of mine. He's done her hair well, hasn't he?'

'You're going to a lot of trouble with my sister.'

'It's about time someone did, don't you think?' Lou

saw Miranda turn scarlet, so changed the subject. 'Do you like our little place?'

'It's . . . nice.'

'It's gorgeous,' Regina corrected. 'I'll be thinking of you living here, when I'm back in rainy old England, Miranda, though they say we're going to have a great summer this year, so maybe it won't be too bad. I never did like searing hot days but English summers can be delightful.'

'On the rare occasions when the weather's fine,' Sebastian sneered. 'Give me Australia any time.'

'Oh, the weather's heated up in the past few years. We get some rather nice summery weather now in England – most years, anyway.'

After some chit-chat, Sebastian changed the subject abruptly. 'I'm afraid you must leave renting the flat to the trust, Minnie.'

Lou looked at her, willing her to respond.

She bent her head and began to pleat her skirt, hunching her shoulders.

He took pity on her. Too much change, too quickly. He turned on her brother, furious at the man. 'You're a mean sod, Fox!'

Sebastian gaped at him and made a few incoherent noises as if he couldn't get any proper words out.

'If you can't treat your sister more generously,' Lou went on, 'I'll consult some of *my* friends about what to do to help her. I doubt they'll approve of your miserly attitude towards her inheritance. Harold Pennington, for one, is going to be very interested in what's going on. He's working hard to build up a reputation for philanthropy, not just for himself, but for his business.'

The senior partner and founder of Sebastian's legal firm wasn't that good a friend, but Lou doubted Fox would test that out. From the man's expression that shaft had hit home. 'Miranda needs help. She's not good at business,' Sebastian said curtly.

'She's not been given the chance to learn. But now she has me and I'm *very* good at business – and at mentoring people. Don't worry. I'll see she rents the flat out advantageously and doesn't waste the money.' He waited and when there was no answer, added softly, 'Or do we need to take that to court as well?'

Sebastian breathed deeply and Lou decided this was as near agreement as he was likely to get, so changed the subject.

He could see the amusement in Regina's eyes and wondered if he'd misjudged her. Maybe she wasn't entrenched on Sebastian's side. He hoped not. Her sister would need allies later.

As the two men stared at one another in a challenging silence, Miranda raised her head, shame flooding through her. Her brother was bristling with hostility; Lou was smiling gently. She'd missed her opportunity to speak for herself, been cowardly again.

After a long silence, Sebastian snapped, 'I don't see what business this is of yours, Rayne.'

'I'm very fond of Miranda.'

'How long have you known her?'

Lou smiled warmly across at her. 'Long enough to become good friends.'

She smiled back, for a moment forgetting the others. 'Very good friends.'

'I shall continue to keep a close eye on what you're doing to my partner,' Lou went on. 'She's upset not only because she's lost her father but also her inheritance.'

Sebastian bristled. 'She has *not* lost her inheritance!'

'We both know she has.'

'Can I use the bathroom?' Regina asked brightly.

Miranda stood up, knowing she was running away, but unable to bear the confrontation for a minute longer. 'Of course. Let me show you the way.'

When they were inside the house she stopped to say bitterly, 'Other people shouldn't have to fight my battles for me.'

'You've always been afraid of Sebastian. I've never understood why. He's not that bad.'

'Not to you. But—' She broke off, swallowing hard.

'But what?'

'He used to thump me when he was younger, always in places where the bruises didn't show. I think he enjoys hurting people.'

Regina gaped at her. 'Why didn't you tell Father?'

'I did. He said I should stand up for myself but I could never get the better of Sebastian. He was so much bigger than me physically.'

'I'm sorry. I didn't realise.'

'You were a lot younger and you always had your nose buried in a book. For some reason he left you alone. When I tried to get help from your mother and she had a word with him, my favourite possessions began to vanish, so I soon learnt to keep quiet.'

'But that was *years* ago, when you were a child.'

'He was even worse after your mother left. I read up on abuse on the Internet and its effects last a long time. I still feel physically sick at the mere thought of confronting him.'

'Oh, Miranda, we've treated you so badly. I feel so guilty about that.'

'*You* haven't.'

'I've been neutral at best. I did have a vague idea something was wrong, but I didn't try to work out what or get involved. I was a selfish little bitch when I was younger.' She laughed. 'Still am, I suppose.'

'You had your own life to lead.'

'Well, you've got Lou to look after you and he really seems to care for you. I'll feel better about leaving you in his hands.'

'He can't look after me for long!' She couldn't hold back a sob. 'He's got cancer and only has about six months to live. What'll happen after that?'

Regina patted her arm, frowning. 'If you take my advice, you'll get right away from Sebastian. Why don't you come and live in England? He'd never leave his precious law practice, so he's stuck in Australia. And you've got dual citizenship, because of your mother, haven't you?'

'I suppose so. I do keep my English passport up to date and I've often wanted to go there, to see where my mother was born, perhaps meet some of her family.' Miranda looked at her wearily. 'But do you think anywhere would be far enough from Sebastian? After all, he'll still control the purse strings.'

'You can always get a job.'

'I've no qualifications, no experience of anything but housekeeping, so I doubt I'd get even a sniff of a job during a recession like this.'

'You are such a defeatist, Miranda. There's always a way if you look for it. And in the meantime you're better off than most, because you've got the trust money to live off. Sebastian won't let you go too short because it'd look bad for him.'

Miranda bent her head, then lifted it to say, 'I am trying to learn to be more assertive.'

But from the look in Regina's eyes, her sister didn't think she was doing very well. Miranda wasn't proud of herself, either.

Nikki packed her things, pausing from time to time to stroke something then lay it aside regretfully. There wouldn't be room for anything extra in such a tiny bedsitter.

When they arrived, Tim helped her carry up her possessions, then put his arms round her.

'I love you, you know.'

She did know but wasn't as sure about her own feelings, so leant against him, hiding her face. 'It's nice being together.'

He whirled her round, laughing.

In the morning she had to rush into the tiny bathroom off the landing to be sick. She rested her clammy face in her hands, then raised her eyes to the spotted mirror above the stained sink. She hated it here already. There was simply no privacy. She was sure the sound of her vomiting would have echoed down the stairwell.

Her brain was foggy and she'd read that it could be an ongoing side effect of pregnancy. She was starting to worry about the exams now. They weren't taking place for a month or two, but would she be able to do herself justice?

Had she been wrong to leave home?

The next day the new cook/housekeeper started work, plus a daily maid, and Jack Bennet joined them as Lou's manservant. He was in his fifties, experienced at caring for wealthy people in their final months; an intelligent man with cool, assessing eyes.

'We're ready to go,' Lou told Miranda.

She was puzzled. 'Go where?'

'Anywhere we choose – as long as it's in Perth. I don't think I can cope with flights, even the five hours to Singapore. No, I meant ready to enjoy ourselves.' He looked at the clock. 'I've got a couple of business appointments this morning, though. Jack can take me. There'll be a lot of hanging round.'

'I don't mind.'

'Well, actually, I've booked you an appointment with a personal shopper. She'll be ringing you on the house phone in about half an hour. You need some more modern clothes to match that hairstyle. And we won't have any arguments. I'm paying.'

She was silent, trying to take this in. 'I do feel awful about how I look, but Dad lost touch with modern prices in the last few years and always grumbled if I wanted new clothes. It didn't seem worth bothering. I didn't go anywhere, after all, except to the shops or the library.'

'Well, you'll go places with me. I'm taking you out to dinner tonight at one of my favourite restaurants, and I expect you to wear one of your new outfits.'

'Won't you be too tired?'

'I'll take a stimulant, if necessary. Don't look so disapproving, Miranda. With such a short time left, I don't want to waste more of it than I have to resting.' He held her gaze for a moment longer, then his smile returned.

She felt tears rise in her eyes. 'How can I ever thank you?'

'Gather up your courage and be the Miranda you should have been. That'll be thanks enough.'

'It's too late.'

'It's never too late to change.'

The phone rang just then and he picked it up. 'Rayne

here . . . Josh, thanks for returning my call.' He blew a kiss at Miranda and made a shooing motion with one hand.

She walked out. He was kind, but sometimes that made her feel like a child who needed looking after. She'd changed but she still wasn't yet her own person by any means – only, who was she?

She glanced back at Lou and remembered the depressed man in the park. He wasn't depressed now. She was doing him good, she knew, and that was one way of paying him back. She squared her shoulders and went to change into her smartest clothes.

'I'm back!' Regina yawned as she walked round the flat, exhausted by the long flight from Australia. She was surprised to find no sign of her daughter. At seven o'clock in the morning Nikki ought to be here.

When she pushed open the door of Nikki's bedroom, she knew immediately that something was different, but it took a moment or two for it to sink in that quite a few of Nikki's possessions were missing. Her computer, the pile of books, the CDs, the clothes she had to be nagged to hang up.

She went across and flung open the wardrobe doors, to find it half empty.

As she turned back she saw the envelope on Nikki's desk. It had 'MUM' scrawled across it. She picked it up, staring at the word, her hand shaking. Nikki hadn't – she couldn't have hurt herself . . .

When she tore it open she found a brief letter.

Sorry about this, Mum, but I can't face more arguments. I don't want to have an abortion and Tim doesn't want me to, either.

We've found a flat – well, a bedsitter, really – and his parents are helping us with the rent. If you could help, too, that'd be great.

Don't worry about school. They know about the baby and are being very supportive. I'm going to study really hard and at least get my A Levels.

The counsellor said you and I could go and see her together. I think that'd be a good idea.

I've taken my mobile phone. Hope that's all right. You can always ring me on it.

Nikki

Regina surprised herself by bursting into tears of relief. Of course she didn't really believe her daughter would commit suicide, but just for a moment . . . She began to feel angry and scrubbed away the moisture. All she'd done for that girl! All the hopes she'd had for Nikki's future, because there was no doubt her daughter was an extremely intelligent girl.

Could Nikki not at least have faced up to her? Clearly not. She was as bad as her aunt Miranda.

Then a terrible thought occurred to Regina, so terrible she froze where she stood.

Was *she* like her brother Sebastian? *Were they both bullies?*

No, of course she wasn't. She was only trying to help her daughter. Sebastian, on the other hand, was trying to keep hold of their sister's money. And succeeding. He didn't give two hoots whether Miranda was happy or not.

When she'd calmed down a little, Regina rang her daughter's mobile phone, but only got voicemail.

'For heaven's sake, Nikki, ring me back or better still, come home and discuss things with me. Running away never solves any problems.'

She ended the call and went to unpack but kept finding herself standing stock-still in the middle of a task, worrying about her daughter.

In Wiltshire Katie Parrish looked at the letter, wondering who could be writing to her. Shrugging, keeping one eye on the clock, she tore it open and began to skim through it. The words seemed to shimmer in front of her as she tried to take in what they meant.

She forced herself to breathe deeply a few times then read the letter through slowly.

Dear Ms Parrish

I believe you've been searching for your birth parents for a while now. I'm sorry I didn't find out about this until recently.

If you're still interested, I may have information about your birth father.

Could you please email me at the above address?

*If you don't now wish to pursue matters, I shall
not trouble you again.*
  Yours faithfully,
  B. Lanigan

She began to shake as she read it for the third time
and had to fumble her way to a chair. She'd given up on
her search because she'd not had a single response on the
two websites she'd found to post such queries.

'Mum? I have to go to school now. *Mum?*'

She jerked upright and stuffed the letter into her
handbag. Ned came running into the room, ready to
leave, so she grabbed her car keys and led the way out.

Five minutes later she sat in the car and watched
him dash into the playground. He joined the other little
boys and she watched them running round, gesticulating
wildly, throwing balls, anything but standing still.
Groups of mothers were chatting by the gates. She wasn't
as good as Ned at making friends and hesitated to join
them. She'd do it soon, but not today.

She drove home, sighing as she went back into
the too-quiet house. Having a husband serving in the
armed forces made life difficult. When he was back
home, life was wonderful, but he was on a tour of
duty in Afghanistan at the moment and she was back
to months of raising Ned on her own. And she wasn't
coping as well as she'd expected to.

If only her parents were still around, she'd be able to
discuss this letter with her father, but he'd died suddenly
of cancer three years ago. Her mother had remarried last

year and gone to live in Cornwall. She could ring Mum up when she needed advice, and they often chatted – about everything except this.

Her mother didn't understand her desire to meet her birth parents and got upset when it was mentioned. Her father had told her to find them, if it meant so much to her. And it did.

She pulled out the piece of paper and read the brief message again.

Should she reply to it, go further? Or would she be opening a can of worms that would put barriers between herself and Mum? If she did open the can and didn't like what she found inside, she might not be able to put the lid on again. Pandora's Box hadn't meant much to her when she learnt about Greek legends at school, but it did now.

Like the mythical Pandora, she was a classic case of curiosity leading to something unknown and potentially dangerous. If she hadn't ferreted through the old papers in the attic when she was a teenager, she'd not have found out she was adopted. Her parents said they'd intended to tell her when she was older, but she suspected her mother wouldn't have done so unless forced.

Since then Katie had become consumed with a desire to meet the two people who had created her and to learn about her birth family background.

She closed her eyes and tried to work out what to do now. Should she reply and risk upsetting Mum still further? After all, her adoptive mother had been good to her and was letting her live in the family home rent-free now that she'd moved to Cornwall with her second husband.

Katie sometimes wondered if she should abandon the quest altogether? Mum thought she'd done that already, but hope had still lingered, even though the searches had been fruitless.

She'd not been adopted through any known adoption agency, but privately, so it was much harder to find things out. There simply were no records, well, not that she'd been able to trace. How had her birth parents managed to do this?

She sighed and began to fiddle with the corner of the letter, folding it carefully at ninety degrees, then unfolding it and doing the same to the other corners.

She was, she decided suddenly, going to reply and ask this B. Lanigan for further information. She'd never be able to forget this now.

Chapter Eight

Miranda spent the next two weeks in a whirl of activity, encouraged and often accompanied by Lou.

At Sally's prompting, Sebastian had signed an agreement to pay her what seemed a substantial sum every month.

'I don't think we can squeeze any more out of him,' Lou said regretfully.

'It's far more than I've ever had before.'

'But the trust is generating a lot more income than they're giving you, so you *ought* to be living more comfortably. If anything happens to you, the capital will go to your nieces and nephews.'

The words slipped out before she could prevent them. 'Unless I can trace my daughter.'

'Have you never tried to do that? There are places where you can register to say you want to contact your child.'

'I know. But it didn't seem fair while she was growing

up and then, well, there was Dad getting grumpier by the day. I have looked online but the Family Tracing Service here doesn't seem to do much if you don't have certain information. I don't even know the date the baby was handed over, or which adoption service they used. I haven't been able to find *anything* out.'

His voice was very gentle. 'We could hire a private investigator.' He gave her one of his wry smiles. 'I know a guy who can work miracles when it comes to getting hold of information. He's saved my bacon a few times.'

She didn't trust her voice not to quaver, because the thought of actually finding her daughter made her feel as if she was standing on a precipice, so nodded breathlessly.

'Right then.' He pulled out his notebook. 'Who handled the adoption?'

'My father.' She explained about the years in a mental hospital and saw horror on his face, but he didn't withdraw from her.

'Your own father had you committed?'

'Yes. And the drugs they forced on me made it feel like being in prison in your own body. It took me a while to recover, even after I came out of that place.' She brushed away a tear. 'He must have forged my signature on the adoption papers and it was all finished with by the time I realised what was happening. I only saw my baby once.'

Breath whistled into his mouth. 'He played dirty.'

'Yes. He always boasted that he played to win, whatever it took. Sebastian's the same.'

'I'll get my guy on to it. We want to speed this up.'

'I can see to all that later, Lou. Just leave me with some pointers.'

'Let me help you now. If you could get in touch with your daughter, I'd not be leaving you on your own and that'd make me very happy.' He held out one hand to her. 'You're the gentlest, kindest person I've ever met, Miranda. I wish I'd known you before.'

She wasn't used to compliments, could feel herself blushing. His skin felt warm against hers, and beneath it there was strength, even now. It was a long time since she'd held a man's hand. She'd forgotten how good that felt.

He gave her hand a squeeze then let it drop. 'Change of subject before we get too maudlin. I don't want to spoil the mood, but I'm afraid there's something else we need to talk about.'

'Oh?'

'If I die suddenly, I don't want any attempts at resuscitation.'

All her joy fled. She hated the way he kept reminding her that he had only a limited amount of time to live.

'I've made what I call a living will, with Sally's help, and given copies to my doctor and Jack. I've got one for you as well. I mean it, Miranda. No resuscitation attempts. If I go suddenly, that's it. It'll save me a lot of pain and is infinitely preferable to a slow exit.'

'Are you . . . in more pain these days?'

'A bit. I'm coping, but I can see that I'll have to start using stronger drugs soon to control it. I hate having my head messed around, which painkillers always do. I'd not be me if I were all doped up.'

'What did the oncologist say last time you saw him?'

'That I'm doing well, better than expected.'

'That's good . . . isn't it? Means you may live longer than predicted.'

'Yes.' Lou lost his solemn look and gave her one of his boyish grins. 'I'll do my best, I promise you. I'm enjoying life so much, thanks mainly to you.'

He waved one arm at their surroundings. 'This is a great place to live and you're great company. I'm just trying to cover all eventualities with this no resuscitation stuff. Being prepared is a good way to face life. So . . . let's get cracking on finding your daughter. And on making plans for what you'll do after I go.'

'You don't need to worry about that.'

'Humour me. I want to be sure you'll continue to build a new life for yourself without your damned brother intervening.'

'I won't let him take over again, I promise.'

He looked at her gravely. 'No. I don't think you will. But he won't make it easy, so it might be good to get clean away from him. How about moving to England?'

'Regina suggested that, too.'

'I don't want you under her control, either, mind.'

She chuckled. 'Regina's not at all interested in controlling me. She has her own life. And she's not in Sebastian's league for control; she isn't even managing her daughter very well. Nikki's left home and is living in a bedsitter with the father of her coming baby. She emails me sometimes. Poor kid. She's finding it hard living in such cramped conditions.'

'You're a rather dysfunctional family, aren't you? Not together emotionally at all.'

'We all have different mothers and there are several years between each of us, so we didn't play together or anything. And it's different, I think, having a much older father. Dad had some very old-fashioned ideas about bringing up children. But Sebastian's happily married.' She remembered Dorothy's bland expressions and added, 'Well, I think he is.'

'You don't sound sure. Are there visible signs of affection between him and his wife? You know, smiles, touches, that sort of thing.'

'We're not a demonstrative family.'

He held out his hand to her again and she took it. 'See. *You* touch me without hesitation, and you pat me sometimes when you're helping me. I think you *are* a touchy-feely person, Miranda – or you could be.'

'I'm sorry if I've been . . . intrusive.'

He rolled his eyes. 'Intrusive-shmoosive! It's normal for human beings to touch one another. I *like* it. They call it skin hunger when you don't get touched by other people who care about you. I've felt that for a while.'

She realised she still had hold of his hand and tried to pull away, but his grasp tightened.

Her thoughts must have shown in her face because he let go of her abruptly.

'No! We're not going there, Miranda. You can't change the facts, you can only change how you deal with them. If you get too fond of me, I'll throw you out. I can't cope with that. Not now.'

His voice was so harsh she knew she'd really upset him. But he was right. 'I'm sorry. I won't . . . annoy you again.'

She'd expected him to smile and return to his old easy tone of voice, but he didn't. Grim-faced was the only way to describe him. Her heart began to pound. What would she do if he threw her out? She might be on her way to independence but she wasn't nearly there yet, needed his help to move on.

'I need a rest now, Miranda. Go and . . . do something.'

When she'd left, he stared blindly at the swimming pool outside. As the flickers of sunlight blurred and ran into one, he raised his hand to flick away the tears but more kept coming. He could so easily have loved her, made a life with her. He'd never met anyone quite like her: soft, utterly soft and feminine, completely without guile . . . Life was cruel.

It was a while before the tears stopped. Only then did he ring for Jack.

'I'm tired. I think I'll have a lie-down for a bit.'

Lou could see from Jack's expression that it was obvious he'd been crying. But Jack was a near-perfect carer and he made no comment, just walked along in front of the wheelchair and opened the lift door.

Pity the man was gay, Lou mused. It'd have been great to find someone for Miranda. No, there wasn't time for that. He must just focus on setting her up to succeed and then trust she'd find her own way in life and perhaps a man to share the future with. He was pretty sure she would. She didn't realise how attractive her gentleness was.

Three days later there was a message from the private investigator now tracing the adoption. Lou called to Miranda to come quickly, so she went hurrying into his computer room, a lavish home office, fitted out in style with the furniture he'd brought out of storage.

'He's found her.'

'Found who?'

'Halliday has found your daughter.'

All the air suddenly vanished from the room and Miranda clutched the nearest thing, which was Lou's shoulder. When things came into focus again, she looked down at him. 'Is she registered with one of the family tracing services? Does she . . . want to contact me?'

He shook his head. 'Not sure. She may be registered. We didn't go that route.'

'Then how . . . ?'

'Halliday traced her through a few unorthodox channels. We know where she lives, but she doesn't know yet that you're looking for her.'

'Oh.' Disappointment seared through Miranda. 'Then she might not want to meet me.'

'No. She might not. That was always on the cards. It's up to you to contact her.'

'She'll be twenty-six now. Is she married?'

'Yes. And has a child, a son.'

Joy blazed through her. 'I'm a grandmother?' Her life wasn't a dead end, then. Something of her would carry on, whatever came of this. Strange, how important that was. Tears of happiness welled in her eyes, but she smiled through them. 'That's such wonderful news.'

'What are you going to do?'

'Think about it, work out the best way to contact her, perhaps take advice about that.'

His voice was as gentle as his smile. 'I'll forward you the information he emailed to me.'

'Thank you.' She bent to kiss his cheek. 'I can't thank you enough, Lou. Would you mind if I went and sat in my room now? I need to get my head around this.'

'Do whatever you wish.'

But before she did anything else, she switched on her computer and opened up the file Lou had just sent her, studying it with wonder in her heart. Wiltshire. Her daughter and grandson lived in Wiltshire. She had been called Katie Brooke, but was now married to a Darren Parrish. Katie. Such a pretty name. At least her adoptive parents hadn't saddled her with old-fashioned, pretentious names like Miranda and Regina. And Katie's son was called Ned.

Miranda swallowed hard. Even to know this much made her feel elated – and yet apprehensive too. What if Katie didn't want to meet her?

The following day was scorching hot and Lou said he didn't want to go out in such weather, even in an air-conditioned car. 'Why don't we go house hunting on the Internet instead, to while away an hour or two?'

'House hunting? But we've got this place.'

'We can look at houses in England, for you.'

He was looking tired and she guessed he wanted an excuse for company, so she pulled a chair across to stare with him at the images on the computer screen. After a while, she said thoughtfully, 'Let's look at rentals instead.'

'Humour me and look at houses for sale. Much nicer to have a home of your own.'

'But I can't afford to buy one. It'll just make me feel envious.'

He gave her one of his cocky looks. 'No, but I could buy one for you.'

She didn't even have to think about that. 'No!'

'Why not?'

'Because it wouldn't be right. I'll ask the trust, plead with them to sell that dreadful flat and . . .' She couldn't finish, because no way could she see Sebastian allowing that to happen.

Lou laid one hand on hers. 'You'll not get anywhere with that brother of yours and we both know it. He's got his hands clamped tightly around your money and he won't let go unless the law forces him to. And since contesting a will takes time, years probably, I'll buy you a house so that you can escape there as soon as . . . as you need to.'

'Lou, I can't let you do that.'

He grinned. 'How can you stop me?'

She stared at him in shock then said quietly, 'I don't need to, because I know you'd never force something on me.' She saw the light go out of his eyes and took both his hands. 'Lou, you've given me so much already. I can't go on taking. It's enough, truly it is. Besides, buying a house would cost a fortune. Your remaining money should go to your family.'

He took her hand. 'Would you let me buy it if you knew I was a billionaire and it would give me enormous pleasure?'

She grew very still, feeling shocked. 'Are you really so rich?'

He shook his head. 'Not quite a billionaire, but a multi-millionaire, yes. Even Hilary doesn't know how rich I really am. Don't worry. There will be plenty to leave to my niece. Let me give you a house, Miranda. Please?'

She sat down on the floor beside his wheelchair, arms clasped around her knees, trying to come to terms with this development. 'I don't know what to say.'

'Think about it, at least.'

She stared down at the expensive new skirt, crumpled

now. 'I shouldn't be sitting on the floor in such beautiful clothes.'

'You can scrub the floor with them if you want! From now on, Miranda, don't do what you think you *ought* to do. Do what you *want*, do what will give you pleasure, or give other people pleasure. I've lived all my life for business. I was married once, but I cared more about money in those days and she wanted a real family. When I found I had inoperable cancer, I knew she'd been right and I'd been wrong. But I've been doing something useful with my money for the past few weeks: spending it, giving it to charities I approve of. And I've enjoyed that very much.'

'And I'm another of your charities, aren't I?' She couldn't keep the bitterness out of her voice. People dreamt of having a fairy godmother to bestow gifts upon them, but the gifts she wanted weren't money. She ached for confidence and independence, preferably won through her own efforts. She was coming to see that, now she'd time to think about her own needs.

'You're not a charity. I was rather hoping you were a friend, a very dear friend.'

She looked sideways and found him staring at her with that wise, other-worldly look. 'Yes, I am. I've never had such a good friend as you, Lou.'

'So you'll allow me to buy you a house?'

She sighed, knowing she couldn't refuse him. 'A small one, then. And I'll pay for the furniture myself by selling those antiques. I can't just take and take.'

He nodded. 'All right.'

As she was getting to her feet, she saw the intense satisfaction on his face. She knew then that she was doing the right thing. For him, anyway.

But was she doing the right thing for herself? Or was she once again letting someone else rule her life?

As Regina walked into the school, she felt nervous. Ridiculous to be nervous of meeting her own daughter, but she was. She'd phoned Nikki, trying to persuade her to come home and talk, but her daughter had refused point-blank.

The counsellor came out to meet her with what Regina considered a professional smile – the same sort of smile she used with customers.

'Do come in.'

She looked round. Nikki wasn't there. 'Where's my daughter?'

'I thought we could have a few words first, Ms Fox.'

'Softening me up? I'm not going to attack her, you know.'

'She's very nervous about this meeting. Thinks you'll try to get her to change her mind.'

'Well, I haven't changed my mind. She has the whole of her life before her and to get lumbered with a child before she's even got her qualifications is crazy. But I can hardly force her into having an abortion.'

'And refusing to accept her wishes gracefully could drive a wedge between yourself and your daughter. Do you really want that?'

'Of course I don't.'

'Treat her gently, Ms Fox. She's not feeling well, which makes her very vulnerable.'

'What's wrong?'

The counsellor gave her another of those meaningless smiles. 'The doctor told her it's just pregnancy sickness. Some women sail through the nine months; others are sick a lot of the time and she's one of them.'

'She's not . . . at risk?'

'She says not.'

'*She* says? Haven't you checked directly with the doctor?'

'No. Your daughter is legally an adult, so she can do what she wants.'

'She may be legally an adult, but she's still a child in many ways. All she knows is school and—'

The counsellor leant back. 'She'll be here in a minute. Please, calm down and go easy on her. If I think you're upsetting her too much, I'll have to end the meeting.'

Regina bit back a protest, recognising a brick wall when she met one. They sat for a couple of minutes in silence and she caught herself drumming her fingers on the arm of her chair. She'd rather have asked a few more questions but the counsellor was staring out of the window, presumably having said what she wanted to.

There was a knock on the door and Nikki came in. She looked pale and had lost weight, but what shocked Regina rigid was that her face had changed. It had a different expression on it, a woman's face now. She was suddenly so afraid of losing her daughter that she stood up, holding out her arms. 'Don't I get a hug any more?'

Nikki came rushing forward and when Regina put her arms round her, the two women clung to one another. Regina couldn't decide which of them needed the hug more. It seemed to say there was still hope, that the situation wasn't so bad things couldn't be mended between them.

As she drew away she reached out to brush away a tear rolling down Nikki's face.

'I'm so glad to see you. So very glad.'

The counsellor cleared her throat. 'I think we're over the main hurdle now. Wouldn't you two prefer to talk in private?'

Regina looked at her daughter. 'I'd like that very much.

What about you, Nikki?'

'As long as you don't go on about abortions.'

'I won't.'

Nikki searched her face and seemed reassured by what she saw there. 'I'll have to be back when lessons end, though, or Tim will be worrying about me. There's a café across the road. It's got booths, so we'll be fairly private.'

Nikki walked out of the school grounds with her mother. That felt strange. Well, everything felt strange lately. Not until they'd sat down in the café did she admit, 'I thought you'd be furious.' 'I'm sad most of all. And bewildered. Not long ago you were a child. Now . . .'

'I'm growing up fast. I don't have much choice about that, do I? I'm going to be responsible for another life.'

'Yes. Will you give me your address? Can I come and see you?'

'You can have the address, but it's a horrid place so I'd rather come and visit you, if you don't mind. A studio flat they call it. Hah! It's a grotty bedsitter.'

'One room. That must be hard. How are you coping with running a house on top of . . . everything else?'

'Tim does most of the housework. He's very domesticated. His mother's always insisted on him and his brother doing their share of the chores.'

'Good for her. You'll need help with the living expenses and I'm prepared to give you some money every week. And perhaps we could look round for somewhere better for you to live? If you'd like to, that is?'

'I would.' Nikki had never heard her mother sound so hesitant. The whole world was topsy-turvy lately, and she sometimes felt as if she was floating in an alien sea, not knowing where the currents would take her. She swallowed hard and added, 'I'm glad we're talking again.'

'Me too.'

'Tell me about Grandfather. I suppose he left you some money.'

Her mother explained about the will and Nikki stared at her in horror. 'They did that to poor old Auntie Min?'

'She's not all that old, only six years older than me.'

'She always seems a lot older, looks it too. Couldn't you stop them treating her like that?'

'No. It was a fait accompli. But Minnie's hired a lawyer to contest the will, a good one too, so I'm hoping she'll get the same as us in the end. If anyone asks me, I'll say she deserves it.'

'Won't that take ages, though?'

'Unfortunately, yes.'

'Poor thing.'

'She's found a new friend, a man. She's moved in with him and he's helping her.'

'*Aunt Minnie!*'

'Yes. Women over forty aren't quite in their dotage, you know.'

Nikki could see she'd put her foot in it. Her mother often got very touchy about her age. She glanced at the clock. 'I have to leave in a couple of minutes.'

'We've hardly begun to talk. About the baby—'

She stood up. 'I don't really want to talk about that yet. Having it's a done deal. But if you can help us with somewhere to live, I'd be more grateful than you know.' She watched her mother bite back words then stand up.

'I hope you know what you're getting yourself into.'

'I hope so too.'

'We'll discuss money next time. Here. This is all I've got on me at the moment.' She thrust something into Nikki's hand.

Glancing down, she saw some folded banknotes. 'Thanks. It's been a bit . . . difficult.'

Nikki watched her mother drive away, glad the meeting was over. It had gone better than she'd expected, far better, but she was exhausted now. And word was out at school about the baby, so she still had to face her classmates. She wasn't looking forward to that, either.

Chapter Nine

Katie looked in the mirror one final time, fiddling with her hair, wondering if she should have had those blonde streaks put in. They masked the fact that her hair was a soft reddish brown, a colour she'd never quite liked because it was so different from her parents' mousy hair.

She didn't know if it was the same as her birth parents' hair. It must be – one of them, anyway. Did she get this strange reddish colour from her mother or her father?

Too late now to do anything about her appearance. She was meeting her birth father for lunch and if she didn't want to be late, she needed to get on her way. She'd chosen one of the gastropubs in the town centre, a place where she'd feel safe and where, she felt, no one would know her.

She hadn't told anyone what she was doing, not even Darren. Well, her husband had enough on his plate surviving in Afghanistan without her adding to his worries. He'd understand. He always did.

She drove into town, narrowly missing running into another car at some traffic lights, which brought her sharply to her senses. Heart still thudding, concentrating on her driving now and keeping her unruly thoughts at bay, she found a parking place and edged the car into it gently.

He was early, far too early. Brody Lanigan paced up and down outside the pub, wondering if his daughter would be early, or if she'd even turn up today. She hadn't sounded enthusiastic about them meeting, very cool, in fact. He couldn't remember being so nervous since he'd grown up, but then nothing had been as important as this for a long time, nothing.

A woman came walking along towards the pub and his heart nearly stopped. Her hair colour was rather like his, except for those blonde streaks, but her features were so like her mother's that he would have accosted her in the street and asked who she was if he'd seen her before now.

He moved forward, taking care not to crowd her too closely. 'Katie?'

She stopped and stared at him. 'Mr Lanigan?'

'Yes.' He held back the impulse to ask her to use his first name at least, and gestured. 'Shall we go inside?'

She hesitated, studying him. 'We could go and sit in the park instead, if you like. It'd be . . . more private. I'm not really hungry.'

'Neither am I. Too excited about meeting you.'

She didn't respond to that one, just stood and waited.

The resemblance wasn't as close to her mother when she spoke, he decided, because her own personality took over, but he didn't need DNA testing to prove who she was.

He realised she was waiting for a reply. 'That's fine with me. I don't know the town, so you'll have to show me the way.'

She turned and he followed, not sure what to say, staying silent when she didn't try to make small talk either, worrying already that this wasn't going as well as he'd hoped.

The park was a public garden, with plenty of people walking about and aluminium benches to sit on. She chose one in a corner, in full view of people, but with no other benches nearby.

He sat down, carefully keeping a distance, but not enough to let someone come and sit between them.

'How did you find me?' she asked.

'I've had a private investigator working on the case for a while.'

She looked surprised, a frown creasing her forehead. 'Why would you go to that length?'

'Because when you were born, I wasn't allowed near you. You were taken away and never heard of again. I found out you'd been adopted, but I was too young then, and too poor, to do anything about it. But I always wanted to find you – and I'm sure I have done. You're so like your mother, I'm having trouble handling this.'

'My birth mother,' she corrected.

He nodded and repeated obediently, 'Birth mother.'

She swallowed hard and began to fiddle with her handbag. 'I'd have to have proof. Maybe we should get our DNA tested.'

He felt in his pocket. 'Or maybe this will convince you.' He offered her the photo. 'This is your mother. That's me.'

She stared at it and her mouth began to wobble. 'She is very like me.'

'Could be your twin.'

Tears began to roll down her face and she fumbled in her bag for a handkerchief, but didn't seem to be finding one.

He thrust his at her. 'Here.'

She mopped her eyes and tried to speak, then the tears started again. 'I'm sorry.'

He risked squeezing her hand. 'Don't be. It's a big thing.' He found she was clinging to his hand, sobbing openly, and pulled her into his arms, shushing her gently and patting her back till she stopped crying so hard.

As she drew away, he released her instantly. 'Sorry.'

'Don't be.' He blinked because his own eyes were suspiciously moist. 'Can I borrow the handkerchief for a moment?'

She gave a shaky laugh and shared it with him, but needed to take it back again. 'I don't know what to do.'

'Whatever you feel comfortable with. I don't want to disrupt your life or upset your adoptive parents.'

'Dad's dead.'

'I'm sorry.'

'Me too. He was a great father.'

'I'm glad for you.' And he *was* pleased about it, but jealous too. 'And your adoptive mother? Is she still alive?'

'Yes. She remarried last year and she's living in Cornwall. I'm married myself but my husband's in the army, in Afghanistan. We have a son.'

He nodded. 'So my PI told me.'

'What happened to my birth mother?'

'I don't know. Her family whisked her away and she wasn't seen or heard of for a couple of years. They'd always insisted on having the baby adopted and she must have given in. She got word to my family just once, a couple of years later, that we'd had a daughter. She gave me your date of birth. That's how I knew about you.'

'She didn't want me?'

Here was the million-dollar question. 'I don't know. Her family was very . . . dominating. They had money, contacts. They made sure I couldn't get a job easily, so I had to move to another town, and I'm pretty sure they got me chucked out of my flat, too.'

'Where were you living then?'

'Western Australia. Perth.'

'My parents lived in Australia for a while. Near Sydney. But they came back here after I was born.'

Silence fell again and he steeled himself to ask the question. 'Would you like to stay in touch? Get to know one another?'

She looked at him with a troubled expression. 'I think so. I'll have to talk to my husband about letting you meet Ned, though.'

'I can give you character references and get a police clearance. You'll want to check up on me and I don't mind that at all. In fact, I'd prefer it if you did.'

Her face cleared. 'That'd be good. I have to be careful, for Ned's sake.'

'That's your son?'

She smiled, suddenly beautiful. 'Yes. He's five, a real handful, in his first year at school.'

'How about that coffee now?'

'Does it show that I've been crying?'

It was his turn to study her. 'I'm afraid it does. Your mother had the same delicate skin.'

'Tell me about her.'

'I can only tell you what she was like then. I haven't seen her, not once, since her family found out about the baby.' But he'd thought about her often, dreamt about her occasionally still, much to his annoyance.

Half an hour later Katie looked at her watch. 'I have to go now and pick up Ned from school. I'll give you my mobile number.'

He didn't say that he knew exactly where she and her son lived, even had a photo of the boy. He didn't want to frighten her. 'I'll give you my mobile number as well. I'd really like to get to know you and meet my grandson, but it's your call when and where.'

'I'll be in touch.'

He watched her walk away, kept his calm as he went to find his car and drive home, but once he was safely out of sight of the world, he wept nearly as hard as she had done. He'd been hunting for her for a while, thinking about her since he'd heard from her mother – who could go to hell and fry there for keeping him from raising his only child!

Why had Miranda done that to him? He'd never understood. He'd wanted to marry her, wanted to very much. She'd said she loved him.

She must have loved her family more.

Miranda hummed as she got herself a bowl of muesli. She was feeling happier than she had for years. Living in such comfort, with others to do the hard work, spending her days with an intelligent man, having time for herself – life didn't get much better. Well, hers never had, anyway.

She knew it couldn't go on for ever, but it was the respite she'd desperately needed and she did think Lou was enjoying them living together, too.

The lift whirred and a minute later he came rolling into the kitchen. 'You look well.'

'I feel well.'

'It's great getting up and seeing your smiling face.' He waved a paper at her. 'I had trouble sleeping and I think I've found you somewhere to live. Here. I printed out the details.'

As she reached out to take it from him, he stiffened and clutched his chest, groaning. 'No! Not yet. Not—'

His eyes rolled up and he slumped in the chair.

'Lou!'

But she'd seen that same look on her father's face, a sudden absence of life and expression, like a wax model of the person who'd once inhabited the body. Dropping the piece of paper she forced herself to feel for a pulse but found nothing.

No resuscitation, he'd said, and it had indeed been an easy death.

Fighting back tears, she murmured, 'Goodbye, Lou.' She bent to kiss his cheek and then stood up, trying to work out what to do. Her brain didn't seem to be functioning properly, so she walked out into the hall and yelled, 'Jack! Jack, come quickly!' There was no answer and she nearly panicked, then realised she could have used the little com-unit Lou had, so went back to press the emergency button on that.

He might have stipulated no resuscitation, but he'd not wanted to die quite yet, she'd seen that for herself. She'd have given months of her own life to buy him a little more time. He certainly deserved it, had so wanted to finish his last work – remaking Minnie into Miranda, a much better person, in charge of her own life.

Could she carry on with his task and do that on her own? She didn't know, but since she owed so much to him, she vowed to try with every fibre of her being. 'I won't let you down, Lou.'

Jack came rushing into the kitchen, took in the situation at a glance and, as she had done, felt for a pulse. He looked at her across the body. 'He's dead.'

'Yes. It was . . . quick and easy.' Her voice broke on the last word.

'I think you'd better sit down, Ms Fox. You're very pale.'

'Am I?' As if that mattered. She let him guide her to a chair, but her eyes kept going back to Lou. Oh, she was going to miss him so much! She realised Jack had been speaking and made an effort to concentrate. 'Sorry. What did you say?'

'I said: he's made all the arrangements, so if you'll leave it to me, I'll do what's necessary.'

'The funeral?'

'All arranged. He didn't want his niece making the decisions about that.' He glanced back at the body. 'I think you'd be better sitting somewhere else because we're supposed to leave him as we found him till a doctor's been to see him.'

'The housekeeper will be arriving soon.'

'I'll deal with Tania. Perhaps you could wait in the small sitting room?'

She let him guide her there, wondering why she wasn't in tears. She'd nearly started weeping when it happened, but now she felt as if her emotions had been locked away.

She went to stand by the window, which looked out on to the patio he'd loved so much. Poor Lou had only had a few weeks in this house, but at least he'd loved being here. And so had she.

She supposed she'd better ring his niece, but she

couldn't face doing that yet, so sat down and thanked whatever kind fate had led her to Lou Rayne. He'd given her so much.

And she *wouldn't* let him down. She would not!

Once the doctor had left and undertakers had taken the body away, Jack came to find her. 'Are you all right?'

Was she? 'I feel a bit numb.'

'Shock. It happened so suddenly. Even I thought he'd live for months longer. Um . . . Mr Rayne told me you should contact Sally Patel if he died.'

'I suppose so.'

He hesitated. 'Are you sure you're up to it? Shall I get her on the phone for you?'

That hit home. No, she wasn't sure she was up to anything, but she was very sure she was going to try. 'I'll be fine. I'll do it straight away.'

She rang Sally's office, wondering if such a busy lawyer would have time for her. But when she explained, the receptionist said, 'I'll put you through to Ms Patel, Ms Fox.'

Miranda took a deep breath and began her explanation.

'Oh, damn!'

'I beg your pardon?'

'Lou was coming in today to sign a revised will. I'd better come and see you so that I can explain how things stand before his niece arrives.'

'*You* are coming to see *me*? Shouldn't I come to your rooms?'

Sally gave a snort that was almost a laugh. 'He wasn't just a client, Miranda, he was a very dear friend. I'll miss him as much as you will. Now, I can't get there till just after eleven, so hold off on informing people he's dead, especially that brother of yours. In fact, don't let Sebastian Fox into the house.'

'I think Lou's manservant has already told his niece.'

'Hmm. Well, in case she comes straight round, remember that the tenancy of that house is in your name not hers, so she can't throw you out.'

'Throw me out?'

'Yes. You must have noticed the way she looks at you. She's been terrified you'd cut her out of Lou's will. I bet she tries to get rid of you today.'

Miranda couldn't believe anyone would be so heartless. 'I'm sure she won't. But surely the contents of the house are hers.'

'Some of them, if I remember correctly. She can't take anything till after we get probate, though. Remember that.'

As Miranda put the phone down the doorbell rang. She sighed. She didn't want to deal with people. What she really wanted was to go and sit quietly on the patio, in the place Lou had loved so much. She walked out into the hall and met Tania on her way to answer the door. 'I'll see to that.'

'Very well, Ms Fox.'

When Miranda opened the door, Hilary Rayne walked in without waiting for an invitation.

'Where's my uncle's body?'

'The undertaker has taken him away, but is bringing him back tomorrow.'

'How dare you call in an undertaker without consulting me? You're not a relative. I'd like you to pack your things and leave this house immediately. From now on, I shall be—'

Miranda's numbness vanished abruptly. '*Leave this house?*'

'Yes.'

'Have you no compassion?'

'You've not known my uncle long enough to grieve deeply, and I'm sure you lined your pockets nicely while he was still alive. Let the thought of that cheer you up.'

Miranda drew herself up. 'Actually, this is my house, so you have no authority here.'

Hilary went white. 'He can't have bought it for you already!'

'He leased it in my name. I wondered why he insisted on doing that; now I know.'

'And the contents?' Her eyes went to the pictures on the walls, the scattering of beautiful ornaments on tables and stands.

'How should I know? We never discussed his will. Presumably his lawyer will be able to tell you that. She's coming round shortly. You're welcome to stay until then.'

'I heard that your brother is a lawyer. Why do you need anyone else?'

'None of your business.' Miranda gestured with one hand. 'No one is using the small sitting room. I'll ask Tania to bring you a cup of tea.'

'Herbal.' Hilary's expression was tight with suppressed hostility but she marched across the hall, heels drumming on the floor.

Miranda walked through to the formal lounge, an elegant space which could comfortably seat twenty people. Lou had loved this room, had hung his favourite paintings here and displayed his favourite objets d'art. She loved it too, but she'd enjoyed his pleasure much more than the beauty of the art works.

She used the intercom to ask Tania to take some herbal tea to Mr Rayne's niece, then went across to the window. Hugging her arms round herself, she stared sightlessly out at the front garden. She hadn't realised how hostile Hilary felt towards her. Lou must have known, though.

Well, they could take away all the furniture and art works. Thanks to Lou's foresight, she didn't have to move out until she was ready. She even had enough furniture of her own to manage here until she'd worked out what to do, though she'd have to let the staff go, couldn't afford to pay them.

Sebastian picked up the phone.

'There's a Ms Rayne on the line insisting she speak to you,' his PA said.

'Who?' Then he recognised the name. Who was this? An ex-wife of that fellow? 'Put her on.'

'Mr Fox, I'm Lou Rayne's niece. I don't know whether you're aware that my uncle died today.'

'No. I wasn't aware of it. Please accept my condolences. When did this happen?'

'Early this morning.'

'Is my sister all right?'

'Your grasping sister has possession of his house and I want you to get her out. I deeply resent her presence here at a sad time like this. And if she's got him to leave his money to her, I warn you, I'm going to contest the will.'

The phone snapped off before he could say a word. So Lou Rayne was dead. Sebastian smiled. Good. He'd be able to bring Minnie back into line again now.

But if Rayne really had left her a lot of money, he'd have to do something about it, and that didn't mean letting Hilary Rayne claim it back. Minnie knew nothing about managing money, nothing at all, and without Rayne's support, she could easily become unstable again.

He glanced at his engagements diary. Fate was on his side, it seemed. Nothing for the next couple of hours. He could go and see her straight away.

Miranda was sitting down when she heard a car pull up to the house. Assuming it was Sally Patel, she hurried to open the front door, horrified to see her brother coming towards her. She tried to close the door again, but he put out one hand and held it open.

'Let me in, Minnie.'

'No. I don't want you here.'

He shoved her back into the house and moved inside. 'Don't be ridiculous. Who else should be here to help you but your family?'

'I don't need your help and I want you to leave.'

'Of course you need my help. You have to sort out your financial situation and plan what to do next.'

She edged towards the intercom and managed to switch it on by feeling behind her, raising her voice, hoping to catch Jack's attention. 'Please leave this house immediately, Sebastian!'

'Where did Rayne keep his papers?'

'That has nothing to do with you.'

With a scornful look, he turned on his heel. 'He must have a home office.'

She rushed after him, grabbing his arm as he started to throw doors open. 'Did you hear what I said? Get out of my house!'

By that time Hilary Rayne had come to the door of the small sitting room and was watching with a look of intense satisfaction on her face.

Sebastian looked across at her. 'I'm afraid my sister is hysterical.'

'I can see that. Do you need my help?'

'Not now. But I'm sure you'll remember what a state she was in.'

'I certainly will.'

Miranda could have wept with frustration.

'I'm going upstairs, Minnie. You're to stay here and try to calm down.'

'I'll calm down completely the minute you get out of my house.'

Ignoring that he started up the stairs.

Someone pushed the front door fully open and a voice said, 'What's going on here?'

Miranda turned round, tears streaming down her face. 'Sally! My brother has shoved his way in and he won't leave, though I've asked him to.'

'She became hysterical,' Hilary said at once. 'I saw it all. Of course he couldn't leave her in that state.'

Sally looked across at Sebastian, who smirked. 'Shall we discuss this in more comfort?'

He walked slowly down the stairs, taking Miranda's arm as he passed and forcing her to walk next to him.

'Let go of me!' She tried to drag herself away from him but he held on so tightly it hurt.

'At this rate, we'll be suing you for assault, Fox,' Sally said in a very crisp, authoritative tone.

'It's not assault to try to calm down a hysterical woman who also happens to be my sister.'

'She wasn't hysterical,' another voice said.

Jack ran lightly down the stairs. 'Ms Patel, I'm very glad you've come before the situation got out of hand. I was just about to ring your office. Since the intercom was switched on, I've heard everything they both said. She asked him to leave, but he refused and started searching the house.'

'I heard everything too.' Tania walked out of the door that led to the service area. 'And I'd have been just as upset as Ms Fox if someone had forced their way into my house like he did.'

Sally smiled sweetly. 'I'm glad to hear that. Won't you both join us? Miranda, dear, come and sit next to me.' She led the way into the formal living room and sat down on Lou's big armchair, which dominated the room.

Sebastian followed, giving the two servants a dirty look as he flung himself down on a couch next to Hilary.

'Now, please tell me what happened this morning, Miranda.' She stared across the rug at the visitors. 'And I don't want any interruptions. You'll all get your turn to speak.'

'This is not a court of law,' Sebastian snapped.

'We can take it before a JP if you prefer. I happen to know that Paul Mawson is playing golf this morning, but he'll abandon his game if I tell him this is an emergency. I can easily send for him.'

Sebastian scowled and leant back, arms folded.

Miranda explained what had happened, managing to speak calmly.

When Sebastian opened his mouth to interrupt, Sally held up one finger and he closed his mouth again.

After everyone had had their say, she stood up and moved to stand in front of the fireplace with its huge flower arrangement. 'I'm holding my late client's will. I'm also aware that this house is rented in Ms Fox's name, so if she asks someone to leave, then that person should do so immediately.'

'I have no intention of leaving my sister to flounder

around without support,' Sebastian said. 'You may not be aware that she had a nervous breakdown and was hospitalised for over a year.'

Sally turned to Miranda. 'Is that true?'

'That was over twenty years ago and I've had no mental health problems since. It was postnatal depression, actually. And if I need support now, it'll be from my lawyer not from my brother, whom I don't trust.'

'Fine. You've made your wishes clear to me. As Ms Fox's legal representative, I'm asking you to leave this house now, Mr Fox, and not to return unless your sister invites you to.'

His expression spoke volumes but after hesitating for a moment or two, he got up and moved towards the door, where he turned to say, 'I shall be taking advice about this.'

When he'd gone Sally turned to Lou's niece. 'If you'll make an appointment to come and see me in my office, I'll explain your uncle's will to you, Ms Rayne. I can tell you now, however, that you're the major beneficiary.'

Hilary's face brightened then her smile faded as she looked across at Miranda. 'Has *she* been left anything?'

'I'm not at liberty to disclose the other provisions Mr Rayne made – and the secrecy is at his express order.'

'If he's left anything to her, anything at all, I warn you I shall contest the will.'

'You're being rather premature and, if I may say so, rather greedy too. Mr Rayne has left you enough to live on in luxury for the rest of your days, but he's also left generous amounts to several trusts and charities as well. I can't see a court finding anything wrong with that.'

'Is she included in that?'

Sally took a deep breath. 'Please keep any further questions for when you come to see me. Do you wish Ms Rayne to leave now, Miranda?'

'Yes, I do.' She looked across at the younger woman. 'I'll get Jack to let you know about the funeral. Lou left him detailed instructions. I don't know what he wanted. It was Lou who organised everything, not me.'

'There you are. You have nothing to worry about.' Sally gave Hilary one of her famous glassy smiles. 'I think you'd better leave now and not come back unless invited by Ms Fox.'

She turned to the two servants. 'Would you mind making statements about what happened today?'

'Not at all.'

When she'd gone, Jack said, 'I know Mr Rayne was going to change his will. Did he not do that?'

Sally sighed. 'Unfortunately he died before everything could be signed. He was going to do that tomorrow.' She looked at Miranda. 'I'm sorry. You'd have been in a better position with the revised will.'

'I'll be perfectly all right. After all, I do still have the money from the trust to live on.'

'And your brother to deal with. He seems to think he can bully you.'

'He always has,' she said in a low voice.

After a moment's sympathetic silence, Sally turned

back to the other two. 'I'll send my clerk later today to take your statements about what happened this morning. You're not leaving yet?'

They looked at Miranda.

'I'd be really grateful if you'd stay until after the funeral, when we should all know where we stand. And I'd like to thank you both very much for standing up for me today.'

'We told the truth,' Tania said. 'It's a good thing the intercom was switched on.'

'I managed to switch it on without Sebastian realising,' Miranda admitted.

'Well done!' Sally said approvingly.

Only after the door had closed behind them did she turn to Miranda and lose the crisp look and tone. 'I'm sorry you had to go through that, today of all days. The scene was like something out of a gothic novel! I can't believe a lawyer with Fox's reputation could behave like that in private.'

'He's always bullied me and when he physically manhandles me, I can do nothing about it, because he's so big. He takes after Father's side of the family and I take after my mother's.'

'Has he manhandled you before, then?'

'All my life.'

Sally let out a huff of anger. 'With your permission, I'll take out an injunction on your behalf that he must stay away from you.'

'I doubt he'll obey it.'

'Oh, I think he will. It would look very bad for a lawyer to be in breach of the law.'

'He'll find a way to circumvent it.' She felt indignation rise. 'Why did he bring up my bout of depression? He talked as if I'd turned into a halfwit.'

'We'll have to keep an eye on that.'

'I shan't feel safe, even if we do take out an injunction. My sister and Lou both said I should get out of the country, as far away from Sebastian as I can, and they were right. Once everything's sorted, I'm going to go and live in England.'

Sally stared at her in approval. 'What a good idea! We'll start working on it after the funeral. I'd like to help you, if that's all right with you?'

'Why should you do that?'

'Because I hate to see people being bullied and because Lou cared about you. There will be no charge whatsoever.'

'Thank you. I can't believe you're being so kind.'

Miranda saw her visitor to the door, then trailed back inside, making for the kitchen because she suddenly felt very thirsty.

Tania turned as she entered. 'I just wanted a cup of tea.'

'I'll make it for you. Oh, and there was this piece of paper under the table. It's something printed from the Internet. Is it yours or should I throw it away?' She held it out.

Miranda took it and realised it was the paper Lou

had been holding, something he'd printed out from the Internet for her. 'It's mine. Thank you. I'll be out on the patio if you don't mind bringing my tea there.' She'd already learnt that the kitchen was Tania's territory during the day, so left her to it.

She went to sit in Lou's favourite spot, feeling desolate and alone. The paper crackled as she clutched it to her chest and she smoothed it out, wondering what he had been so excited about. If he'd gone to this much trouble, she was certainly going to read it. But not now. Now she just wanted to sit in peace for a while.

Chapter Ten

The day of the funeral dawned with intermittent clouds and sunshine, a typical late autumn day in Western Australia. As Miranda got dressed, she couldn't help remembering her father's funeral, when she'd looked so shabby. It seemed a long time ago and yet it was only a couple of months. Today she was wearing some of the beautiful clothes Lou had bought for her and her hair had been properly cut and styled.

The woman in the mirror stared back at her, looking a little anxious, but also very elegant. That still surprised her every time she saw herself. The only garment Lou hadn't seen and approved was the hat, an elegant confection in black mesh with a wide brim and one black silk rose sitting in a spray of leaves that curved around the crown of the hat. He'd have liked the hat. She'd known that as soon as she put it on in the shop.

Regina had emailed to offer condolences, wish her

well and bring her up to date about Nikki. Something about her sister's email was different, less confident perhaps. Miranda didn't have time to think about it just then. She hadn't heard from Nikki herself for a while and would make an effort to get in touch with her niece once this was over.

The funeral was to be held at the crematorium without any clergyman officiating, by Lou's express wish. His instructions said that his beliefs were his own and he didn't want a stranger, priest or not, pontificating about him.

Hilary got out of a sleek black vehicle just as the limousine carrying Miranda and Jack drew up. They got out and waited. She turned to glare at them and took the lead position in the line of people waiting to follow the hearse from the gathering point to the chapel.

The funeral director came to escort Miranda into the second position in the line, leaving Jack to go to the rear. She tried to demur, but he said that Mr Rayne had worked it all out and left them a list, so she stayed where she was. If Lou wanted her here, then here she'd stay. She felt a lot better, however, when Sally fell into place beside her.

There were more people there than Miranda had expected and more arriving all the time. These people exuded money: men with confident faces and perfectly fitting suits, dagger-thin women dressed in what she was sure were designer clothes, all nodding familiarly to one another.

'Lou was well liked,' Sally said quietly as people continued to arrive.

'Why did he never see any of them?'

'They knew he had terminal cancer and didn't intrude. Some of them have flown in from the eastern states or overseas.'

Eventually the hearse came along, moving very slowly, and they walked behind it to the chapel. The tears Miranda had been holding back overflowed and ran down her cheeks, so she bent her head a little, hoping the hat would hide them.

To her horror, cameras flashed and journalists kept pace with the women at the head of the line of mourners.

'Ignore them,' Sally said.

'Why are the media here? And why on earth do they want to photograph me?'

'Lou was a very rich man and you were his last known companion.'

Miranda looked at her in horror. Hilary thought she was a gold-digger and now everyone else would.

'They're not important,' Sally repeated firmly.

The service was brief and consisted of a short piece written by Lou and read by Sally. He thanked everyone for attending, but especially thanked Miranda, who had brightened his last days, and his niece, who had looked after him when he was incapacitated.

Sally looked out at the mourners, not trying to hide her tears. 'I shall miss him very much.'

Hilary stood up and Miranda braced herself for

some pointed remarks, but his niece said very little, only regretting that she'd lost her uncle. She called down the Lord's blessing on his soul, the only mention of religion in the whole service.

Finally the coffin slid out of sight.

Hilary led the way into the reception area and Miranda tried to find a corner out of the way, as she usually did at social events. But Sally stayed by her side and people came up to speak to them, so this time she wasn't left to watch the others. She was grateful for their kind words and treasured the remarks they made about Lou.

Other people gave her curious glances but saved their condolences for his niece.

'There's a proper reception in town afterwards,' Sally said. 'You should attend.'

'I know. Jack told me, but I really don't think—'

'It's Lou's farewell. He wanted them to have a party, eat well, drink well, reminisce about him. You can't let him down.' With a sigh Miranda got back into the limousine and endured another hour or two of chatting to strangers in a luxury suite in a hotel.

'I'd better go and deal with the will now,' Sally said. 'I've seen Hilary and she's ready.'

'I'll take a taxi home, then, and leave you to it.'

'You're needed. He's left you something.'

Miranda looked at her in dismay. 'His niece will say I only stayed with him for the money, and I didn't.'

'As long as you know the truth, what does her opinion matter?'

'It'll matter if she says it publicly.'

'That won't matter once you're in England, and it'll only be a two-day wonder, anyway.'

She said it confidently, as if going to England was a fait accompli.

Another sweeping change coming into her life, Miranda thought. And such a big one. She just wanted to stay in that lovely house for a while and . . . and what? She didn't know, felt herself to be drifting without Lou's support and encouragement.

Sally settled Hilary and Miranda in her office.

'I've asked my legal representative to join us,' Hilary announced. She looked at her watch. 'He won't be long.'

Another lawyer was shown in five minutes later. Sally nodded a greeting, introduced him to Miranda and indicated a chair which he brought across next to Hilary's.

Sitting down behind the desk, Sally picked up some papers. 'These give details of the other bequests in the will, and I have copies for you. What is more pertinent today, I feel, is how the will affects the two beneficiaries here, Lou's niece and his partner. The major beneficiary is his niece, Hilary, to whom he's left approximately ten million dollars in today's terms. It would have been more but for the recent crash in the share market. However, if you hold on to the shares, as he advises in a note he wrote to you only last week, their value should rise again.'

Hilary nodded.

'He also left you the contents of his house, except for those items specified in the bequest to his partner, which I shall detail later. My client left separate bequests to five charities which he had supported with regular donations for many years. These amount to approximately two-thirds of what you've received.'

Hilary nodded again, though there was a sour expression on her face. Could she not be satisfied? Miranda wondered. She was rich now. Imagine having all that money! How free you would feel!

'And finally, to his partner Miranda Fox, he left the contents of his home office, including his computer, and everything in the big sitting room in the house they were sharing. In addition there are a few more pieces of art, which are still in storage, and his car.'

'I want to know what they're all worth!' Hilary said at once.

Sally stared at her, not hiding her disgust. 'Why?'

'Because if they're valuable I'm going to contest the will. *She* wormed her way into his life very recently and she doesn't deserve any bequest at all.'

The lawyer put his hand on his client's arm in a calming gesture and she subsided with an angry twitch of her shoulders.

'If I may suggest it,' he said quietly, 'I could arrange to have the bequests to Ms Fox valued.'

Miranda surprised herself. 'Certainly not! It's none of your business.'

Sally smiled at her but quickly schooled her expression into calm neutrality. 'I can see no need for that.'

'What if the pieces of art are extremely valuable?' Hilary persisted.

'That's irrelevant. You've been left a generous legacy and I doubt any court would consider that you'd been slighted by your uncle, who has left a statement with me that though you helped him after his heart attack, you've never been close and are not dependent on him in any way.'

Hilary ignored her lawyer's attempts to silence her. 'We'll see about that. I'm not taking your word for anything. That woman' – she jerked a head angrily in Miranda's direction – 'is mentally unstable. I have that on her own brother's authority. She only stayed with my uncle for the money and because she doesn't know how to fend for herself. It's downright immoral for her to receive so much.'

'Ms Rayne, please!' Her lawyer tugged at her arm.

'No! I'll have my say. I could have accepted those things going to charity, but not to *her*.'

Sally sighed. 'I'll overlook your harsh words today, Ms Rayne, because you're clearly upset about your uncle's death. But please be careful how you speak about my client in future.'

The other lawyer said in a colourless voice, 'Perhaps *you* might have the pieces valued, then, Ms Patel, and let us know the amount?'

'Why should we?' She saw Hilary open her mouth

and added, 'If your client makes any more threats or insinuations, it'll be we who are considering litigation.'

He inclined his head.

Hilary bounced to her feet. 'In that case, I insist someone goes back to that house now and itemises the things in the rooms that *she* has been left. I don't trust her, not one inch.'

Miranda had had enough. She looked at the clock. 'You can send someone today or not at all.'

'I'd prefer to come myself.'

'I'll not have you in the house unless someone else is there too.'

There was dead silence, then Hilary's lawyer said, 'I could send my clerk to accompany Ms Rayne – if that's acceptable to you, Ms Fox?'

She looked at Sally, who nodded.

Miranda sighed. 'Very well. But the two of them are to stay together at all times.'

'What do you think I'm going to do, steal your possessions?' Hilary yelled.

Miranda glared at her. 'No, you'll harangue me. And I won't have it in my own home. If you start shouting, I'll ask you to leave at once.'

When the other two had left, after arranging to meet Miranda at the house, Sally said, 'I'm sorry about this. Wills often bring out the worst in people. Who'd have thought a niece of Lou's would be so suspicious? What are you looking so surprised for?'

Miranda smiled. 'That's the first time since I was

twenty-one that I've stood up for myself in an argument and yelled back. I enjoyed it.'

Sally grinned. 'Good. Keep practising. You must do it again if anyone threatens you. Lou would approve. Now, to change the subject, you *are* going to move to England, aren't you?'

'I think so. If I can scrape enough money together.'

'Oh, I think you'll find the stuff Lou left will give you a decent nest egg. Sell it and take off on your adventure. Do you have friends there?'

'My sister and niece. Regina and I have never been really close but my niece is pregnant and I think I may be able to help her, so I'm going to live somewhere near them, not too close, though.'

'Good.' Sally glanced at the clock. 'I have another appointment now, I'm afraid. Will you be all right, Miranda?'

'Yes. And thank you for your help.'

'Don't let her upset you.'

Easier said than done, Miranda thought. And actually, she too felt she didn't really deserve a big bequest. But on the other hand, it was Lou's final wish that she have these things, so she wasn't going to give into Hilary's bullying.

And it had been quite exhilarating to yell back. She smiled at the memory.

The clerk and Hilary didn't leave until ten o'clock that night. Lou's niece had checked every item that might have a value, questioned whether Miranda's own antiques really did belong to her, because Lou had forgotten to mention them in the will, and insisted on the clerk making a complete list of them, just in case.

Miranda wished they hadn't brought the antiques over from the flat, but they'd looked so silly there and she'd wanted to have them nearby.

She closed the front door behind her unwelcome visitors and leant her back against it for a moment, rubbing her aching forehead.

Jack's voice made her jump. 'Tania left you something to eat and said I had to make sure you had a proper supper.'

'I'm not hungry.'

'When did you last eat?'

She tried to work it out. 'A few bits and pieces at the funeral feast.'

'Then have something light, just to get Tania off my back.'

She looked at him ruefully. 'Taking care of me, now, Jack?'

He smiled. 'I like taking care of people.'

She went with him to the kitchen, ready to force down some food to appease him, but found herself suddenly ravenous and consumed the whole plateful of meat and salad, then downed the glass of white wine Jack had poured for her.

When she woke in the morning, Miranda didn't even remember getting into bed. She looked at her bedside clock and gasped because it was after nine. She'd slept in again.

It was as she was clearing up her clothes, which she'd dropped everywhere the previous night, that she found the crumpled piece of paper Lou had been holding when he died. She smoothed it out and this time read it carefully. It contained information about a picturesque cottage in the country, in a village a few miles away from where Regina lived.

She looked at the price and almost screwed up the paper. She couldn't afford that unless the trust allowed her to sell the flat, and she was sure they wouldn't do that. But she didn't throw it away, because the cottage was very pretty. And anyway, she could *ask* the trust to sell, couldn't she?

After a breakfast substantial enough to gratify Tania and Jack, whom she found sharing a tea break in the kitchen, she wondered what to do, then decided to go and check Lou's computer. As far as she could tell, she'd be the one who had to clear up his emails and anything pending. That must be why he'd left her the contents of his office. He'd given her his password a while ago as part of his 'preparations for departure', assuring her that there was nothing on the computer that she couldn't see. But she still felt as if she was prying when she switched it on and clicked on the email program. His laptop was a much faster and more modern machine than her elderly one, slimmer and sleeker too.

She checked his emails, sending replies to several

people to tell them he'd died, cancelling an order for some books that just needed a final confirmation and also stopping his subscriptions to several email newsletters.

Then she went on to check his recent documents. To her surprise there was a draft will there, with different clauses from the one that Sally had read. This looked like a new one that he'd been intending to sign. It left her money as well as the furniture and works of art. Well, too late now. And she didn't mind, really, because she wasn't a greedy person, whatever Hilary said, and he'd been more than generous with her.

She went to her bedroom, where her own computer was set up and used that to write a letter to Sebastian and Mr Tressman about the trust, asking if she could sell the flat and buy a house in England instead. She'd grown quite keen on the idea of moving to England. After all, her sister and niece lived there, and she'd got on better with Regina this time than ever before. And it was as far away from Sebastian as she could get. The idea of that was very appealing.

She didn't expect the trustees to agree, but was going through the motions in order to leave a paper trail of what she wanted, in case she ever decided to challenge the trust. Not that she thought she would. How was she to win against an experienced lawyer like her brother, for goodness' sake?

Given the current situation, she'd probably have to rent somewhere in England. She couldn't sell any of the things Lou had left her yet, but she was going to sell her own antiques and use what she got for them as living money until she found a job, any sort of job.

On consideration, she sent the letter to Sebastian by courier, to be sure it'd get there quickly, and sent a copy to Sally Patel as well.

She was pleased that Lou's laptop belonged to her now. She could take it to England with her. Hers was four years old and was developing a few eccentricities that hinted it was coming to the end of its useful life.

When she felt like a break, she couldn't resist going back on line for another look at the cottage Lou had found for her. He was right. It looked lovely, exactly the sort of place she'd dreamt about buying in her years of looking after her father. She'd done too much dreaming and not enough standing up for herself. That would change now.

While Miranda was reorganising Lou's email system to suit her own needs, another message arrived. She opened it to find it was from the detective he'd hired to trace her daughter. Her heart started to thud as she read the message, then read it again to make sure she hadn't misunderstood what he was saying.

He'd found her daughter in England!

She printed the message out, holding back the tears, because she'd done enough weeping. This seemed like another sign that she was doing the right thing in going to England.

She wasn't going to tell anyone else in the family about finding her daughter, though, not even Regina. She didn't want anyone interfering.

Regina came home from work to a quiet, tidy flat. She'd been longing for her own space for years, looking forward to the day Nikki left home, and now that she'd got it, she knew she'd been fooling herself. She could have gone out tonight with people from work, but hadn't felt in the mood for socialising. She'd just ditched one guy and wasn't up to hunting for another yet. In fact, she was growing tired of the dating game.

She must be getting old!

She switched on the TV, checked the newspaper programme listings and found nothing worth watching.

Giving into an impulse, she rang her daughter's mobile. 'Hello? Nikki, it's me.'

'Can I ring you back, Mum? We're just in the middle of something.'

'Yes, of course. I'll be in all evening.'

She waited for the call but it never came, which left her worrying about Nikki, who hadn't sounded her usual chirpy self all week. Or was she fooling herself about that as well?

She went to fiddle with emails, then rebelling against the idea of growing too old to date, she trawled the Internet for a dating site she'd seen advertised on the television. But when she got there, the men all looked so young, with that silly haircut that stood on end like the cartoon character Tintin, or those unshaven cheeks which scratched horribly when they kissed you.

They said forty was the new thirty, but she felt nearer fifty tonight. She should take up knitting or do charity work. If she caught herself saying, 'Things were better when I was young . . .' she'd throw herself off the nearest cliff.

Would Nikki even miss her if she did?

Did she deserve to be missed?

Chapter Eleven

Katie Parrish looked at the letter, wondering who was writing to her from Australia. She gave into curiosity and, keeping one eye on the clock, tore it open and skimmed through it. The words seemed to waver in front of her and she had to force herself to breathe deeply a few times before she could calm down enough to re-read the letter.

Dear Ms Parrish
I believe you were searching for your birth parents last year. I have information about your birth mother, who is looking for you. If you're still interested in pursuing this matter, please let me know, and I'll get her to contact you.
   J. Halliday

She froze for a moment, unable to believe this was happening. She'd given up hope, then first her birth father and now perhaps her birth mother had turned up. She wasn't prepared for another encounter, not yet.

Impossible to reply to the letter that night, she just

couldn't. Instead, after she'd put Ned to bed, she wrote a long, loving email to Darren, attaching a photo she'd taken of their son kicking a football around.

But she kept stopping to wonder what she was going to do. She was still tiptoeing on ice with her birth father, whom she'd met twice. He didn't push for anything more than she was willing to offer. She wished he would. She couldn't tell how he was feeling, not really, because he was always calm and pleasant, keeping his feelings under control. He was sharing facts about himself, at least.

He worked as an IT consultant, offering software solutions for company systems, was divorced with one child, a son of twelve – which meant she had a brother, well, half-brother, but still – a brother! His clothes were always casual, usually jeans and tops that had seen better days, but his leather jacket was so beautiful it must have been expensive and his car was a late model. She didn't know what to think about him, how to understand what he really wanted from her.

He spoke of her birth mother only with bitterness. If this Miranda had been so bad, why had he made a baby with her?

But Dad had always said not to pass judgement until you knew both sides of a story, so she was trying not to close any doors between them.

Now a further dilemma hovered: should she wait for Darren to finish his tour of duty and then tell him about her birth parents and ask his advice about contacting her birth mother? No, that wasn't how a self-reliant modern woman behaved. Katie prided herself on coping with anything and everything. A soldier's wife had to.

It took her three days to bring herself to the point, but in the end she wrote back to the anonymous Mr or Ms Halliday saying she would like to know more and perhaps meet her mother one day. The return address on the letter was a post office box number in London.

After much thought she gave them her home address. It'd be stupid to hire a PO Box just for this and, anyway, she was in the phone book now. They could easily trace her on the Internet.

It took five days for Miranda to get a reply from the PI about her daughter. She saw another email from him when she switched on her computer in the morning and opened that one first.

Your daughter is willing to meet you. When will you be coming to England?
Jeff

'As soon as I can,' Miranda said softly. 'As soon as I possibly can.' She told the PI to say she'd be coming to England once she'd finalised a few things in Australia.

She loved her daughter's name. 'Katherine, familiarly known as Katie.' She'd always loved that name, found herself murmuring 'Katie' at intervals. It seemed like a good omen. Or was she reading too much into things?

She got on the phone as soon as places opened for

business, first contacting an auction room which had a good reputation to ask to have her possessions valued. Surely they'd sell for enough to provide the money to pay her fares and start renting a place in England? That was her first priority at the moment.

They'd not got probate on Lou's will yet, but she could sell her own antiques straight away. Thinking of them made her angry all over again. Sebastian had refused to confirm to Hilary's lawyer that they were indeed hers, forcing her to go through another series of hoops to prove that to the stupid woman's satisfaction.

Although Miranda stressed the urgency of her wish to sell, the auctioneer said they were very busy planning a special auction of rare antiques. He asked what exactly she had for sale, and she mentioned one or two pieces, especially the eighteenth-century chest of drawers and one of Lou's paintings, which was by a well-known Australian artist.

There was dead silence at the other end of the line, then he said, 'I'll send someone round this afternoon. It'll not be till about four o'clock, but if it's urgent, I'll make an exception for you.'

He was doing it for himself, not her, she thought, putting down the phone, because he scented something valuable. That thought lifted her spirits a little. She went to look at the chest of drawers, running her fingers across its beautiful gleaming wood. Perhaps it was worth more than she'd thought? She didn't really want to sell it, but hardened her heart, reminding herself she had no choice.

The rent money from the trust's flat would make a big difference in England, too, helping with her daily living expenses. And surely she'd be able to get some sort of job?

She kept copies of all the business correspondence, printing out emails, photocopying letters and sending backup copies of everything to Sally, who had offered to remain her lawyer. Miranda had offered payment for this.

'No need. I'm doing this for my own satisfaction, and for Lou,' Sally had said, grinning as she added, 'And just a little bit for women's lib. Don't let the cause down, Miranda Fox. Get out there and make a new life for yourself. That'll be payment enough for me.'

'I will.'

Miranda smiled at that memory and went home full of enthusiasm, sure she was well on the way to a new life, only to find a letter waiting for her from her father's lawyer, Mr Tressman, to say that he and his fellow trustee didn't feel it right to sell the flat when real estate prices were so depressed.

Knowing Sebastian, she'd expected that but was still disappointed. All right. She would manage without their help and if she ever got together any spare money, she'd take them to court about how they were managing the trust.

The valuer arrived at half-past four and went through her possessions carefully, not quite managing to hide his excitement at what she showed him. He refused to give her a valuation estimate, however, until he'd called in a colleague.

'Now?' she asked in surprise.

'Right now. If what I suspect is correct, we don't want to leave them uninsured for even an hour longer.'

There was only one conclusion to be drawn from that and excitement began to bubble up inside her.

The valuer and his colleague didn't leave till eight o'clock that evening, phoning for insurance before taking the chest of drawers with them, carefully wrapped and secured. By that time Miranda was exhausted but elated. Some of the objects were definitely valuable then. It looked like she would have more than enough to live on and even buy a decent car.

She wished she could ask Lou if she was doing the right thing, though, or had someone to share her jubilation with. How had she let herself get to this age without making any real friends? Why had she let her family trap her in such a cloistered existence?

Since Jack was out and Tania had found herself another job, Miranda went into the kitchen to find something to eat. She'd have to go shopping for food soon, but only for herself. Jack was going to start looking for a new job next week and seemed confident that it'd only take him a day or two to find one. After that she'd be completely on her own here.

She made a sandwich and afterwards walked slowly round the house, room after room, at least half of them unfurnished. Ridiculous of Lou to move in here, only he'd not had time to wait for somewhere else suitable for a wheelchair to come vacant, and as it turned out, she was glad he'd had the pleasure of spending his final days in a beautiful home by the water.

She might as well close the place up and go to England straight away, or at least as soon as the auction was over.

That made her wonder about the year-long lease. She hated the thought of wasting the money that had gone into it. A place like this cost a fortune. The mere thought of how much made her cringe. Could she let it temporarily? She went into the office and made a note to ring up the rental agent the following morning.

Although she stayed up late, reading in bed, she didn't hear Jack come home and felt a little nervous. She was grateful for the security system, but even that wasn't enough to give her a peaceful night. She kept starting awake, wondering if she'd heard a sound.

In the morning she woke with a dull headache and a fierce determination, born of the long wakeful hours, to get out of here as soon as possible.

Nikki watched Tim set off for school then she put the kettle on again. She was free first period and had a special dispensation to come in late, because of her condition. The kitchen was more like an alcove, and a dark one at that. You had to switch the light on to work in here.

Tim had left everything neat and tidy, he always did, but she looked round with loathing. She hated this place, especially the cockroaches that sometimes crawled out of crevices. She'd lost interest in Tim, in making love, in everything. What was mainly keeping her going was a grim determination to get the best possible results in her exams. After that, she'd re-evaluate the whole situation.

On an impulse she rang her mother. 'I thought I'd pop round to visit you tonight. If you'd like, that is . . . if you're free.'

'Nikki, I'd love it. Come for tea. Um . . . do you want to bring Tim?'

'No. He's got some studying to do. I'll see you around five-thirty then.'

'You still have your key. Come straight after school. I'll run you home afterwards.'

'All right.'

As she got ready to leave for school, Nikki looked down at her stomach, which was beginning to swell. Not much but *she* could feel the difference. She hated that, was dreading looking like a beached whale. She was excused from games now, more because the sports teacher wasn't taking any risks, she suspected, than because she couldn't keep up with the others. Instead she had to walk briskly round the games field or gym on her own, because everyone kept saying it was still important to exercise. She'd rather have found a hole and crawled into it during games lessons because she wanted to join in. She'd always loved sport.

At school she tried to keep in with her old group of friends, but they chatted about boyfriends, clothes and pop music, all of which had lost their appeal to her at the moment. If she mentioned anything about being pregnant, there was an awkward silence and they'd ask half-hearted questions then quickly change the subject. She listened to them making arrangements to go out clubbing, or to sleep over at each other's houses. No one invited her to sleep over any more.

The counsellor and nurse were keeping an eye on her, so she tried to appear cheerful when she was with them. She wasn't sure she'd fooled them, though.

Let's face it, she wasn't sure about anything anymore, except that she didn't want to spend her life with Tim – and didn't know how to tell him that. He was a really nice guy, like a happy, bumbling puppy, and quite good-looking too – but that sort of thing wasn't enough for a whole lifetime.

She didn't know what she wanted, just not to be with him all the time. His perpetual cheerfulness was driving her mad, and she was sick of hearing him talk about soccer.

Miranda had timed things well. There was a fine antiques auction the week after she'd had her things valued. The auctioneers set a reserve price on each item. The amount they set on the chest of drawers took her breath away and it was a moment or two before she could speak.

'It *can't* be worth that much, surely? I mean, it's just been standing around full of rubbish for years.'

The auctioneer smiled at her. 'We'd have put a higher

reserve if you hadn't been so eager to sell quickly, or we might even have sent it to London. Western Australia is a bit of a backwater as far as antiques of that calibre are concerned.'

She frowned, trying to do the sums in her head, then said slowly, 'Put a higher reserve on it, then. I should have enough to get me to London without that.'

The second valuer smiled. 'Good.'

Heartened by this, Miranda called to see the estate agent who'd rented them the house and explained that she wanted to terminate the lease and get some of her money back.

He frowned at her. 'We couldn't refund the whole amount. There are expenses to be incurred in trying to let that house again.'

'But you could give me some of it back?'

'If we manage to let it. Not everyone can afford such an expensive property. It might just sit there for months. Do you want us to try?'

'I certainly do,' the new Miranda said and proceeded to bargain them down on what would constitute 'expenses'.

She'd not paid much attention to the weather in her eagerness to get things moving, but now she found herself caught in a heavy shower, one of the first of the rainy season. She took refuge in a café, saw Dorothy sitting on her own and hesitated.

Her sister-in-law beckoned her across.

As she took her seat, Miranda said, 'I wasn't sure

whether you'd want to speak to me after I took out an injunction to keep Sebastian at a distance.'

Dorothy shrugged. 'That's none of my business. It certainly put him in a foul mood, though.'

Miranda was surprised. Her sister-in-law didn't usually say anything critical about her husband.

Dorothy gave her a wry glance. 'He's not the easiest of husbands.'

'No. I imagine not. I'm sorry.'

'I cope. I'm not brave enough to defy him, as you've been doing lately.'

'Brave? Me? I don't think so.'

Dorothy smiled. 'In your own way you are. And you coped all those years with your father – how, I don't know. Tell me what you're going to do with yourself now.'

'Go and live in England. I'll have to rent somewhere, since the trust refuses to sell that horrible flat.'

'It's a dreadful place, isn't it? I told them at the time it was too small and they'd get a better return from a larger place, but Sebastian overruled me. Where are you going to live? Somewhere near Regina?'

'Probably. I don't know. Depends on rental prices and what's available in her area.' Miranda suddenly realised she was being skilfully pumped for information and decided to offer some for free. 'You have excellent taste, by the way.'

'Do I? In what?'

'Furniture. That chest of drawers you've always

admired turns out to be very valuable, and so are my aunt's other antiques. Strange, how it all works out. If I hadn't had all this upset, I'd not have had to sell them and would never have realised what a fine legacy she'd left me.'

'May I ask how valuable?'

'Go to the premium antiques auction at Peabody's next week and find out.' As the rain seemed to have eased up, she finished her coffee and stood up. 'Have to rush. There's a lot to do.'

She looked back into the café as she passed the huge window and saw Dorothy already speaking on her mobile phone. No doubt calling Sebastian.

Suddenly Miranda laughed aloud, not caring whether people stared at her. She was doing it, coping, planning her escape, and to hell with Sebastian.

She ought to have done this years ago, and maybe she would have if she'd realised how long her father would live.

Nikki let herself into her mother's flat, kicked off her shoes in the hall and walked slowly round her old home. She'd thought it a terrible place to live, with no garden and only her own bedroom when she wanted to have her friends round. Now, living here would seem the height of luxury.

Her former bedroom was nearly as big as the whole of the studio flat she and Tim were living in, and had its own modern shower room. She was surprised to find her things as she'd left them, and couldn't resist picking up one or two of her favourite books, comfort reads, and stuffing them into her school bag.

In the kitchen she found a note saying 'HELP YOURSELF' with a smiley face beside the scrawled words. She made a mug of drinking chocolate, an old favourite when she got home from school, and sat at the table drinking it slowly and eating one of the coconut snacks her mother loved and always had in.

When she looked at the clock there was still an hour before her mother got home, so she went to sit on the comfortable sofa, leaning her head against its velvet softness just for a minute or two. She'd do some of her homework after that.

Regina let herself into the flat, saw Nikki's shoes in the hall and frowned to see how scuffed and worn they were. There was no sound coming from the living area, so she opened the door tentatively, wondering if Nikki was lost in her homework.

When she saw her daughter fast asleep on the sofa, long lashes resting on her cheeks, hair looking ragged and in need of a cut, she moved quietly into the room. Nikki's face looked thinner and there were dark circles under her eyes. Her stomach was pushing against the school skirt, and she'd been biting her fingernails, too, something she hadn't done for years.

This wasn't the face of a happy person.

Regina moved across to the kitchen and switched on

the kettle, trying to keep quiet, but soon heard sounds of Nikki stirring.

'Oh, you're back, Mum. I must have dozed off. I was going to do some homework while I waited for you.'

'You can do it later. I thought I'd cook a chicken stir-fry, if that's all right with you.'

'Sounds wonderful. No one does chicken stir-fry as well as you. Can I do anything to help?'

'You can do the onions. You know how they make me cry.'

They worked together, as they had done so often. 'I've missed having you around,' Regina said softly.

'I've missed being here.'

'Are things not working out? Is he . . . not treating you well?'

'You couldn't find a nicer guy than Tim, but . . .'

'But what?'

'It doesn't matter.'

'It does to me.'

'I don't want to spend my life with him. I don't want to be tied down at all.' She suddenly burst into tears. 'I've made such a mess of things!'

'It's too late now for an abortion.'

'I still wouldn't have one. I told you. I can't face that. Oh, you don't understand!'

As she swung away, Regina caught hold of her and pulled her into a tight embrace. 'I do understand. Truly, I do.'

'How can you?'

She hesitated. She'd kept the secret for so many years. 'Let me finish this and I'll tell you something. You're old enough now.'

She served up the food, which she hadn't the slightest desire to eat, and gestured to her daughter to begin eating. But neither of them showed any great appetite.

'What were you going to say?' Nikki asked at last, pushing her plate away.

'I suppose you can't have a drink. Would you mind if I had a glass of wine? This isn't going to be easy for me.'

She'd wondered whether one day she'd reveal all to her daughter, and now she knew the time had come.

Chapter Twelve

Brody tried to arrange to meet his daughter a third time, calling and getting her voicemail, so was only able to leave a message. It seemed like a very long time till she replied. He wondered if he dare push to see his grandson this time, but she was so cool with him he only dared take things slowly.

At their meeting he asked casually, 'What did your husband think about you meeting me?'

'I haven't told him yet. He's serving in Afghanistan, so I don't like to worry him.'

Would it worry him? Brody hoped not. 'It must be hard being a soldier's wife.'

'I can cope!'

She said that so defensively, he wondered whether she had to keep convincing herself as well as others. 'I'm sure you can.'

He hated feeling like a stranger. When you fantasised about meeting your daughter, you imagined making a warm connection, *feeling* as if she was a close relative as soon as you saw her. Katie felt more like a business acquaintance, no, not even that – the wife of a business acquaintance, doing her best to keep a conversation going between two people with nothing in common.

He looked at her in despair and the words tumbled out before he could stop them. 'Look, nothing can make up for the years we've missed, but surely we can do better than this for getting to know one another?'

She choked on her coffee and put it down hastily, her expression wary. 'I think we're doing pretty well. I don't want to rush things.'

He backed off quickly. 'All right. If that's what you want.'

Her mobile rang. 'Excuse me answering but Ned wasn't feeling well this morning and I said I'd keep in touch with his school.'

She listened, her face quickly betraying that something was wrong. 'I'll come straight there.'

'What's wrong?'

'Ned's in hospital. He collapsed at school. I've got to go.' She dropped her phone when she tried to put it into her handbag. Her hands were shaking as she picked it up.

'You can't drive in that state, Katie. Let me drive you to the hospital.'

She looked at him as if he were speaking a foreign language, then suddenly what he'd said seemed to sink in and she nodded. 'Yes. Yes, that'd be a help. I can get a taxi back to the car park afterwards.'

At the hospital she said, 'I'll be all right now,' and rushed inside. He went off to hunt for a parking space because he wasn't leaving her like that. When he went into casualty, there was no sign of her, so he asked at the desk.

'Are you a relative?' The woman gave him a suspicious look.

'Yes. I'm Ned's grandfather, Mrs Parrish's father. I've just been parking the car.' It was the first time he'd said that to anyone else and in other circumstances, it'd have given him a thrill.

'Ah. Well, your daughter is in Waiting Room Two along that corridor.' She waved one hand to the left. 'They're prepping your grandson for an operation. He's got acute appendicitis.'

'I'll go to her.' He went into a room where two couples were sitting on hard plastic chairs looking anxious and Katie was on her own in the corner, her face chalk white, her hands clasped so tightly her knuckles were white too. He went across to her.

'I told you, you didn't need to stay,' she said. 'I can manage. I'm sure you've got more important things to do.'

'I can't think of anything half as important as this. Please let me stay with you. I may be able to help, if it's only to bring you cups of tea.'

She hesitated, then gestured to the chair next to hers.

'They've taken him up to the operating theatre. They think his appendix may have burst. That can be . . . quite dangerous.' Her voice wobbled on the last word.

'Oh, my dear!' He put one arm round her and though she stiffened at first, she suddenly collapsed against him, sobbing. 'I don't know what I'll do if I lose him! I haven't been able to get pregnant again.'

He patted her back and made soothing noises, trying to hide his own fears and work out the best way to help this stranger-daughter of his. He'd never been good at people and relationships, not since he'd had to leave Perth, hating the world, and taking refuge in computers.

His brief marriage hadn't changed his opinion about that. Even his son from that marriage seemed more like a stranger.

Once Katie had stopped weeping and settled down to wait, he said gently, 'Tell me about Ned. I've been dying to meet him.'

'You have?'

'Yes. Of course I have. He's my grandson. I can't tell you how happy it made me to find out I had one.'

'I wasn't sure what you wanted from us. You never insisted or asked for much, not about anything.'

He could only offer her the truth. 'I didn't dare insist. I've been terrified of you rejecting me.'

She clung to him, fingers digging in. 'I lost the best father on this planet to cancer, and Ned lost his grandfather. No one can ever replace Dad. But because of him, I'd like to try to get to know you. I know how rewarding a father–daughter relationship can be.'

He found he was stroking her hair, found that his own cheeks were moist, and he didn't care if the other people in the room were staring at them. 'I'll try my hardest to live up to your dad,' he murmured and felt her nod against him.

The day of the antiques auction was rainy, with storms forecast later. Miranda got there early. She wanted to see what happened to her furniture and would be sad to lose some of the pieces, particularly the chest of drawers that was apparently so much more valuable than the other things. She'd loved it for its grace and beauty, not its value.

When she got to the auction rooms, she found Dorothy waiting there, and wasn't surprised. As a lawyer, Sebastian wouldn't breach the order to stay away from her, but he'd sent his wife in his place. Miranda couldn't help hoping the furniture would sell at top prices, not just for the money but to show him she wasn't totally dependent on his goodwill as her trustee.

She had a sudden image of him as a huge black spider spinning its web and trapping her, as her father had trapped her before. Only she wasn't going to let that happen a second time.

She went to sit down at the other side of the room and when Dorothy got up and came across to ask if it was all right to join her, she just shrugged. She was too tense to play games and pretend they were two friends meeting by chance. 'Be sure to take notes for him.'

Dorothy nodded, the bland half-smile with which she usually faced the world not slipping at all.

This was like no auction Miranda had ever seen before. It had been advertised as a fine and rare antiques furniture auction and the online catalogue had displayed one beautiful piece of furniture after another, including all of Miranda's pieces. The people here today were, on the whole, exquisitely dressed and spoke in soft, educated voices.

'You're selling all your antiques, aren't you?' Dorothy said abruptly.

'I don't want to but I've got no choice. The trust won't allow me to do anything but live on a pittance in that horrible little flat. I'd suffocate there.'

Dorothy was silent, then said suddenly, 'I'll deny I said it, but you go for it, Miranda. Get as far away from him as you can, like our sons did!'

Miranda looked at her sister-in-law in surprise. 'I thought you were here to keep an eye on me and report back to Sebastian, not to encourage me to rebel.'

'That's why he asked me to come, but I do have my own views, you know.' A bitter expression flitted across Dorothy's face as she said that. 'I just don't think it worthwhile broadcasting them.'

'Why did you say something today, then?'

She shrugged. 'In case you needed encouragement now that nice man is dead.'

'Oh.'

The auction started just then. Miranda got out her pencil, ready to note the prices in the catalogue, and noticed Dorothy doing the same.

When the first of her items came up for sale, she felt quite sick with apprehension. To her astonishment, it sold for considerably more than the reserve. She'd memorised every single reserve price. Closing her eyes for a moment she felt relief sweep through her, then wrote the price down. Of course she'd be paying a commission on that, but still, it was very cheering to know you had some money coming to you.

One by one, her pieces sold well. Only one didn't go higher than its reserve price. She heard someone nearby say that this was a 'good buying crowd not like last time' and thanked whatever fate had helped her to sell now.

'He'll hate this,' Dorothy murmured.

She'd spoken so softly that Miranda wasn't sure whether the remark was meant for her, so didn't respond.

Two hours later the last of the items came up for sale, the chest of drawers. The price went up and up, and soon passed the first reserve price that had been suggested, then the higher reserve price they'd settled on. It sold for twenty thousand dollars.

Dorothy was looking at her in amazement. 'I'd no idea they were so valuable. They've just been sitting around your father's house, being used all the time. They could have got damaged.'

'They were quite safe. I was there to take care of them, and Father wasn't the sort to damage anything.'

'He might have had a fall and knocked one flying. Did *you* know how much they were worth?'

'I had no idea. My aunt always said she had some nice pieces, so I knew they'd fetch something, but not how much.' She might have escaped from her father sooner if she'd known. Or perhaps not. She'd retreated into herself, she knew, thankful for the Internet. It had needed both the unfair will and Lou to push her out of retreat mode.

She stood up. 'I'm going home now.'

'Thanks for not being nasty today.'

She turned to Dorothy. 'I'm not the sort. I never was. Perhaps I'd have had a better life if I had fought back.'

'And perhaps you wouldn't be the same person if you had. I envy you.'

'Envy *me*?'

'Yes.'

'Whatever for?'

'Being yourself. Not hurting other people. I bet *you* sleep well at night.' On that she walked off.

Miranda was baffled by this. Did Dorothy not sleep well at night? Why ever not?

Regina went to sit in her favourite place, the recliner chair, putting up the footrest with a tired sigh. She waited until Nikki was curled up on the sofa, then took a deep breath.

'I've not quite told you the truth about your father.'

'Oh?'

'He's not dead. At least, I think he isn't. I don't know where he is, though.'

'*What?*'

'And I understand perfectly well what you're going through at the moment because I was never married. Your father just . . . didn't hang around once he found I was pregnant – and even if he had, I'd not have married him.' She paused, looking at her daughter. 'It was hard, managing on my own in a country where I knew no one. But it was better than going back and letting Dad take over, as he had done with Miranda. I'd have done anything rather than run back to him.'

She took a big slurp of wine. 'When she first came out of hospital, he treated Miranda like a slave, and a half-witted one at that. And Sebastian was equally nasty.' She explained in some detail about Miranda's baby.

'That's why—' Nikki broke off.

'Why what?'

'Why she rang me up and told me to keep the baby if I wanted. She offered to help, too.'

'She's changing. She became so quiet and . . . and colourless after having the baby. I was glad I was able to come and work in England, be away from them all. I liked it here. I still do. My mother was English like Miranda's – Father seemed to go for English wives, after the first one – and I had a British passport, so I could come and settle here. I saw my mother a couple of times when she came to Europe on holiday, but she had a new husband younger than her and wasn't interested in presenting him with a stepdaughter of my age.'

Nikki was watching her open-mouthed. 'I can't believe what I'm hearing!'

'It's the truth.'

'Who was my father?'

'A guy I met. He was from New Zealand but working in London. He was fun, but definitely not husband material. When he found out I was pregnant, he vanished overnight. Literally. He needn't have bothered to run away. I'd not have been stupid enough to marry him.'

'Did you never try to trace him? I mean, you could have claimed maintenance, at least.'

'Then *he* would have had rights. He was a no-hoper.'

'Why did you go out with him then?'

'I was lonely and he was fun, I'll give him that. Great in bed, too.' She saw her daughter blush at that. The young always seemed to think parents didn't do sex any more.

'I do understand what you're going through, Nikki. And I'm sorry, but I still can't face a baby living here. There isn't room and I'd have no privacy.'

'You've always guarded your privacy very jealously.'

'Yes. I know. I'm sorry if that's hurt you. It's how I am. I can't take people non-stop, have to have regular peace and quiet. But I will help you financially and I'll even babysit for you from time to time.'

Nikki looked at her very solemnly, in the way that had been so endearing when she was a small child, then gave her a faint smile. 'I do understand, Mum. After living with Tim for a few weeks, I'm longing for some privacy myself. Only I can't afford it.'

'Why don't you stay here tonight? It's Saturday tomorrow. You don't have to rush off to school and I don't have to rush off to work.'

She watched as Nikki closed her eyes and let a few tears leak out. 'Oh, darling!' She moved quickly across to take her daughter in her arms. 'Don't cry. We'll find some way of coping, and you definitely don't have to marry Tim. In fact, I hope you won't. Not because I don't like him, I do. He seems a really nice guy. But because you're too young to tie yourself down.'

'I've come to that conclusion myself.'

She gave Nikki another hug then stepped back. 'I've got some ice cream in the freezer.'

'Chocolate toffee chip?'

'Yes. Our favourite. If ever we needed comfort food, it's now.'

When a nurse came to the waiting room door and called, 'Mrs Parrish', Katie hurried forward. Brody followed more slowly.

'Your son's just been brought back to the ward, Mrs Parrish. Perhaps you'd like to sit next to him and be there when he wakes up properly?'

'Yes. Oh, yes.'

'Can I come too?' Brody asked.

The nurse frowned.

'He's Ned's grandfather,' Katie explained, 'and as my husband is overseas he's . . . supporting me.'

'That's all right, then.'

The figure on the bed looked so tiny, Brody's heart seemed to stop beating for a moment. He let Katie take a seat by the bed and pulled a chair up beside hers, staring down at his grandson. 'He's got my family's red hair; a bit darker, perhaps.'

'Yes.' She took hold of the child's hand and bent to kiss his cheek. 'I'm here with you, Ned darling. You're in hospital.'

His eyes fluttered open for a moment but there was no real comprehension in them.

She kept hold of his hand, her eyes fixed on the child's face, as if she was willing him to get better.

Time passed slowly. Brody usually hated being inactive, but somehow today, it felt right simply to sit there with his daughter. Together. After an hour or so, he whispered, 'How about I fetch you something to eat?'

'Just a coffee. Black, no sugar.'

He came back to find her talking to a very drowsy child and when he stood at the foot of the bed, he was stunned by their resemblance to one another – and to Miranda. Same eyes, same facial structure. His genes seemed to be taking a back seat when it came to the physical looks of his descendants, except for the hair. Well, the child looked like the Miranda he had known as a young woman. He didn't know what she looked like now, and didn't want to, either.

'This man is a new friend,' she told her son. 'Brody's been helping me. See. He's just brought me some coffee.'

The boy's eyes lingered on Brody for a minute, then fluttered shut.

'He seems all right.'

She beamed at him. 'Yes. The surgeon popped in to tell me they'd got the appendix out in the nick of time. I'd love that coffee now.'

He realised he was still clutching it to his chest and smiled as he passed it to her.

'I'm going to be staying the night,' she said, 'just to be sure he's all right. I have to go home and get my things first, though.'

'I'll drive you.'

'You can take me back to my car, but I won't impose on you any longer.'

'It's not imposing. I want to help in any way I can.'

She gave him a long, solemn look. 'You have. But now I know Ned's all right, I'll be fine driving my car, I promise. I'll give you our address. Once he's home, you must come and have tea with us. I'll tell him who you are tomorrow. He'll be excited, because he doesn't have any grandfathers and all his friends do.'

Since she was very firm about it, he dropped her off at her car, treasuring what she'd said all the way home. He had their address, an invitation to visit.

At his own house he tried and failed to concentrate on his favourite TV programme. He wasn't hungry, was simply happy. He felt as if he and his daughter had turned a corner, as if she'd really accepted him as her father. And that was a wonderful feeling.

Miranda went to answer the door and found a policewoman standing there with another woman who looked like some sort of official.

'Ms Fox?'

'Yes.'

'Can we come in?'

'May I ask who you are and what this is about?'

She held out a photo-identity card. 'We've had a deposition about you. Your brother is worried that you're . . . um, not in a rational mood, that you might need help.'

'I'm in a perfectly rational mood and I don't need any help. I can't believe he's doing this.'

'Perhaps we could come in and chat for a while?'

She remembered the 'chatting' to the doctor last time. It had led to them locking her away for a very long time. 'I don't think so.'

'Ms Fox, it'd be better if you cooperated.'

'I'd like to call my lawyer first. She can tell me how much cooperation I need to give you.'

She closed the door in their faces, even though the woman tried to hold it open. Then she ran for the phone, calling Sally's rooms and telling the receptionist about the urgency of the situation. But Sally was in court that morning and wouldn't be available until lunchtime.

'Tell her it's really urgent,' she repeated.

As she put the phone down the doorbell rang again and she hesitated. She had a bad feeling about the presence of the police with the social worker. She didn't know what rights they had and might just be imagining she was in danger, but wasn't going to risk letting them in.

Without stopping to think it through, she grabbed her handbag and fled, leaving the house by rear doors that led out on to the riverside patio, hesitating for a moment near the swimming pool, then taking the path to the servants' quarters, to which she had a key.

She fumbled in her handbag, dropping the bunch of keys, and anxiously looked over her shoulder as she picked them up. She didn't dare go out on to the road and knew her car would be easy to follow, so waited in the housekeeper's flat out of sight. She saw them walking round the house, but though the patio door was open, they didn't go inside. It seemed a very long time until she heard their car drive away. She peered out of the window, which overlooked the road and was dismayed to see that they stopped the car about a hundred metres away, no doubt waiting for her to emerge.

All the old fears came back in a cascade of terror, the dread of being helpless and locked up again foremost. She took out her mobile and rang Sally's rooms once more, explaining that she'd had to go out, so could be reached only on this mobile.

Then she settled down to wait, making herself a cup of coffee from the neatly arranged supplies in the cupboard.

She wasn't hungry. She was just . . . terrified. Surely it couldn't happen to her again? Not in this day and age.

It had taken her years to work out that her father had pulled strings to have her locked away and, when she'd confronted him, he'd been unrepentant. She'd so nearly left him then; would have done so but for the minor stroke he'd had while they quarrelled. By the time he came out of hospital, a shadow of his former self, pathetically grateful that she was still there, she'd known she was trapped.

People might say the mental health system was better now – foolproof, but she still didn't trust it. No system was foolproof. Sebastian was just as powerful as her father had been, and knew all the ins and outs of the law.

Three hours passed, by which time she was so anxious she couldn't keep still. She paced the floor, taking care not to be seen from the window, made another coffee and waited . . . When her mobile rang, her heart felt as if it was stuttering and she dropped her phone as she tried to answer. She scrabbled for it, pressing the button and saying, 'Yes?'

'Miranda? Is that you?'

'Sally! Oh, thank goodness!' She burst into tears.

'Calm down and tell me what's wrong.'

She explained.

'Oh, my dear! I'm so sorry this has happened. Look, I'll come and get you myself. Tell me exactly where you are hiding.'

It was twenty minutes until a car drew up and Sally got out. It seemed more like two hours. Miranda ran down the stairs and opened the door, not daring to step outside yet.

'This has really upset you,' Sally said gently.

She could only nod.

'Come on. We'll go back to my rooms. You'll be safe there.'

As the two women walked outside, however, a car crept forward slowly and parked across the gates.

'This is outrageous!' Sally said. 'Get into my car and leave this to me. I'm going to lock you in, so that no one can pester you. Are you all right with that?'

Miranda nodded and slid quickly into the front passenger seat of the car. She watched Sally turn to face the same two people who had come to the door. She couldn't hear what they were saying, but she could tell that Sally was furiously angry.

It took longer than she'd expected for the conversation to end and, at one stage, Sally pulled out her mobile and rang someone.

When she eventually got into the car, she said, 'I need you to hold yourself together now, Miranda. We'll only get through this if you keep your cool.'

'What's happening?'

'We need to go straight to the surgery of a psychiatrist I know. I'm afraid the only way they'll let this drop is if some medical expert certifies that you're all right. It seems your dear brother has been on to your family doctor, who's prepared to swear that you've been mildly depressed for years and that your father's death followed by Lou's has thrown you over the edge.'

'I'll never speak to Sebastian again.'

'I'll have trouble being polite to him myself.'

A sudden thought occurred to her. 'What doctor is that?'

'Dr Grant.'

'But he was my father's doctor, not mine!'

Sally stared at her. 'Say that again!'

'Father's former doctor was my doctor until they put me inside. After I came out he insisted I had to keep taking anti-depressants, so after a while I went to a woman doctor and she helped me come off them. Father was absolutely furious. It was one of the few times I stood up to him. I'm still her client officially, but I'm rarely ill, so I haven't seen her for a couple of years.

'When Father's doctor retired, he found Dr Grant, another chauvinist who talked down to women. I've met him when he's been visiting Father, but I've never been his patient, so how he could know whether I was depressed, I can't understand.'

'It should be quite easy to prove that you're not his patient, then.'

'Yes.'

'And will your doctor back you up that you're no longer clinically depressed?'

'Yes. She's nice.'

'Leave it to me. Just tell my friend the truth. He may

be a psychiatrist, but he's very easy to talk to and not at all a chauvinist.'

Two hours later, Miranda thanked Sally. 'I'm off the hook for the moment but I'm worried about what Sebastian will try next. He can be very . . . tenacious when he wants something and for some reason he wants to control me.'

'The money, I should think. You are still going to challenge the trust, aren't you? I'm becoming increasingly eager to win that case.'

And Miranda found herself doing something she hadn't expected – smiling. 'Go for it.'

'It'll probably take years, so I think you should go to England immediately,' Sally said thoughtfully. 'Do you have a current passport?'

'Yes. A British one, actually. Father was very insistent that I maintain my right to British nationality, even though I've always lived in Australia.'

'He was right.'

'But I can't just take off. There's too much to do here. It'll take me weeks.'

'We'll fix that. Have you enough money to go now?'

'Yes.' She explained about the auction. 'I'm sure they'll give me some of the money straight away.'

'Then if you take my advice you'll vanish. Make a list of everything that needs doing and I'll pass it on to my nephew. He's a law student and desperate for money. He's as sharp as they come, and I'll vouch for his honesty.' She frowned. 'You'd better stay at my place tonight, I think.

No use giving them the slightest opportunity to play any more dirty tricks.'

'I can't impose on you like that.'

'Think of it as avoiding making future trouble for me. I'm going to book you on the first available flight and see you on to the plane myself. We'll call at your house on our way home to my place and you can pack.'

The first flight with a seat free was at eleven o'clock that night.

'I can't be ready by then!' Miranda gasped.

'Yes, you can. I'll help you.'

'I'm bound to forget things.'

'They do have shops in England, you know!'

The first time Miranda stopped for breath after that was when she sank down on her aeroplane seat, closed her eyes and leant back.

She opened them to find her neighbour smiling at her.

'Bit of a rush, was it?'

'Yes. Last-minute decision. I only decided to come this afternoon.'

He blinked. 'Now, that's what I call impulsive. Unless . . . I'm sorry, it's not for a bereavement, is it?'

'No. It's for a new start away from my interfering family.'

The admiration in his eyes surprised her. She wasn't used to that. He was a year or two younger than she was, she guessed, but she didn't care about that. It was, she realised, the first time she'd attracted a man's attention, if only to flirt, since she'd moved in with her father all those years ago.

But it wouldn't be the last!

She smiled at him and he smiled back. She'd lost a good half of her life, but she was going to make the rest of it count.

When she got back from the airport, Sally checked the time differences and rang Miranda's sister. She'd been given the number in case she needed to contact her client urgently, but she wasn't going to wait for that.

'Hello? Regina Fox?'

'Yes.'

'I hope I didn't wake you, but I'm calling from Australia. I'm your sister's lawyer.'

'Is Miranda all right?'

'Yes. But your brother's been rather a nuisance, so she's on her way to England as we speak.'

'*Miranda is?*'

'I hope you'll keep this information to yourself.' Sally quickly brought Regina up to date on what had been happening. 'I thought it might be nice if you could meet her at the airport. She's not been to England before and it can be a bit confusing at first. Though I'm sure she'll cope.'

'Right. I'll be there. Give me her time of arrival and flight number.'

'You won't tell your brother?'

'No. I wasn't comfortable with him myself. Can't think what's got into him that he has to boss everyone around. Have you any idea what Miranda intends to do here?'

'I don't think she knows yet. But I'm sure she'll enjoy a little holiday before she settles in.'

When Regina put the phone down she frowned and wandered into the kitchen to finish off her breakfast. She was delighted that Miranda had kicked over the traces. She wasn't sure about having her to stay for long, because Nikki might need to come home again and there were only two bedrooms, but they could deal with that if it happened.

What the hell had got into Sebastian? How did Dorothy put up with him? She wouldn't.

She smiled as she got ready to leave for work. She wished she could see his face when he found out that his meek and mild sister had rebelled and come to England.

Chapter Thirteen

Miranda was exhausted by the time the plane landed in England and the twenty-hour journey felt more like twenty days. But at least she was small enough to find the seat reasonably comfortable and had even managed to sleep for a few hours, unlike her much taller neighbour. He had started the journey smiling and chatting, but had finished it in grim-faced endurance.

She'd had time to think things through on the journey; well, a little. She knew what would happen if she contacted her sister. Regina would take over – from the best of motives, but still, she'd take over. Fearful as she was about sorting things out in England, it seemed to Miranda that she had to do it herself, or she'd be letting Lou down.

She collected her luggage and showed her passport, not quite sure what to expect. The passport said she was a British citizen but she didn't feel like one. To her surprise, the customs officer started chatting to her.

'Not used this passport yet.'

'No. I've lived in Australia for most of my life.'

'Here for a holiday, then, or coming back to stay?'

'I thought I'd try living here. I've got a sister and niece here. I've been caring for my father, but he died a few months ago.'

'Well, I hope you have a nice stay – however long it is.'

With a smile he closed the passport, handed it back and sent her on her way.

As she wheeled her luggage out of the restricted area she felt her stomach churning. She was here, land of her forefathers, but it felt alien. She walked forward out of the arrival area and stopped to look round. She saw an automatic teller machine and went across to that to get some British money, using her credit card. She felt a lot better after that.

A sign saying 'Taxis' caught her eye, so she turned in that direction. Only where was she to go in her taxi?

She'd left in such a hurry that she'd not even gone online and booked a hotel. Oh, how she wished for ten minutes with her computer! She was carrying it, but would have to find a way to get online here.

As she passed a car rental stand, she stopped. Should she hire a car instead of taking a taxi? That'd give her some independence, at least.

What would Lou have advised?

But the voice in her head remained silent and people were pushing past her, knocking her luggage trolley, making her step instinctively sideways.

She should have spent more time during the flight working out exactly what to do when she arrived instead of chatting then sleeping, and only having approximate ideas about her future actions.

In the end she moved towards one of the car rental desks, joining a line of people seeking vehicles. When she arrived, she asked for a small automatic car and took out her Australian driving licence and passport for identification.

It wasn't cheap, but at least she had wheels. She had to wait again for the courtesy bus to take a group of hirers out to where they would pick up their vehicles. Beside her a man in a business suit was talking earnestly on his mobile phone, not seeming to care who heard what he was saying. She'd have to get herself a mobile that worked here. She pulled out her little notebook and started a list. Mobile phone. Buy car. Find somewhere to live.

There! She felt as if she was making a start already. That felt good.

Warned by Sally, Regina set off in good time for the airport. But there was an accident on the M4 motorway which held her up for over an hour, then the traffic on the M25 was even slower than usual.

She parked and made a dash for the arrivals area, but to her dismay the plane had landed nearly an hour ago. She couldn't believe she'd missed her sister.

Where had Miranda gone? What was she doing now? Someone was bound to take advantage of her.

Feeling guilty that she hadn't set off earlier, Regina turned and made her way back to her car. She could only hope her sister would contact her. Surely she would?

Nikki saw Tim waiting for her at morning break and sighed. She just wanted to sit in peace and drink some orange juice now that her stomach was starting to settle down.

'Hi, there.' He planted a kiss on her cheek.

'Don't do that here!' she hissed. 'I've told you.'

'I can't help it when you look so pretty.'

'Well, I don't feel pretty.'

'I missed you last night.'

'I was tired. When Mum suggested I stay over, it seemed a good idea. Did you . . . um, sleep well?'

'Yeah, sure. You know me. But I missed having someone to chat to this morning.'

She looked at her watch. 'I've got to go.'

'I'll wait for you after school.'

'No. I've got some studying to do. I'll work in the library and come back later. Can you fix something for tea?'

She watched him walk away, saw the admiring glances other girls gave him. He was a hot guy. Only . . . she was no longer a hot chick. She'd changed, was still changing. If only her mother would help her financially, she'd move to a place of her own, even if she had to live in the tiniest flat ever built.

The trouble was, Tim would be hurt and he didn't deserve that. He was too nice for his own good, much too nice for her.

Katie found another email from her mother's representative waiting for her when she got back from the hospital. Ned was so much better, he was fretting to be let out, which made her feel good. The email took the edge off that.

She read it, wondering why her mother didn't make contact in person.

> *Hi, Katie*
> *Your mother's asked me to tell you that she's delighted you're willing to meet her. She's coming to England and will be in touch personally when she gets there. She has your email address.*
> *Cheers*
> *Jeff Halliday*

'Oh, no!' She closed her eyes for a moment. She hadn't said she wanted to *meet* her mother, just make contact, surely? She had enough on her plate at the moment, what with Ned and Brody, and Mum kicking up a fuss that she was contacting her birth parents at all, not to mention her part-time job, without which she'd go mad from loneliness.

And Darren hadn't emailed her for days. That happened sometimes when he was on a mission. She always worried more at those times. You kept hearing on the TV news that another British soldier had been killed in Afghanistan, and you wondered if it was your husband. Only the newsreader's words, 'The family has been informed', kept her sane. And even so, she found tears welling in her eyes as she thought how upset those poor families would be.

How would she face it if anything happened to Darren? He said it wouldn't, and she didn't contradict his cheerful optimism, because if ever a man loved his job, he did. She'd been glad to move out of army quarters, though, away from other people's worries.

They showed pictures on the TV news of the bodies being brought back – repatriated, they called it. She hadn't realised she'd be living close to the place they brought them when she moved to Wootton Bassett, and she always checked that no coffins were due to be driven through the town before she went shopping.

It was good that such a small town was showing a wonderful example to the rest of the country about respecting the soldiers who'd lost their lives, but she avoided the repatriations. It'd kill her to be involved in that slow procession along the main street, because it'd be Darren she'd be imagining in the coffins beneath those flags.

It was good, though, that the Queen had named the town Royal Wootton Bassett, only the third town ever to receive that honour; not good that the repatriations were going elsewhere.

Being a soldier's wife was beginning to get to her,

Katie knew. If she hadn't had Ned to look after, she didn't know what she'd have done.

Books were lifesavers too. She'd never read so much in her whole life, mostly romances or cheerful chicklit that was guaranteed a happy ending. They helped her feel better, somehow. She wasn't reading anything miserable or heavy until Darren came back safely.

And now she had a new father to deal with, a man sparing with words, who didn't usually let his emotions show, but who'd been there for her when Ned was rushed to hospital. That meant a lot.

She did hope Mum wouldn't come up from Cornwall to see Ned and check up on them, which she did periodically. It might damage Katie's growing relationship with Brody because Mum wasn't noted for her tact and excelled at putting her foot in it big time. It was a good thing Sam, her mother's new husband, found that amusing. Other people got upset. Katie smiled at the thought of Sam. He was such a nice guy. He'd taken a lot of the emotional load of keeping her mother cheerful off her.

And now, to top it all, her birth mother was going to be in England. She couldn't refuse to see a woman who was coming all the way from Australia to see her. But from the way Brody talked about the woman, she didn't sound trustworthy in relationships.

And anyway, Katie wasn't sure she could forgive her for giving her baby away. Her father said he'd not been consulted, which amazed her. He said he'd explain about her mother's family another time.

But how could you form a relationship with someone who'd given you away? She had a child of her own now and if anyone tried to take Ned away from her or hurt him, she knew she'd fight tooth and nail. Whatever it took.

The traffic lights were all green, so Brody got to the hospital before Katie that evening.

Ned was sprawled on the bed scowling at a book. He said a grudging hello to his grandfather.

'Something wrong?'

'This one's too hard for me. But it's got dinosaurs in it.' The child's face brightened. 'Can you read it to me?'

'Sure.' Brody found he had to keep stopping to discuss the illustrations and listen to Ned's views on dinosaurs.

Katie came rushing in late, with only fifteen minutes left before visitors were chucked out. 'Sorry. I was at work and got held up in the traffic.' She hugged Ned, hesitated, then planted a quick air kiss near Brody's left ear.

As they were walking out of the hospital together, he risked it. 'Would you like to have dinner somewhere?'

Her response was instantaneous. 'I'd love to. The house seems empty without Ned. If his temperature stays down, he can come home tomorrow. I'll have to phone you and let you know.'.

'What sort of food?'

'I don't mind.'

'I know a nice little Indian restaurant.'

'Great. Let's go.'

It wasn't far and once they were settled at their table, he asked something he'd been wondering about. 'What's your husband like?'

'Tall, dark but not handsome. He has lovely twinkly eyes, though.'

Brody managed to keep the conversation going by asking about her life, then she began fiddling with the edge of her plate and shooting him worried glances. 'Is something wrong?'

'Yeah. Well, not wrong. It's just . . . my birth mother's been in touch. Or rather her representative has. She's coming to England to meet me. Why can't she email me herself? Why is someone else doing that?'

'Miranda's coming here? I didn't think her family would let her off the leash for long enough.'

She looked at him in surprise.

'Sorry. I shouldn't say things like that.'

'You sound as if you hate her sometimes.'

He picked up his wine glass and took a sip. 'I didn't mean to. I just . . . hate what she and her family did to me.'

'What's she like?'

'I've not seen her for twenty-six years. She'll be forty-seven.' He paused, unable to imagine Miranda looking old. Had she put on weight? Was her hair grey? Did she wear glasses now?

'What was she like when you were together?'

'Small, fair-haired, old-fashioned in many ways. I

used to tease her about that. It came of having such an elderly father, I suppose. James Fox should have been born in the nineteenth century. I'm sure he didn't believe in votes for women!'

Katie laughed. 'She'll probably have grey hair now. Mum dyes her hair because it's gone sort of iron grey and she hates that. But she's older than this Miranda. Mum's sixty now. She says she doesn't feel old and gets mad if I tease her about it even. You're forty-seven as well, aren't you? Do you feel old?'

He looked at her in surprise. 'Old? I'm not old. I suppose I must seem old to you, but I don't feel it inside.'

'How did you and my mother meet?'

'We met at university. We were in the same year. She was studying English and I was doing IT, which was less common then. Miranda was living at home. My family were in the country, so I was a bit lonely, I suppose. She was lonely because she was shy and didn't know how to mix.'

'Did you fall in love with her straight away?'

He'd forgotten how he'd felt about Miranda because the anger had taken over once the family had closed ranks on him and kept him away from her. 'I suppose I did. Well, quite quickly, anyway.'

He changed the subject, didn't want to remember those days and the pain of losing Miranda – losing his unborn child, too. Why had she taken everything away from him? She'd not only stopped loving him but had caved into her family about having the baby adopted.

The only possible conclusion to draw was that she couldn't have loved him, not in the way he'd loved her, anyway. Or maybe she was just a coward, unable to stand up to people. How could he have been so mistaken in a person? It was a question he'd asked himself many times over the years because, whatever he did, he'd never been able to forget her and the few short months they'd been together.

That was what had ruined his later marriage. But at least he saw his son regularly and was on reasonable terms with his ex.

He wasn't on any sort of terms with his first love.

Miranda hired a car for a week. Surely in that time she'd be able to buy a vehicle of her own?

She sat behind the wheel, deeply relieved that the car had a satellite navigation system because she hadn't had time to study the map of England in detail. Now all that remained was to decide where to go and program in her destination.

Should she go straight to her sister's? She was fairly certain Regina would put her up for a night or two. But she was afraid Regina would tell Sebastian where she was, afraid he'd find some way to get to her.

And most of all, she was afraid of not managing, not standing on her own feet.

There was a folder of brochures on the seat beside her. She flicked through them, wondering what they were about. To her relief, a couple were from hotel chains, offering accommodation at what seemed a reasonable price. She looked at the map and found one in Wiltshire, in a town called Swindon.

The instructions for using the satellite navigation system were clear and she programmed in the postcode of the hotel she had chosen. A woman's voice, sounding very upper-class English, told her to take the first left.

Taking a deep breath she drove out of the parking area, waving back to the cheery attendant. Cars whizzed past her, all seeming intent on breaking the speed limit. She'd been driving for years, but suddenly she felt like a learner. Was it her imagination or did people drive more quickly here in the UK?

She could only hope that the satellite navigation system knew where it was going because she didn't. Cars, roads, junctions, motorways loomed at her in quick succession. They were well signposted but what saved her from panicking was the pleasant-sounding electronic voice guiding her.

The motorways were absolutely crowded and traffic was slow at first. She didn't mind that. It gave her time to get used to the car. When she saw a sign for Services, she turned off and found her way into a crowded car park. She sat over a large cup of coffee and a croissant, watching people, something she often did, quite used to being on her own.

The caffeine perked her up and she made her way out to the car again, feeling quite proud of herself. She could do this.

By the time she got to the hotel, she was so exhausted she was worried her driving might be affected. She hired a room and took her luggage up, staring round it and pulling a face. Why did so many hotels choose neutral colour schemes? Still, the room had everything you really needed and there was a café where she could get meals.

She sat on the bed, wondering what to do next? She was too tired to drive anywhere, didn't want to ring Regina yet.

In the end she gave into her sleepiness and lay down on the bed.

She woke five hours later in mid-afternoon, furious with herself for sleeping so long. Not stopping to unpack, she grabbed her handbag and went down to the café for a snack. She managed to chat to the waitress, who was happy to tell her where to go to do some shopping.

Only when she got out of the hotel grounds, she found the directions didn't work. Lost, she had to stop to ask directions and program her satnav.

In the end she got herself to a big shopping centre and bought herself something to read and a couple of casual tops, plus new jeans. The clothes Lou had bought her were too smart for everyday use – well, too smart for her. Prices seemed very reasonable and she had plenty of choice. She also bought some fruit and snack food.

Then, feeling very happy with her purchases, she made her way back to the car, to stare in dismay at a smashed window and the space where the satnav had been fixed to the bottom of the windscreen.

A woman came to the car next to hers. 'Oh, dear! I don't know what the world's coming to when you can't even leave your car here in safety. Lost much?'

'Just the satnav system.'

'They're always after those. You'll have to ring the police.'

'I can't. I've only just arrived in England from Australia and I don't have a mobile phone yet.'

By this time a man had joined them. He thrust a mobile at her. 'Here. Use mine, love. Dial 999.'

She held back tears only with an effort. 'Thank you. You're very kind.'

It was two hours before the police let her go and she then had to wait for the car rental firm to bring her another car and help her program this new satnav system with her hotel, because without that, she had no idea how to get back.

She was way beyond tears by the time she entered her room, having unplugged the satnav system and brought it inside with her this time. She dumped her shopping and went down to the café, ordering a glass of white wine first and then, almost as an afterthought, a proper meal.

First day in England and she'd already been robbed. Fine start that was. What would her family say?

It wasn't till she'd taken a sip of her second glass of wine that she realised that, even so, she'd coped with the emergency. She hadn't panicked or fallen to pieces. She'd done what was necessary and got a new car to drive.

That was good, wasn't it? Yes, of course it was. She raised her glass in a toast to herself.

But she wished she wasn't on her own. She envied the couples sitting chatting, smiling sometimes, touching one another without realising it.

Oh, she was being stupid, wishing for the moon. *Get on with it!* she told herself. She finished her wine and went to her room. She'd go car hunting tomorrow morning.

Then what? Her daughter? Was she ready to face Katie? Not yet, no. Definitely not.

Chapter Fourteen

When Regina picked up the phone at work, it was her daughter.

'I won't keep you a minute, Mum. Just wanted to know how Auntie Min was. I'm really looking forward to catching up with her tonight.'

'I don't know how she is, I'm afraid. There was an accident on the M4 and by the time I'd got to Heathrow the passengers had disembarked. She didn't know I was coming so she didn't wait around.'

'Oh, no! You mean she's all on her own in a strange country? Poor Auntie Min.'

'I'm afraid so. And if she has a mobile for use here, I don't know her number, so I've no way of getting in touch with her. I don't know why she hasn't rung me, though.' After a short silence she changed the subject. 'Do you and Tim still want to come to tea tonight?'

'If you don't mind.'

'If I minded, I'd not have asked you.'

Silence and a sniffle.

'I'm sorry. I shouldn't have spoken sharply.'

'I'm sorry too. I cry for nothing these days. It's not much fun being pregnant, is it?'

'No.'

'How on earth did you cope on your own?'

'I coped because I had to.'

Another silence, then, 'I have to go now, Mum. Another test to do.'

Regina stared at the phone after her daughter rang off. She kept forgetting how fragile Nikki must be feeling. What on earth was she going to do about her daughter? She wasn't going to look after another baby, or have her life upset by one coming to live with her, but she didn't want to leave Nikki in such a horrible slum, either.

Only, there was Tim to think about too. His parents were moving north soon and he'd be on his own as well. Nikki might not want to marry him, but she'd not want to hurt him, either, by moving out to a place on her own.

Regina frowned. She could use some of her father's money to buy a small flat or house for her daughter to live in. She'd earmarked it for a retirement fund, which was a boring thing to do with a windfall like that, but once an accountant always an accountant. It'd be sensible to make sure she was financially secure when she got older. After all, she had only herself to rely on.

She'd been wrestling with this problem of how to use her inheritance ever since she got back from Australia. It must be wonderful to have someone to share your problems and toss ideas around with. She'd never been that fortunate. But she'd coped, and coped well, too, if she did say so herself.

Miranda woke at two o'clock in the morning, wide awake, because it would be early morning in Australia. She had trouble getting back to sleep and hoped her internal clock would adjust to the northern hemisphere quickly.

Should she call Regina? she wondered, quailing at the thought of what she had to do today. No. No, she was going to do this on her own. Had to, if she was to regain her self-respect.

After she'd finished breakfast she questioned the hotel's concierge about where to go to look at cars, and with his help found some postcodes to enter into her satnav system. It seemed as if everything went by postcode here.

She visited four car yards and could find nothing she felt certain of, though several cars she'd looked at would do at a pinch. She didn't particularly take to the salesmen, though, so didn't trust them not to palm off a lemon on her. What did she know about English cars?

She wasn't going to try anywhere else because jetlag had kicked in again and was making her feel dopey, but as she turned a corner she found another car yard straight in front of her, a smaller one, so pulled over to the side of the road. It'd be stupid to drive past. She might not find it again

This time the salesman was less pushy and more understanding of her problems.

He laughed at her when she said she'd only driven automatics because hardly anyone in Australia bought manual gear changes any more.

'No fun having the car do it all for you,' he teased.

'I'm happy to leave it to the car. I'll have enough trouble dealing with the crowded roads here. People drive faster than in my part of Australia. Um . . . where do I find the rules for driving?'

'I'll give you a copy of the Highway Code, whether you buy a car or not. From what I've heard, it's not that different from the Australian one. And of course you can find it online, once you get a computer connection.'

He steered her towards a Renault Modus and gave it an affectionate pat. 'This one might suit you nicely. It's automatic and has air conditioning. Some people say you don't need air con with our climate, but park your car in the sun and you'll soon find how useful it is. Here. Sit in it. Because they're higher than a normal car, they're easier to get in and out of. I bought one for my wife, who's got a bad back. She loves it.'

She slid into the car and found it very comfortable. 'Can I have a drive?'

'Sure.' He fumbled in his pocket and fitted the key for her. 'I'll sit beside you since you don't know the town. My name's Don, by the way.'

'Mine's Miranda.'

'Nice name.'

'Do you think so? I've always hated it.'

'You should be proud of a pretty name like that.'

Which was a different and more positive way of thinking about it, at least. 'Can you take me somewhere that isn't narrow and crowded?'

Half an hour later she signed the papers to buy the car and gave him a small deposit by credit card. 'Now I have to find a bank and open a UK account.'

Don grinned and pointed across the road. 'Couldn't be more convenient, eh? You can have the car as soon as the money comes through.'

She felt pleased with herself for sorting out a car so quickly. It took over half an hour to arrange for her bank account to be transferred and she paid extra to have her money sorted out quickly. She went back to give the news to Don.

'It must be hard,' he said suddenly.

'What?'

'Coming to a new country on your own.'

She made a non-committal noise. It would have been harder to stay in Australia but she wasn't going to tell people about Sebastian. As far as she was concerned, he was out of her life for good.

'Do you have somewhere to stay?' Don asked.

'Not yet. I'm going to buy a house later, but I don't want to rush into anything so I thought I'd rent.' Even though she liked the looks of the pretty cottage whose details Lou had downloaded from the Net, she was going to hold back, look at others, and make absolutely certain she got something that suited her.

He frowned. 'Look. I have an idea. My wife's cousin is going to Canada for three months to visit her daughter and meet her new grandson. Hazel's worrying about leaving her house empty. Maybe you could stay there and pay her a bit of rent? She lives in Wootton Bassett. I could get my wife to ask her if you like.'

'That'd be wonderful. Do you want me to get references? My sister lives there too. She's an accountant, very respectable.'

He chuckled. 'With a face like yours, you couldn't possibly be a criminal, but maybe it'd be a good idea. We'll see what my wife finds out from Hazel, first.'

Feeling hopeful about this possibility, Miranda made her way back to the hotel.

It was exhilarating to sort things out from her list of things to do, she thought when she got back to her room. Some were big tasks, others small, but each one was a step that she'd taken without help. She was more than coping, she decided. She was making progress.

But she was tired again now. Should she ring Regina? No. Not yet. She wanted some time absolutely on her own. She was going to prove to her family that she could manage her own life, because even Regina always treated her in a protective way.

The only person she was going to contact for the time being was her daughter. For that she had to find an Internet café because there was no Wi-Fi in this hotel.

She yawned. Tomorrow.

Sebastian had been trying to contact his stupid sister all day, but it seemed as if Miranda had disappeared from the face of the earth. In the end he was forced to contact her lawyer.

'Ah, Sally. I'm really worried about my sister.'

'I thought Regina had gone back to the UK.'

'Not that sister. Why would I worry about her? Regina is a capable woman.'

'So is Miranda.'

Stupid bitch! he thought. She was just trying to needle him. 'That's a matter of opinion. Anyway, as I was saying, I can't find her anywhere. Do you have any idea where she is? You may not realise how fragile she is. She shouldn't be left without support.'

'She's not at all fragile.'

'I think I know her better than you do.'

'I doubt it. Anyway, I know where she is. She's left the country and – Are you all right?'

He controlled the choking with some difficulty. 'Where has she gone?'

'That's not your business.'

'I think it is.'

'We'll have to agree to disagree about that. Now, if that's all you wanted, Fox, I'm a busy woman.'

She put the phone down on him before he could answer. He glared at the handset and slammed it down into its holder. No doubt Miranda had gone to Regina's. Well, they'd see about that. He checked the clock. Regina would just be getting up. A good time to ring.

'Ah, Sebastian here. Could I speak to Minnie, please?'

'Minnie's not here. I've not seen her since I left Australia.'

'If you're hiding her from me—'

'Why would I want to do that, Sebastian?'

'Has she stopped over somewhere on the way to see you?'

'As far as I know, she's not on her way to see me. She hasn't contacted me at all.'

He stared at the phone in shock. 'Are you telling me the truth, Regina? If I find you've been hiding her . . .'

'Firstly, I'm not hiding her. Secondly, don't threaten me, Sebastian Fox. Thirdly, why is it your business what Miranda does, anyway?'

'Because I'm her trustee.'

'The trustee of that stupid fund, you mean. You're not her guardian or her jailer. She's an adult with every right to do what she wants.'

'She needs someone to support her, look after her.'

'Rubbish. I can't believe you're hounding her like that. Have you run mad?'

He slammed the phone down and sat there with his head throbbing. They were all ganging up on him now. He had no doubt whatsoever that Minnie was in England at Regina's. Well, he had the purse strings, and though she'd got some money from selling those damned antiques, it'd not last for ever then she'd have to come to him for more. With a smile, he picked up the phone again and rang his fellow trustee.

'Tressman? Fox here. Look, Miranda's gone off to England so I think we should stop her payments.'

'Why should we do that? She'll need the money for her holiday.'

'I haven't authorised a holiday.'

Silence, then, 'I'm not aware that we need to authorise what she does, Fox. We deal with the money only, and I'm not agreeing to cut that off.'

Sebastian slammed the phone down and began to massage his aching forehead. Why had he arranged to have both signatures required? To make sure Tressman did nothing without his say-so. Only it had backfired on him. Well, Tressman was going to regret crossing him like this.

These headaches were getting worse. He might have to consult the doctor. If people would only do as he told them, he'd not have half these problems to contend with. Even Dorothy was being rather irritating these days. She'd said last night she thought Miranda could cope perfectly well. He'd soon set her straight.

He began to put his papers together. He had no more appointments today, so he'd go home. It was good to check up on one's wife from time to time.

Sally picked up the phone and rang a woman she knew in the Social Services Department, explaining the hassles her client was getting from a brother who seemed to be paranoid about controlling her. She could have rung several people but knew Danielle had had problems in the past with a manipulative husband, so would be more sympathetic.

They had a nice chat about men who thought they owned women, and women who thought they owned men, too, then Danielle went off to check out who was dealing with this case.

Two hours later, just as Sally was getting ready to leave for the day, Danielle rang again.

'I've sorted that little matter out. A Ms Dean will be ringing you to ask for confirmation of what I've told her, but there should be no problem. It was only a general inquiry anyway, and they'd not have done anything about it if your client hadn't been involuntarily committed to a mental hospital some years ago . . . and if her brother hadn't made such a fuss and threatened legal action . . . What . . . ? Yes, it's hard to believe, isn't it? They did some dreadful things to women in the old days, didn't they? Fancy locking someone away for having postnatal depression!'

Sally was smiling broadly as she left the building, but as she thought it over on the way home, she began to wonder if it was Sebastian Fox who had a psychological problem that needed help. His behaviour was going beyond what was rational, a long way beyond.

Nikki was right, Regina thought as she served the meal. Tim was like a big, friendly dog. But at least he did care about her daughter. That shone out in the way he looked at her, spoke to her, touched her.

She made too much food on purpose, so that she could give them the leftovers. The way Nikki looked at her when she made the offer said that her daughter had seen through that.

'Thanks, Mum. That'd be great. We'd better get back now. I've got some studying to do.'

Tim looked at her solemnly as he stood on the doorstep. 'I will look after her, Mrs, um, Ms Fox. If it was up to me, we'd get married straight away.'

'I know you'll look after her, but you're both a little young for getting married, don't you think?'

'Not me. I'm the homebody type. I really want to settle down. I don't care how hard I have to work to set up a home.'

Behind him Nikki rolled her eyes and tugged his sleeve. 'Come on! Mum'll be freezing standing on the doorstep in this wind. It's more like winter than late spring.'

Regina went inside, shaking her head, sadly. She could see heartbreak ahead for that poor lad.

She'd often wondered why she hadn't hankered to settle down with someone, but had never met a man for whom she'd give up her independence. Seeing poor Miranda trapped by Sebastian and their father had probably driven her to the opposite extreme, total independence. And that wasn't a bad thing, surely.

Regina rang Sally to let her know she'd still not heard from Miranda. 'I'm really worried about her. Why hasn't she contacted me?'

'I don't know. But I'm sure she would if she was in trouble. Perhaps she's enjoying being on her own.'

'She's never been on her own.'

'Precisely.'

'I don't think she'll cope. And it's so silly to try when I could help her get settled in here.'

'I'm sure she'll be in touch when she's ready.'

Regina put the phone down and forced herself to concentrate on her job. It had never been so difficult. She didn't know how she'd wound up as an accountant. OK, so she was good with figures. But they could pall on you if that was all you dealt with, day in, day out. Even a high salary didn't altogether make up for that. What she enjoyed most was the contact with clients but, since her last promotion, she was dealing with big, corporate accounts and the people she dealt with kept changing.

Oh, she was being silly lately. Security of employment was even more important these days, and she'd proved that she'd made a wise choice by going into accounting, hadn't she? There might be a recession on, a lot of people might be hurting, but her job was secure for as long as she wanted it. Her firm had let a few people go, but her manager had told her how pleased they were with her work and was hinting at further promotions once the recession was over.

The trouble was, she sometimes wondered whether she wanted to play company politics and climb any higher up the corporate ladder. She was even toying with the idea that as soon as the economy settled down, she might look into making a change. Not moving into something too risky, but just . . . something different. The money she'd inherited meant she didn't have to put up with a job she didn't like, but could look for one that gave her more satisfaction.

That was a wonderful thought.

Miranda went back to complete the deal on her car purchase two days later. She was being very careful with her money because she'd been looking through the property pages of the local newspapers and knew she didn't yet have enough to buy a decent house in a decent area, and she couldn't see anyone giving an unemployable woman a mortgage. She wasn't going to live in a tiny box of a house in a rough area, though.

She just hoped they'd get probate soon and then she could sell Lou's pieces. They might fetch a few thousand dollars more, which would make a big difference.

At the car yard Don greeted her with a smile. 'Got it all sorted then?'

'Yes.' She handed over a bank cheque, signed her name to various bits and pieces, refusing his offer of arranging car insurance when she found out how much it'd cost.

'I can get it much cheaper than that. I've been checking on the Internet. I'll make a phone call before I leave to set it up, if that's all right with you.'

He sighed but didn't take offence. 'Time was when I

could make a nice bit of extra money through insurance, now you've only got to go online to find a better deal than the insurance companies will allow me to give.' He pushed the car keys across the table but didn't seem in a hurry to move. 'Thought any more about my cousin's house?'

'I was waiting for you to tell me if it's available, Don. Then I'd have to go and see it, and, of course, your relative would want to meet me.'

'Well, Hazel is interested, especially if you can pay her the rent on the quiet.' He looked at his watch. 'How about I take you to meet her now?'

'Won't your boss mind?'

He grinned. 'I am the boss. This place might not be as large as some, but it's steady and independent. I've got customers coming back time after time for cars.'

She wasn't surprised. He was good to deal with and seemed honest to her. 'I need to return the hired car today, I'm afraid, so I can't take up your kind offer of taking me to meet Hazel. I don't want to pay for more days' hire than I need to. I'll take the car to the depot I picked it up from, then get a taxi back here.'

'Where's the place you hired it from? . . . Oh, no worries. We can drop it off on the way.'

She beamed at him 'That's great. It'd be such a help.'

He held the door open for her and gestured towards a Mercedes. 'That's mine. Can't miss it, can you? I love red cars. If you follow me in your car, I'll show you where the depot is.'

'I'd better program it into my satnav first, just in case we get separated. I don't know what I'd have done without that. Oh no! I won't have one in the new car. I need to buy myself one.'

'We'll do that too on the way back. I know a good place.'

'Do they happen to sell mobile phones, too?'

'Yes. And if they don't have one that suits, we can go elsewhere.'

'I just need something simple. I've got to be a bit careful with my money.'

'I like the fancy ones, myself. Good fun to play with.'

'I think I'm going to be too busy to play with gadgets. For a while, anyway. You're very kind. I can't tell you how grateful I am.'

'If we can't help one another, it's a poor lookout, don't you think?' He waved to another man and called, 'I'll be out for an hour or two.'

She followed Don's car through the town, a confusing part of Swindon which she had trouble getting straight in her mind, even though she'd studied the street map. To her relief, she didn't lose him because the only time they were separated he waited for her, parked illegally on double yellow lines.

After she'd handed over the car, she sank down in his expensive Mercedes, which smelt of new leather, and enjoyed the luxury of being driven.

He pulled up in front of a picturesque thatched cottage just outside Wootton Bassett. 'There it is. Pretty, isn't it?'

'It's gorgeous.'

Hazel was a motherly looking woman but her gaze was shrewd as she shook Miranda's hand and began to show them round. The cottage had only two bedrooms, and a tiny bathroom with an uneven wooden floor in between. Downstairs was a living room and kitchen. It was lovingly over-furnished, with ornaments crowded on every surface.

'Don said you had a sister in the district. All right if I ring her?' Hazel asked.

'Of course it is. You'd better wait till the evening because she'll be at work just now. She works for Dalton and Carrick.'

'Good company, that,' Don said approvingly.

'She's been with them for years. She's some sort of fancy accountant.'

'I was thinking of asking a hundred and fifty pounds a week,' Hazel said hesitantly. 'That'd cover electricity and all that, as long as you didn't go mad with it. And of course, I'd want you to look after the garden. A neighbour mows the lawn for me, so you'd not need to worry about the grass, just keep the weeds down and deadhead things. How does that sound? That'll save me hiring a gardener.'

'It sounds just fine to me. I love gardening.' She fumbled in her bag. 'I've written down my sister's name and phone number. She lives in Summerhey.'

He pulled out a fancy mobile phone that looked more like a computer than a phone and started fiddling with it. 'Here we go . . . Yes, there she is! That proves she exists and lives in a respectable place. So that's the first step taken, eh, Hazel?'

His cousin smiled. 'I didn't expect otherwise. Your friend doesn't have a dishonest face.'

That was the second time someone had commented on her face, Miranda thought. Did she look soft or what? 'I'll pay a month in advance each time. How does that sound?'

'It sounds fine to me. I must say the extra money will come in useful. Since my George died, I've had to be a bit careful. My daughter's paying my fares, but it's nice to have a bit of spending money to treat the grandchildren, isn't it?'

'Yes. I'll need to get online while I'm here, but that's only a question of getting broadband connected. Is that all right?'

Hazel smiled at her. 'You don't need to do that. I've got broadband already. I don't like computers, but my son set mine up and helps out when something goes wrong. I must say it makes it a lot easier to keep in touch with my daughter and her family. Why don't you just use my computer?'

'I'll pay the broadband costs for each month, then. I insist.'

After they left the cottage, Don whisked Miranda off to a shop to buy a satnav. When they got back to the car yard, he smiled at her. 'I'm sure we'll have no difficulty with your sister. Shall I help you program the hotel into your new satnav, so that you can find your way back?'

'Thanks. You've been very kind to me.'

He shrugged. 'Well, you're a sale, aren't you? And perhaps in a few years, you might come back for another car.'

'I definitely will.'

'My wife and I were saying last night, she'd not dare move to a strange country on her own, whether she had a sister there or not, so you're a brave woman.'

As Miranda drove off, she felt happier than she had for a long time. Things were going really well. She even had a home lined up. And now, to ice the cake, someone thought her brave. That compliment had boosted her confidence enormously.

Chapter Fifteen

The phone was ringing as she got in. Regina nearly didn't pick it up because she was tired. 'Hello . . . ? Min – sorry, I mean Miranda! Where on earth are you? I tried to meet you at Heathrow but I got held up and missed you.'

'How did you know I was coming?'

'Sally told me.'

'I wish people would just leave me to get on with my life, however well-meaning.'

Regina didn't know what to say to that and was surprised at how sharply her sister had spoken, so moved on. 'Are you coming to stay with me? I'd really like that.'

'No. Thanks for the offer, but I've found a place of my own. It's quite near you, though.' She explained that Hazel would be phoning tonight to check up on her.

Regina laughed. 'I'll tell her you're perfectly respectable, I promise you. If you won't come to stay, how about coming to tea one day?'

'I'd like that.'

'Oh, and I don't want to upset you, but Sebastian rang.'

'Did he?'

'He was absolutely furious at you for leaving Australia.'

'He can be as furious as he wants. It's none of his business and I'm not going back, not as long as he's around, anyway.'

'I don't blame you. How about coming to tea tomorrow?'

'Fine.'

'Want me to pick you up?'

'No. I've bought a car.'

After they'd finished chatting, Regina put the phone down and went to make herself a cup of coffee, amazed at how her sister was coming out of her shell. She even sounded more . . . more definite. Good for her!

The next afternoon Miranda found an Internet café and sent an email to her daughter, saying she hoped they could meet and explaining that she'd moved to England now and would soon be in a house, rather than a hotel.

She sat staring at the screen for a long time after the email had gone. Would Katie agree to see her? It would be hard to bear if she refused.

Her mobile phone rang, making her jump because she still wasn't used to carrying it around. It was Hazel.

'I spoke to your sister last night. She sounds a lovely person. Look, I wondered if you'd like to move in tomorrow so that I can show you how things work before I leave. Seems a waste you paying for a hotel room, when you could sleep here.'

'I'd love to! Thank you.'

'You're welcome, dear. We're helping each other, aren't we? Come at about ten o'clock, or whenever suits you after that. I'll be in all day.'

After she'd finished the call, Miranda did a little dance round the hotel room, feeling as if she could almost fly. The euphoria faded as her mind returned inevitably to her major remaining worry.

Surely her daughter wouldn't refuse to have one meeting? If she could just see Katie, talk to her, it'd make her so happy. But of course she longed for more than one meeting.

Her father and Sebastian had a lot to answer for.

Katie stared at the email message from her birth mother. It was short, only a few lines, and didn't give away much about the personality of the sender. Did she really want to meet this woman? It'd upset Mum, but she had to do it, at least once.

'What's she like as a person, my birth mother?' she asked Brody again that evening, and couldn't help noticing how rigid he suddenly went.

Then his expression softened slightly. 'Gentle. Too soft for her own good, I used to think. Her older brother used to trample all over her. I told her she needed to stand up to him, but she never did. Why do you keep asking? If you arrange to meet her, you'll find out for yourself.'

'I'm scared to. What if I don't like her?'

'Then you don't have to see her again.'

'That's not so easy if she's come all this way to meet me.'

He thrust his hands into his jacket pockets and scowled into the distance. 'I've said all I'm going to say. You must decide for yourself. Just make sure you don't bring her anywhere near me.'

'Do you hate her that much?'

'I don't want to wake the dead.' He changed the subject. He didn't know what he thought about Miranda now. This was stirring up all his old feelings, and maybe they weren't as dead as he'd thought.

Katie was left to sort out her dilemma alone. It was all too much because she still hadn't heard from Darren. It was the longest time her husband had been out of touch. She prayed every night that he was safe and would come safely home to her and Ned.

In the end, she decided to give her birth mother a chance. It was only fair, because she'd agreed to see Brody, hadn't she? She couldn't think of him as Father or Dad, especially not Dad. No one would ever replace her own Dad. Brody was much younger and quite with it, really, considering he was in his late forties.

She'd arrange to meet Miranda – what an old-fashioned name! – somewhere public and not give her a phone number or an address. That way she didn't need to see her again if she didn't want to.

If that was cruel, well, it was the best she could manage.

Oh, Darren, I really need you. Why are you so far away?

Regina watched the car pull up, surprised at how different her sister looked. She went to open the front door and they paused awkwardly then gave one another air kisses, as if they were mere acquaintances.

'Well, come in and sit down. Can I get you a glass of wine?'

'Better not. I've got to drive and I'm still not used to the traffic here.' Miranda looked at her, hesitated, then blurted out, 'Do you mind?'

'Mind what?'

'Me not coming to see you first.'

'No. I was surprised, I must admit. I thought you'd *need* my help, but you sound to be doing just fine. You were lucky to get a house to rent so cheaply.'

'Yes. It's a tiny place but big enough to have friends round. Perhaps you'd come for a meal one night once Hazel has left? And if you want to have a few drinks, you could stay over. There's a spare bedroom. Nikki might like to come too. What do you think?'

'I'd love that and so would she. She rang up to ask about you.'

'I emailed her today, told her where I was living, gave her my phone number, but I haven't heard back. How is she?'

'Managing. Just. She doesn't look all that well, but the school nurse is keeping an eye on her. She'll be due her twenty-week scan soon, then we'll get photos of the baby.'

'I wasn't well the whole time I was pregnant,' Miranda

said. 'The family doctor told me to snap out of it. Dr Grant was an unfeeling brute.'

'Why didn't you go to someone else?'

'Dad got furious when I suggested it. He said Dr Grant had known me since childhood and it'd be stupid to go to a stranger. And afterwards, well, you know what happened.'

Regina reached out to squeeze her sister's hand. 'I'm so sorry for what they did to you. I wasn't much use.'

'You were only fifteen. What could you have done with Father and Sebastian both ranged against me? Never mind that, tell me more about Nikki and her guy.'

'He's fine. Nice lad. They're living in this ghastly bedsitter and she hates it, but it's all they can afford. I don't know what to do. She's eighteen. An adult. I can't force her to do anything now.'

'She'll be all right. She's an intelligent girl.'

'Mmm. Anyway, what are you going to do with yourself now? What will you live on?'

Miranda wondered how much to tell her sister. She still wasn't used to thinking of Regina as on her side. 'Who knows what I'll do? But my aunt's antiques sold very well and there are the things Lou left me as well. They might be quite valuable. So don't worry. I'm not short of money. I don't have enough to buy a decent house, though.' She also had her mother's jewellery with her, but didn't say anything about that. She hadn't even had it valued, so maybe it wasn't worth as much as she hoped.

They ate a meal that was utterly delicious. 'Did you cook this? It's marvellous.' Miranda closed her eyes in ecstasy as she spooned up every bit of the wonderful dessert, a concoction of fruit and ice cream with a tangy sauce.

'Yes. Don't sound so surprised. I love cooking. I've been to all sorts of classes. Food is my big weakness. It's a good thing I don't have a weight problem.'

'I've never really gone beyond plain cooking. You know Father.'

'Yes. Meat, potatoes and two sorts of boiled vegetables.'

Miranda laughed. 'Don't forget the gravy, dark brown or light, never a creamy sauce. He'd have thought the world had ended if he didn't get his gravy. But I can cook a few other things. I'll give you a call to work out a date once I've settled in.'

'And if you get lonely, well, you know where I am.'

Miranda drove home thoughtfully. Regina always made her feel inferior; she was so elegant and self-assured. As for that superb meal, well she'd never be able to make anything half as good as that. She was going to buy a cookery book and learn a few new dishes, though. She never wanted to eat roast lamb, her father's favourite meat, again as long as she lived.

When she got home, she had a chat with Hazel, then checked her emails. She froze as she saw the list of senders. Her daughter had replied!

'I'll just go up to bed now,' Hazel said.

'What? Oh, yes. I won't be long.'

'Be as long as you like. You won't disturb me. Once my head's on that pillow, I'm gone for eight hours.'

Miranda waited until the bed above her had creaked and silence reigned before opening Katie's email.

We could meet for coffee, if you like. How about tomorrow, two o'clock, in Carey's Café? It's in Wootton Bassett near the Post Office. Do you know the town?
    Katie

Tears welled in Miranda's eyes. It was a very terse email, but it offered hope. Surely her daughter wouldn't close the door on her after this meeting?

She wrote back immediately to say she'd be there. Then she shut the email system down and got ready for bed. She couldn't concentrate on anything else tonight.

The next morning Miranda waved goodbye to Hazel, who had decided to visit a cousin in London on her way to Canada, now that she had someone to look after the cottage. It was a relief to see her hostess go. Hazel was a lovely woman, but she never stopped talking and Miranda simply wasn't used to that.

She walked round the house, relishing the silence, wondering if she dared put some of the ornaments away. No, better not. She might forget where they went and they were clearly much cherished pieces. Hazel had dusted them all every day. Miranda was definitely not going to do that. Life was too short.

She went across to Hazel's computer, which sat

at one end of the cosy room that covered the whole ground floor except for a small kitchen. The cottage was as small as the flat Sebastian had bought her in Australia, but it felt incredibly different. People had been happy here, she was sure. Generations of them, because the cottage dated from about 1780, with thick stone walls and a thatched roof.

Living here even for a couple of days had changed her mind about what sort of house she intended to buy. If she was going to spend her life in England, she wanted far more space. The cottage in the advertisement would probably be small, too, however picturesque it might be. And she preferred somewhere lighter. The windows here weren't big enough for her.

Sorry, Lou, she told the shade of the man who'd saved her. *Your cottage won't do.* Lou seemed still to be hovering at the edges of her life. She even found herself talking to him. Oh, she did miss him!

She'd have to study local house prices on the Internet. Today she couldn't settle. She was meeting her daughter in a few hours and the butterflies had moved into her stomach and were practising for the Olympics there.

Nikki went to sit at the back of the classroom in case she had to dash out. She wasn't feeling at all well. She realised someone was standing beside her and looked up to see her friend Aysha staring down at her.

'You're as white as that piece of paper,' Aysha said with her usual bluntness. 'Should you be here today?'

'I should if I want to pass my A levels.' She made an effort. 'But thanks for caring.'

The door opened and Aysha turned away. 'See you at break.'

But Nikki felt the world spin round so fast a short time later that she had to raise her hand and tell the teacher she was ill.

'You'd better go to the sick bay,' he said.

When she stood up she felt so dizzy, she fell down and couldn't get up again. She didn't protest when they brought along a stretcher on wheels, didn't even care that she'd be the talking point of the school for this.

'You're going to hospital, young woman,' the nurse said. 'This is more than just pregnancy sickness.'

She tried to sit up and failed. 'No. I can't miss any more lessons. If I just lie down for half an hour, I'll be all right, I'm sure.'

The nurse took hold of her hand. 'Look, Nikki, you're not at all well. Sometimes a pregnant woman needs medical help and this may be one of those times. We're not risking anything.'

'I've never even been in hospital before.'

'There are no dragons there.' She kept hold of Nikki's hand as she punched in a number and spoke quietly to someone on the phone.

Nikki tried to listen to what she was saying, but couldn't seem to concentrate, drifting in and out of consciousness. She felt so tired, she couldn't be bothered to protest any more. They'd just keep her in hospital for an hour or two, then send her home, she was sure. She'd researched it online. Some pregnancies were like that. Some women never felt well. It didn't usually affect the baby.

The paramedics checked her blood pressure and asked her questions. She hoped her answers made sense. It was hard to think straight when you felt so spaced out. She probably needed a day or two in bed. She'd be all right after that.

When she came to again, she was lying in a cubicle. She stared round in surprise. She must be at the hospital. How had she got here without waking up?

A man in a white coat came into the cubicle. 'So you're conscious again, young lady. How long have you been feeling ill?'

She tried to think. 'Weeks. Most of the time since I've been pregnant.'

After a few more questions, he said gently, 'We're going to have to admit you.'

'No! No, I've got to keep up with my school work.'

'You can study better if we find out what's wrong with you. And they can send work to the hospital. We have someone here who manages that sort of thing.'

He was right. They'd probably find she was short of iron or something. She put one hand protectively on her stomach. This was the best place for her baby, too.

There were footsteps outside and a nurse peeped in. 'Her mother's here, Doctor.'

He turned round. 'I'll have a quick word. Can you get

Nikki admitted to the gynaecology wing ASAP.'

'I'll see to it.'

He turned back to Nikki. 'I'll send your mother in shortly. She can fetch your things to hospital for you.'

Outside he found an attractive woman who looked far too young to be his patient's mother. 'Mrs Fox?'

'*Ms* Fox.'

'Could I have a word before you see your daughter?' He didn't wait for an answer but led the way down the corridor.

Regina stared at the doctor as he walked away, suddenly fearful for Nikki, then hurried after him into a tiny room with a sagging old couch along one side and a couple of hard chairs facing it. She took a seat on the couch and waited.

He sat down, frowning. 'Your daughter's quite ill, I'm afraid.'

'How ill is "quite ill"? Is something wrong with the pregnancy?'

'Yes. We'll need to do some tests and then we'll know better how to treat her. I suspect pre-eclampsia. In the meantime she'll have to stay in hospital. Whatever you do, don't let her persuade you to take her home. It could put her life in danger.'

Shocked, she tried to take this in. 'Nikki is that ill?'

'Yes. Are you all right?'

'Sorry. It's just . . . a shock. Nikki's never had a day's illness in her life, except for the usual childhood ailments.'

'Could you bring her some things in?'

Regina just managed to stop herself saying her daughter no longer lived with her. 'Yes, of course.'

'Good. We'll go back and see if they've found her a bed. I don't suppose you have private medical cover?'

'No, I'm afraid not.' It had seemed a waste with them both being so healthy and she'd never bothered with it.

Regina followed as they wheeled her daughter up to a ward, calmed Nikki down when she objected to being put into a hospital gown, and promised to go and get the girl's own things. 'There's a key to the flat in my school bag. Did they bring that in with me?'

'I don't think so, but I can easily get it from school.'

'Sorry to be such a nuisance.'

'You're not doing this on purpose and, anyway, what else are mothers for?'

'Thanks, Mum. Tell Tim, won't you?'

'Yes, of course.'

With a sigh, Nikki closed her eyes again and Regina went to the nurses' station. 'I'll be back in an hour.'

'Can you just give us a few details first?'

She helped them fill in the forms then hurried off.

The school nurse had her daughter's things and summoned Tim.

He looked horrified when they told him Nikki would have to stay in hospital and declared he was going to see her at once.

'Why don't you come back to your place with me first

to pack Nikki's things, then you can ride to hospital with me?'

'Yeah. Great. She's going to be all right, isn't she? And the baby?'

'They're both in good hands.'

The flat, to which Regina had not so far been invited, shocked her rigid. It was a hovel situated in a slum, there was no other way to describe it.

Tim shot her a quick look sideways. 'I know it's not much but it's all we can afford just now. As soon as I've finished school, I'll get a job and we'll find somewhere better.'

'I'm sure you will. Now, let's sort out some clothes for Nikki and maybe a book or two. What was she reading? I can't remember a time when she didn't have a novel in her hand.'

'She picked up some books from the charity shop a couple of days ago. I'll get them.'

He was silent all the way to hospital and he looked so anxious there could be no doubt he loved her daughter. But he also looked young and a little afraid.

They were both far too young for this.

Brody was worried. What the hell was Miranda doing here? Not only in England but in Wiltshire, of all places. He felt to be making progress with his daughter and didn't want anything interrupting that.

Nor did he want the past stirring up again. He'd loved Miranda deeply – more fool he! – and she'd let him down, though what her family had had against him, he'd never understood. He'd dreamt about it all last night and the night before, living through it again, feeling the anguish and frustration . . . then the fury at being driven out of his home town.

It had been hard to carry on studying when he was both angry and upset, but he'd figured if he ever found her again and they got back together, as they surely would, he'd at least have a decent job to support them. He'd got a first-class degree. Miranda hadn't finished hers.

After the child's expected birth date, he went to see her father again, asking about the baby. He found himself facing the brother instead. Arrogant sod!

'She had it adopted,' Sebastian said.

'It's my baby too. I'll take you to court about that.'

'What? Did you think you could suckle it yourself and raise it? They'd laugh you out of court. Anyway, you can't prove you're the father. She put "Father unknown" on the birth certificate.'

'I want to see her, talk to her.'

'Well, she doesn't want to see you. And anyway, she's not here.'

Within the week, Brody was sacked on the most spurious of excuses and, for all his excellent grades, failed to get even a sniff of another job.

Then one evening he met his former boss, John, in a café where he was doing some casual work. He scowled but said nothing.

John hesitated, then said in a low voice, 'Meet me in the gents in a couple of minutes.'

When Brody slipped inside, John said, 'You've offended someone, Lanigan! The word is out around Perth in the sort of firms where you're likely to look for jobs that you're not to be trusted.'

'Who did that?' As if he didn't know!

John tapped the side of his nose. 'Not wise to ask. Some people have friends in very high places.'

'I can't believe this is happening in this day and age.'

'It's happened in every age. Money and power can talk very loudly. Look, if I were you, I'd get out of the state and look for work elsewhere. Western Australia is a small place; you can do better for yourself anyway. Tell future employers you've been enjoying a holiday since you graduated and don't try to provide anything but academic references.'

'Could you give me a private reference?'

'Sorry. I'd like to keep my job.' John walked out.

Brody stood there in silent humiliation, then pulled himself together to finish his shift. A week later he moved to New South Wales and never went back to Western Australia.

Ten years after that he accepted a transfer to the UK and stayed on. It had been a good move. He felt free of his past here.

After a few years, he'd had a little luck, developed some small software programs that filled useful niches and would keep selling well. They brought in steady royalties, and he was quite comfortable financially now; could pay the necessary child support for his son, afford decent holidays, whatever he wanted.

He wasn't rich, had no desire to push harder financially. Comfortable was quite enough for him.

After his marriage broke up, he hadn't looked for another long-term relationship, except for the ones with his children. Nothing, but nothing was going to mess up his fledgling relationship with his daughter . . .

He realised he'd slipped back into thinking about the past again, something he'd vowed to stop doing. He got up to pour himself a whisky and sat down, scowling at some stupid-looking woman on the television. He had no idea what programme had been showing. The one he'd started to watch must have finished.

How many people were sitting on their own tonight feeling lonely? Why was he so often on his own, anyway? Because he was no good at relationships, that's why. He raised his glass and took a big mouthful. 'To hell with the past!'

But he choked on the whisky. He wasn't really a drinker.

What was he now? Not the bright-eyed lad who'd loved Miranda, that was sure. What would she see when she looked at him now? If they ever met again.

What would he see when he looked at her?

Chapter Sixteen

Miranda arrived at the café early, feeling extremely nervous. She chose a seat from which she could observe the door and sat down, ordering a latte. When a young woman walked in, she had no need to ask if this was her daughter. She was shocked at how much the newcomer resembled not only herself but also her mother in the old photos she regarded as some of her treasures. She stood up and waved.

Katie threaded her way slowly across the jumble of tables in the café and stopped just before she got to the table, studying her. 'Miranda Fox?'

'Yes. And I'm sure you're Katie. You look so like your grandmother at the same age. Won't you join me?'

After the slightest of nods Katie sat down, ordering a cappuccino from the hovering waitress.

Miranda tried to keep her voice steady, tried not to stare too much. 'Thank you for agreeing to meet me.'

'I thought it was only fair. You . . . um, look younger than I'd expected.'

'My mother's side of the family is noted for its baby faces. It's a problem when you're young, but a blessing when you get older.' She stopped, realising she was babbling, forcing herself to wait.

Katie could hear the nervousness in her mother's voice and it disarmed her a little. If Miranda had been confident and brassy, she'd have had a lot more trouble relating to her, she was sure. But this woman was tense and on edge – just as she was herself.

'I'd like to hear about my birth family, baby faces and all. It's important to know where we come from, don't you think? That's why I posted my details on the adoption lists.'

'I didn't find you through those lists. A dear friend contacted a private investigator. He knew how much it mattered to me.'

'He must care about you.'

'He died recently. I miss him.'

The naked pain in her face disarmed Katie still further.

'I've brought you some copies of family photos that I'd scanned in.' Miranda fumbled in her handbag with hands that shook visibly.

Katie stared at those hands as she took the photos, then looked up at the gentle face with its over-bright eyes. Oh dear, being unkind to this woman would be like smacking a baby for crying. She swallowed hard and bent her head to study the photographs.

'I've written on the backs who they are. This one is my mother. Can you see the resemblance to yourself?'

'Yes. She died young, didn't she?'

'How did you know that?'

She didn't want to tell her about Brody, not yet, and he definitely didn't want to be brought into things. 'I've been doing some research.'

'She was very young when she died, only twenty-eight. In fact, my father's first two wives both died young. The third one left him. So I have an older half-brother and a younger half-sister. My sister lives in England, near here, actually.'

'And your brother, my uncle?'

'He lives in Australia and is best forgotten. He's an arrogant bully.'

Katie stared at her in surprise.

'I'm sorry. I didn't mean to say anything about him.'

'It's all right. I'll probably never meet him.' She had to wonder, though, why a woman as gentle as this hated the man so much. 'Tell me about my father, how you met him, why you parted.' To her amazement, she saw her mother wipe away a tear.

'He was called Brody Lanigan and I met him at university. I loved him very much. My father ... separated us forcibly and I never saw Brody again. He was very intelligent and good-looking, at least I thought so.'

This didn't sound like a woman who'd callously abandoned her lover and child. Katie was puzzled, but didn't dare ask anything else in case she revealed too much.

'Would you tell me about your son, Katie?'

She smiled involuntarily. 'Ned's five, into mischief all the time. He's intelligent – well, I think so – and tall for his age, like his father. Here, I have a photo.' She held it out.

'I can't believe I'm a grandmother. I never hoped for that.'

Katie watched Miranda's forefinger touch the photo lightly, tracing out Ned's face, and that gesture further weakened her resolution not to see her mother again, as did the tears that had welled in the other woman's eyes when they were talking about Brody.

'And your husband, Katie? What does he do?'

'He's a professional soldier, a captain. He's serving in Afghanistan at the moment.'

Her mother looked shocked. 'That must be hard on you.'

'I've grown used to being a soldier's wife. I knew what it'd be like when I married Darren. It's just . . . sometimes, like now, he's out of touch for a while, then you can't help worrying. But I cope. You have to.'

That was the word she always used. Cope. It was as good as any to describe how it was. But it was getting harder and harder to say it with confidence. She finished her cappuccino. 'I have to go soon. I deliberately kept the time short in case—' She broke off, not wanting to hurt her mother. Oh, dear, she'd intended to be so businesslike!

'In case you didn't take to me,' Miranda said quietly.

'Something like that.'

'And now you've met me? Can we see one another again? Or did I fail the test?'

She could see how white-knuckled her mother's hands were. 'You passed it. And yes, we can meet again. Here, if you like. How about in two days' time, but half an hour earlier, so that we can talk for longer? I'll bring a few photos for you.'

'I'd love that.'

Katie stood up. 'I have to pick Ned up now.'

'Yes.'

She hesitated, not knowing how to say goodbye, whether to air kiss her mother or not. But it seemed false, so she just nodded and tried to smile. Didn't quite manage it.

When she was outside, she glanced back into the café and saw that her mother had turned her back to the room. But her shoulders were shaking visibly and she was mopping her eyes.

This wasn't a woman who didn't care about people, who abandoned them without a word.

What had really separated her birth parents?

When Regina and Tim got to the hospital they found Nikki sleeping, and the nurse who took her things from them didn't encourage them to linger.

'Best thing she can do is sleep undisturbed.'

Nonetheless they waited for half an hour, then Regina said briskly, 'Come on. We're doing no good here and I'm sure we've both got better things to do.'

Tim shook his head stubbornly. 'I'm staying. She might wake and need to see someone she knows.'

'OK. She was upset to be in hospital. Will you be all right? Have you money for a taxi home if you leave after the buses stop running?'

'I can walk.'

'It's too far. Here.' She stuffed a couple of notes into his hand and patted his shoulder.

He looked at her earnestly. 'I do love her, Ms Fox. I know you think we're too young, but you can truly love someone at any age.'

'I know. Been there, done that.'

She felt sad as she walked out to her car. She felt pretty certain that Nikki didn't have the same depth of feeling for Tim.

When she stopped the car, she looked at Miranda's cottage in surprise, because she hadn't made a conscious decision to come here. Then she pulled a wry face and got out. Why not?

Her sister came to the door, beaming at her, then the smile faded. 'What's wrong?'

And Regina, who prided herself on being sensible and practical in all situations, burst into tears.

Sebastian sat at his desk, drumming his fingers, unable to concentrate. He didn't know when he'd been as angry as he was now – with Miranda, of course, always with Miranda. She had given the family nothing but trouble over the years.

Dorothy said it wasn't worth getting so het up and he should just concentrate on other things, but the anger wouldn't go away, nor would the image of Miranda letting the family down by acting foolishly in England.

He'd spent years planning how to manage that money and make sure it came to his sons in the end, and was anyone grateful to him? No. His sons hadn't been across to visit him for several years now, nor had they been particularly welcoming when he suggested going to visit them in the eastern states; a plane flight of nearly five hours, so not a journey to be undertaken lightly.

And whatever anyone said, if Miranda had slipped into depression once, she could do it again at any time. She needed someone to keep an eye on her for her own protection, as his father had agreed.

She'd sold most of the antiques and Dorothy had told him the prices she'd got. Miranda would waste the money, he was sure. And she'd presumably taken the jewellery with her to England as well.

And now the final straw, the cause for his fury escalating steeply, he'd been required to attend a meeting with an official mediator to discuss the will and the application to have it overset. Sally had been quick off the mark in lodging an application for this and must have pulled a few strings, because a judge had ordered them to try that path first.

The letter said that since one trustee was in favour of over-setting the will's provisions, it seemed worth trying to come to an agreement rather than going the more expensive route of a court case when the courts were overloaded with more important work.

He had no intention whatsoever of oversetting the terms he'd worked out so carefully, not under any circumstances. He would have refused even to attend, but Robert Courtenay, the head of his firm, was big on mediation and was making a name for himself in that area. He'd told Sebastian how important it was to try this route first.

Sally Patel must have got at Courtenay, since there was no other way he could be au fait with the case. Case! There was no case to answer. Minnie wasn't getting hold of that money. He'd make damned sure of that.

When she got home, Katie went straight to her computer to check her emails, but there was still no word from Darren.

She knew better than to contact anyone about her husband. If he'd wanted her to know what was happening he'd have told her. And if anything went wrong, if he was – her thought skittered away from the word 'killed' and she substituted 'injured' – well, the unit welfare officer had her mobile phone number and would contact her personally. That was how they did it these days.

No, she just had to carry on. Somehow.

She was glad when Brody rang to ask if he could drop by for half an hour after tea to see Ned. Her guess was that Brody also wanted to find out how she'd got on with Miranda. She wished she'd had more time to get to know her mother before discussing her with him and would have pretended to be busy.

Unfortunately Ned overheard the call and guessed who it was, jumping round her in delight, so she couldn't say no to Brody dropping in. Ned was getting very attached to his grandfather.

Brody turned up with flowers for her and a wooden puzzle game for Ned, who seemed to have an affinity for twisting and manipulating shapes.

'You're looking a bit strained. How did it go today?' he asked.

'Better than I'd expected.'

'Oh?'

'She seemed nice. As you said, she's a very gentle sort of person.'

He hitched his shoulders slightly, which could mean anything, but his lips pressed tightly together.

'She hurt you badly, didn't she?'

Another shrug. He stared across the room to where Ned was fiddling with the puzzle.

'She was in tears today.'

He looked straight at her then.

'After I'd left, I looked back and she was sitting there in the café, all on her own, crying. I nearly went back to comfort her, only I had to pick Ned up, so I couldn't, but I felt awful leaving her in that state. I'm seeing her again in two days' time. I wondered if you'd like to join us?'

'No.'

'Shouldn't you ask her what really happened? I mean, all you have is what her brother said to you, and she didn't speak very well of him today. In fact, she called him an "arrogant bully".'

'She's telling the truth there, at least.' He changed the subject, so Katie didn't press the point.

'Do you want to take Ned to the zoo at the weekend? If the weather's fine, that is.'

Ned must have been listening because he rushed across the room. 'Say yes, Mummy. Say yes!'

'As long as the weather is OK. I'm not tramping round zoos in the rain and nor are you.'

'It'll be fine,' Ned said confidently.

Regina rang the hospital a couple of times, leaving messages, and went to see her daughter during her lunch break.

'You're still looking pale.'

Nikki's voice was sharp. 'Thanks for that compliment!'

'Have they decided what's wrong with you?'

'Pre-eclampsia, they think.'

'That's not good.'

'Tell me about it. I can understand now why you wanted me to have an abortion. Having a baby stuffs up your whole life. How am I to get good grades in my A levels when I'm like this, Mum?' She rubbed away a tear.

'I'm sure the doctors will be able to help you and then, once you're feeling better—'

'They said I needed bed rest for the time being. In

other words, lie here and go mad.'

'Oh.'

'And all Tim could say was we had to do what they said because of the baby. I'm doing it because of me, because I don't want to die of eclampsia. I'm starting to hate the baby, hate it!'

There was a gasp from the doorway and Regina turned to see Tim standing there looking horrified.

'Go away!' Nikki screamed at him. 'I told you to go away and not come back till tomorrow. Why will you not give me some space to get my head round this?'

He looked at her pleadingly.

'Go – away!'

Her voice was so high pitched, a nurse came running.

Regina waved Tim away and he disappeared, but when she went to look out of the door, he was still standing at the end of the corridor.

The nurse was taking Nikki's obs and frowning. 'You've got to calm down,' she said quietly. 'I told you earlier it doesn't do you any good to get agitated.'

'Then tell him to go away.'

'I'll do it,' Regina said. She went out and joined Tim, not mincing her words. 'You're upsetting her and making things worse. You have to go home and leave her in peace.'

'You'd think she'd want me here with her.'

'I don't think she wants any of us here. Most of all she doesn't want to be here herself, hasn't come to terms with that yet.'

'How can she hate the baby?'

'She doesn't. She just hates feeling helpless. Don't we all?'

'What should I do, Ms Fox?'

'What Nikki said: go home. Give me your mobile number and I'll ring you when I get back from the hospital.' As he still hesitated, she added, 'You know that's all you can do, Tim. I've brought in her mobile, so she can ring you herself if she wants you here.'

'I suppose so.' He walked off, shoulders hunched, looking so young and beaten her heart ached for him. She walked slowly back to the ward.

'Has he gone?' Nikki demanded.

'Definitely gone home, I promise you. He only wants to help. You shouldn't shout at him.'

'Well, he's not helping. No one can help me now. I'm trapped.' She began sobbing.

The nurse shook her head and mouthed, '*I'll get the doctor.*'

Regina waited. A tired-looking woman in a white coat came and checked Nikki. 'I think we'll give you a sedative. What you need more than anything is rest.'

Nikki didn't protest, which made her mother realise how ill she was, but let them give her an injection and then lay back with her eyes closed.

'You might as well go home too, Mum.'

'I'll stay till you get to sleep.'

She opened her eyes and glared at Regina. '*Go – home!* What's with everyone? I do not, repeat, not, want to be on view every minute of the day. I want you all to leave me in peace.' She threw one arm across her eyes, her lips pressed together in a thin, pale line.

Regina could do nothing but leave.

Miranda was enjoying living in the cottage, loving the peace of being on her own. She was happy to have a garden again. She'd missed her garden so much.

When the time came for her to see Katie again, she wasn't as nervous as she'd been before. Her daughter seemed as friendly as could be expected, given the circumstances, so Miranda didn't feel the situation was hopeless.

She found Katie waiting for her and hurried across the café. 'Am I late?'

'No. I'm early.' She looked down at a gadget she'd been fiddling with. 'I've just been picking up my emails. I was hoping—' She broke off with a sigh.

'That you'd hear from your husband?'

Katie nodded, then forced a smile. 'Never mind. We army wives get used to this sort of thing. Tell me where you're living and what you're doing with yourself. Did you come to England because of me?'

Miranda explained that her half-sister Regina lived nearby and there was a daughter, too.

'It's good to think of having more relatives. Mum and Dad don't have any close ones.'

'Yes. Unfortunately Nikki is in hospital at the moment. She's pregnant and there seem to be complications.'

'Poor thing. Her husband must be worried sick.'

'She hasn't got one. She's only eighteen and in her last year at school. So is the father.'

'Ooh, that must be hard. Is your sister very upset?'

'Yes. So is the baby's father. I thought I'd pop into hospital on my way home, see how Nikki is. We email one another fairly regularly. She knows I understand how she feels about the baby.'

'You had me adopted. Is she going to do that?'

'No.'

The phone rang just then and Katie said, 'Excuse me a moment.' She checked her phone and looked at Miranda in horror. 'It's the Unit Welfare Officer.' Her voice changed, became firmer. 'Yes, it's Katie Parrish. No, I'm in a café, with a friend. Yes, I can rely on her. Look, just tell me what's happened!'

She listened again, then one hand came up to cover her mouth and her eyes filled with tears. 'I see. But he's going to be all right . . . ?' She switched off the phone and sat with it in her hand, tears rolling down her cheeks.

In the end, Miranda laid one hand gently on hers. 'I can see it's bad news. Can I do anything to help?'

'It's Darren. He's been shot. In the leg. He's being sent to the UK for another operation. It's serious but it's not likely to be life-threatening.' She gulped and struggled to keep calm, clasping Miranda's hand now without realising what she was doing. 'I've been dreading this happening. I planned what I'd do, how I'd manage, only I can't remember now.'

'It's shock. You'll calm down gradually. In the meantime, you're not on your own. I'll do anything you need to help you.'

Katie looked at her blindly for a moment, then seemed to see her properly. 'I . . . can't ask you to help. We've only just met.'

'What has that got to do with anything? The tie that binds a mother and child is not something you can switch on and off. It's just . . . there . . . even when the child is invisible.' She looked at her watch. 'What time do you need to pick Ned up?'

'Not for half an hour, but I want to go and get him now, tell him. He keeps expecting his father to phone us, you see, keeps asking.'

'I'm sure they'll let him out of school early but I don't think you should drive. You might not be calm enough. Will you let me drive you? We'll come back for your car later, once you've had time to grow used to . . . the news.'

She had to wait for Katie to think about this and then nod. It was as if the younger woman could only process information slowly.

And still their hands were joined, still Katie was clinging to her. Reluctantly Miranda disengaged her hand. 'I'll go and pay the bill. I won't be a minute.'

She came back to see that Katie had a little more colour in her cheeks. 'Shall we leave now?'

As they walked Katie stumbled and Miranda put an arm round her. 'It's all right. They said Darren wasn't in danger, so it's all right.'

She nodded, but didn't speak.

When they were in the car, Miranda asked, 'Can you direct me or should I programme the satnav?'

'It's not far. I'll tell you where to go.' Having to give directions seemed to help Katie and when they stopped in front of the school, she said, 'I'll go to the front office.'

'I'll come with you, just in case you feel faint again.'

'All right.'

As they walked, Katie gave a laugh that turned into a hiccup. 'Is something wrong?'

'Ned was rushed into hospital to have his appendix out. Brody helped me then.'

Miranda stopped walking. '*Brody?* He's here in England?'

'Yes. I was going to tell you. Anyway, he was a big help. And now *you* are here just when I need more help. It seems as if fate has brought us all together at the right time, doesn't it? I was feeling . . . very alone.'

'It must be hard when your husband's overseas.'

'Yes. Very. Even with the support groups.' She sighed and fell silent.

Miranda didn't say anything, couldn't. She was trying to take in the thought that Brody was here in Wiltshire. Brody, whom she'd never expected to see again.

Did he hate her? Would he turn away from her or would he let her explain how they'd taken her child away from her? Could she hold herself together to tell him? The years of virtual imprisonment had left their mark on her, she knew.

She shivered, trying not to show how afraid she felt. Even the thought of facing him made her want to run and run till she could run no more.

But at the moment, her daughter needed her. She must focus on that.

Chapter Seventeen

Nikki opened her eyes as someone started taking her blood pressure. Why would they not let her sleep in peace?

'Sorry, love,' the nurse said gently. 'We have to do this. I'll be finished in a minute or two, then you can go back to sleep again.'

'Am I going to lose the baby?'

'Not if we can help it.'

'It doesn't seem real, all this.'

'It's the sedative. If I were you, I'd just let myself sleep and give my body time to recover.'

But when the nurse had gone, Nikki opened her eyes and stared round. She wished she hadn't sent her mother away. She didn't want to talk but she didn't want to be alone with her thoughts, either.

How could she have said she hated the baby? She'd seen Tim's shock and wished the words unsaid, but it was too late now. She'd said them. It was all too much lately: the baby, the horrible little flat, being with Tim all the time as he fussed over her like an elderly aunt.

Nothing was fun any more, nothing, and there seemed little hope of life getting any better.

Her mother had been right. She should have had an abortion. Tears welled in her eyes and she turned away from the door so that they'd not see. The nurses meant to be kind, but they were just doing their job and didn't really care about her.

At least it was quiet here . . . peaceful . . .

They went into the reception area of the school and when Katie seemed to be having difficulty producing an explanation, Miranda intervened, which helped her get over the fact that Brody was in touch with her daughter. She'd deal with that later.

'I'll go and get Ned,' the secretary said at once. 'You stay there, Mrs Parrish. I won't be a minute.'

They went to sit on some well-used red plastic chairs and within two minutes there was the sound of running footsteps. A little boy hurtled through the door and ran to his mother.

'I thought you'd prefer to explain it to him,' the secretary said, handing over a backpack.

'Why do I have to leave school early, Mummy?' Ned asked. 'Is Daddy back?' He shot a curious glance at Miranda, jigging from one foot to the other.

'Um, no. I'll tell you in the car, darling.'

He looked at his mother as if puzzled by her tone, but

obediently took the hand she held out. As they stopped by the car he frowned and looked up at her. 'This isn't our car.'

'I wasn't feeling well, so Miranda drove me here and now she's going to take us home.'

'Can I ride in the front?'

'You and I will both ride in the back.'

'Aww.'

Miranda followed instructions and they turned off the main street of the little town, threading through a series of side streets that had her wondering how she'd find her way round if she didn't have a satnav system. She kept thinking about Brody, unable to believe he was here, that she might see him again. If he wanted to meet her. He'd still think she'd dumped both him and their child. How he must hate her!

'This is it,' Katie said. 'Park behind that green car.'

As she slowed down Miranda realised in horror that she'd been driving automatically, lost in her thoughts. Thank heavens there hadn't been an accident! The house they stopped at was a semi, very like its neighbours, old-fashioned with a tiny, useless garage at one side.

Katie got out and led the way up the garden path, with Ned jumping and skipping along beside her, gesticulating wildly as he continued telling some involved tale about what had happened at playtime. She turned at the front door and seemed surprised not to see Miranda behind her. Beckoning her mother to follow them, she went inside, standing in the small square hall with one hand on her son's shoulder to wait for her visitor.

'We'll go into the front room.' Once inside she stopped moving again, not seeming quite sure what to do.

Still in shock, Miranda thought. Join the club. But she'd had years of hiding her feelings, so only said, 'Do you want me to make you a cup of tea? It's supposed to help when you're upset.'

Katie shook her head. 'No, thank you. I'll just . . . explain what's happened to Ned.' She sat down and took a deep breath. 'It's your father, darling. He's—'

'He's not dead! He can't be dead.'

Even young children of serving soldiers have this fear, Miranda thought. How brave they all are!

Katie took her son's hand. 'No, of course he's not dead. But he's been shot and is in hospital, so they'll be sending him back to England.'

He sat still then said in a tight, anxious voice, 'Is it hurting Daddy?'

Seeing Katie struggling against tears, Miranda said quickly, 'The doctors will give him something to stop the pain.'

His face cleared. 'Like they did when I was in hospital. I had my appendix out two weeks ago.' He patted his belly and added with some relish, 'They had to cut me open to take it out because it'd gone bad, and then they stitched my skin together. I haven't got to do anything rough yet. Will they have to cut Daddy open?'

Katie went white again but managed to say, 'I'm sure they've sewn him up again by now. Why don't you get your biscuit and milk, Ned?' After he'd left, she leant back and closed her eyes. 'I didn't cope very well, did I?'

'You didn't do too badly,' Miranda said encouragingly.

'I thought I could cope with anything, even that. I'm a soldier's wife. I *should* be able to cope.'

'No one's perfect and that's a good thing. It'd be terrible living with someone who was perfect in every way, or even someone who thinks they're perfect.' An image of Sebastian floated into her mind, with his scornful way of looking at others as if they were all inferior to him.

Katie managed a faint smile. 'That's one way of looking at it. Darren seems pretty perfect to me, though.'

'You obviously love him very much.'

'From the first moment I saw him. He's not good-looking, but he is attractive – or he would be if they didn't cut his hair so short.'

'You don't think you're a teeny bit biased?'

That brought a genuine smile. 'Totally biased.'

'Well, and so you should be. Why else would you have married him? Now, what about that cup of tea . . . ? No, you stay there. I'm sure Ned will show me where everything is. You'll probably appreciate a few minutes' peace.'

'How did you know?'

'I'm a bit like that myself. I need to be on my own to pull myself together.' She walked out and moved towards the rear of the house without waiting for an answer. In the kitchen doorway she hesitated for a moment as her grandson – *her grandson!* – gave her a beaming smile from a face decorated by a milky moustache.

'I didn't spill a drop.'

'That's very good. Look, your Mummy's tired and she'd like a cup of tea. Can you show me where everything is, then we'll make it together? My name's Miranda Fox, by the way, and I know yours is Ned.'

The fact that her name was Fox made him laugh heartily, after which he seemed to accept her presence without question. He showed her where everything was, chattering all the time about a fox that had run through their garden a few days ago.

Wonder filled her as she watched his expressive face. She stopped him from sending the remains of his milk flying as he flung out one arm, and answered his questions as best she could.

Her grandson!

When the tea was brewed she poured two mugs, feeling quite sure that Katie wouldn't begrudge her a drink, and carried one through into the front room, leaving Ned to empty out his backpack, which he said he had to do before he was allowed to play out in the garden.

'He's a gorgeous lad,' she said as she handed her daughter a mug of tea. 'I hope that's all right. He said one sugar.'

Katie took the mug and sighed with pleasure as she took a sip. 'Yes, that's just right. Thank you so much.'

'It's no trouble to make a cup of tea.'

'I meant for your help and for the few minutes' peace you've given me. I can't tell you how much I needed it.'

'It must be difficult to be the only one looking after a child.'

'Is that why you had me adopted?'

'No! Never! I wanted to keep you, only they—'

Just then someone rang the front door bell.

Miranda stood up. 'I'll answer it. You'll be able to hear whether it's someone you want to see. Unless you call out, I'll say you have a headache and are lying down.'

She opened the door and found herself facing the last person she'd expected or wanted to see today. He looked older, harder and just as attractive as ever.

'Brody.'

He turned away as if to stride down the path and she grabbed his arm.

'Wait! You might not want to see me, but Katie needs our help.'

Brody stared down at her, wanting to pull away but then her words sank in. 'What's wrong?'

'Darren's been shot.'

'He's dead?'

'No. Injured. But she was so upset she wasn't fit to drive, so I drove her home. Only somehow we have to get her car back from near the café. She's still a bit shaky.'

He looked beyond her to see Katie standing in the sitting room doorway, holding Ned back. 'You need your car fetching back?'

'Yes. Miranda was kind enough to—'

'Give me your keys and I'll get it for you. I can catch a taxi there.'

'That'd be stupid, when Miranda can drive you.'

He hesitated, deliberately not looking at the woman standing beside him. He didn't want to speak to her and he definitely didn't want to be shut up in a small car with her.

'I'll get my car keys.' Miranda went to fetch her handbag.

Her voice was as low and musical as he'd remembered, even though she sounded strained today. She'd wormed her way in quickly with their daughter. Well, he'd not make the same mistake twice. Miranda was a Fox and that family was not to be trusted an inch. She seemed to be taking a long time to fetch her handbag.

'Brody!'

He realised his daughter was speaking to him. 'Sorry. I was miles away.'

'I couldn't have managed without Miranda today. And if you can't sit in a car with her and be polite for ten minutes, if only out of gratitude for that, I shan't think much of you.'

He looked at her face. Her eyes looking bruised, her distress visible. He'd already guessed she didn't find the role of an army wife easy, for all her brave words. She was an affectionate woman, you only had to see her playing with Ned to realise that. It must be hell to be separated for long periods, even worse when your husband's life was on the line each time.

'Very well. I'll go with her to fetch your car. But after that, I don't want to see her again, so make sure you don't invite us round here at the same time.' He knew his voice sounded stiff and ungracious, but it was the best he could manage.

'I'm ready.'

He turned to Miranda, realising she must have overheard him. Well, too bad. He couldn't help staring at what the years had done to her, surprised at the deep sadness that seemed ingrained in her face and the way she seemed to have folded up into herself. This wasn't the Miranda he'd known. In spite of himself he couldn't help wondering what had done this to her.

Not what, *who*, he corrected himself. Old man Fox and that damned brother of hers, that was who.

'I'll be in touch,' Katie told her mother.

Miranda hesitated, then said, 'Not if it upsets you.'

'Don't you want to see us again?'

'Of course I do. But the last thing I want is to cause trouble for anyone.'

'You won't be causing me any trouble,' Katie said firmly.

When Miranda walked down the garden path, Brody followed. She unlocked her car and he got in without a word.

She just missed scraping a van as she pulled out and by the time she'd got to the corner, she was shaking so badly she had to pull over to the side. 'I'm sorry. I don't cope well with stress. Can you drive, please?'

'How are you going to get home after we pick up Katie's car?'

'I'll sit and wait till I've calmed down.'

He got into the car and set off, driving very carefully because he didn't know if her insurance covered him. When he parked behind Katie's car, he turned to look at Miranda again.

She was staring blindly into the distance. There were a few silver hairs among the fair ones and her hair was now jaw length, which suited her better. She'd always worn her hair long before because that old skinflint of a father had kept her short of money.

'How come your father let you travel all this way?'

'He's dead.'

'And your brother? I'd have thought Sebastian would still be keeping you on a tight leash?'

'Not any longer. Look, I don't know why you're bothering to make conversation, Brody, if you can call this conversation. You clearly don't want to speak to me. The car is over there. Take it back to Katie.'

He got out, feeling suddenly like a brute. There had been no need to talk to her like that.

Behind him he heard the car start up and he swung round to see her weaving an erratic course down the street. His heart was in his mouth by the time she turned the corner. She shouldn't be driving. She was too upset.

If anything happened to her, it'd be his fault.

It had been such a shock to see how little she'd

changed. It had thrown him.

But he was still angry at her. Furious. Well, he was angry with quite a few people, himself included for feeling like this.

Regina went to see her daughter that evening and to her relief Nikki smiled, seeming glad to see her this time. 'How are you?'

'Dopey. They keep giving me something to keep me calm.'

'They must know what they're doing.'

'Well, that's more than I do lately.'

'Oh, darling, it'll be all right, I promise you it will.'

'How can it be? My whole life's been torn apart. I don't know where I'm going – or who I'll be with.'

'No one does, really. We make plans but life has a way of chucking a wobbly every now and then. I brought you some grapes. That's obligatory, isn't it?'

Nikki gave a faint smile. 'Yes. And at least you're not eating them for me. Mum – when I get out, can I move back home till the exams are over?'

She hadn't expected this and gaped at her daughter.

'All right, never mind. It was worth a try.'

And Regina found herself doing something she'd not intended. 'Yes, of course you can come home. I was just surprised that you'd asked. What about Tim?'

'It's not working. You don't really know someone till you live with them, do you?'

'No. And even then, they can surprise you.'

'Is that what happened with my father?'

'No. We never lived together.'

'Oh.'

She saw Nikki's eyelids fluttering and realised her daughter was falling asleep again. 'You get some rest. I'll come in again tomorrow.'

In the corridor she met Tim, carrying a bunch of flowers. He fumbled in his pocket and held out some banknotes. 'I didn't need them. I hitch-hiked home.'

'Keep them. I'm not short of money. Nikki's just fallen asleep.'

'I'll sit and wait. I want to be with her.'

He was still holding out the notes, but she ignored them, not saying anything as she walked away. Not for her to interfere. If Nikki came home again, it'd be by her own choice.

Regina sighed as she walked out of the hospital. She wasn't sure she wanted her pregnant daughter living at home again, with all the emotional turbulence that was bound to occur. But she could never refuse to have her, for all her previous threats.

Brody drove the car back to his daughter's house, not hurrying because he was still trying to make sense of seeing Miranda today. He'd been unkind to her, but he hadn't been able to help himself. The mere sight of her had brought back so many memories of their time together, the hopes they'd built, the closeness he'd thought they shared.

It had also brought back memories of the cruel abruptness of her disappearance from his life.

He rang the doorbell and waited for Katie to open the door.

She was wiping her hands on a small, frayed towel. 'You should have come straight in. I'm just getting Ned's tea. He's been invited to play at his friend's for an hour afterwards, thank goodness.'

Brody followed her into the kitchen, which was also the eating area, raising one hand to wave to Ned who was eating what looked like pasta and sauce, then turning back to Katie. 'Are you all right now?'

'As right as I'll be until I've seen Darren and know he's on the road to recovery.'

'Did they tell you what happened?'

'No. Only that he'd been shot in the leg. Someone will phone when he gets back to let me know where they've taken Darren, and they'll pay for me to go and see him.'

'Do you want me to look after Ned while you do that?'

'I don't know. It's a kind offer but, until I find out exactly what the injuries are, I'm inclined to think Ned should come too.'

'Well, the offer's there if you need it.'

'Miranda was just starting to tell me why she had me adopted when you arrived.'

'Oh?'

'She'd got as far as saying "I wanted to keep you, only they—" when you rang the doorbell.'

'She wanted to keep you!'

Katie nodded.

'Wanting clearly wasn't enough. She always did have trouble defying them. That father of hers was like a . . . a behemoth or a dinosaur and he'd browbeaten her from childhood. She used to hate to go home from university.'

'She looks as if life has beaten her around quite a lot.' Katie stared at him. 'I'm going to give her the benefit of the doubt until I've heard her story, and you should too. Ask her to explain next time you see her. Listen.'

'If I have my way, I'll not be seeing her again.' He stared right back at his daughter. 'I *don't* want to revive old memories. I've moved on and I'm not going back. So don't get any ideas of inviting us here together, because I'll walk out if I see her.'

'I see.'

He nodded. 'I'd better go now.'

'Yes, I think you had.'

He knew she was disappointed in him, but some things were not negotiable. He'd sworn to have nothing more to do with Miranda and that was one promise he was going to keep.

But he kept seeing her all evening, remembering how she'd looked, what she'd said. She had never been beautiful but there had always been something special about her. It was still there. Not because she was better dressed, but because she carried herself with a quiet integrity that hinted at a woman who'd learnt some hard lessons in life. If he'd met her for the first time now, he'd have found that look intriguing and would have asked her out.

That sudden resurgence of interest in her frightened him more than anything else. He didn't want to go there again, didn't want to be attracted to her. Definitely not.

Chapter Eighteen

Sebastian got ready for the first mediation meeting, feeling aggrieved that he had to go through this ridiculous charade. Over breakfast he tried to discuss it with Dorothy, who usually had sensible views on life.

'I don't want to get involved in this,' she said. 'You'll do what you want anyway, so it'd be a waste of my time arguing with you.'

He looked at her in amazement. '*Arguing* with me! Surely you don't think Miranda should have full control of that money?'

'You and Regina have full control of your shares.'

'What has that to do with the matter? *We* haven't spent time in a mental hospital.'

'As I said, it's not worth discussing.' She got up and tried to leave the room.

He caught her before she reached the door. 'Don't you dare walk out on me!'

'You're hurting me.'

He squeezed her shoulders more tightly and pinned her to the wall. 'I will hurt you if you ever walk out on me again. Come and finish your breakfast.'

He walked her forcibly to her place and shoved her down, feeling intense satisfaction that someone at least was under his control.

'Now, listen to me carefully.' He went over the arguments against allowing Miranda to handle her own money, arguments that had worked well with his father.

Dorothy sat mute, not eating, not responding, and in the end he stopped talking. 'Are you even listening?'

'How can I help but listen when you're speaking so loudly?'

'Then why aren't you agreeing with me? You usually see the sense of my arguments.'

There was a fraught silence, then she snapped, 'I usually don't think it worthwhile disagreeing, because you never change your mind once it's made up. And you certainly never listen to me. Sometimes if I disagree, you hurt me, as you have today.'

'How have I hurt you?'

She slipped her top off one shoulder and he saw the bruise.

'I didn't do that.'

'Who else could it have been?'

'You must bruise very easily.'

'You always say that.'

He wasn't getting into this. He pushed his plate aside and stood up. 'I have to get going.'

When he'd gone she rubbed her shoulder, then went up to their bedroom and took off her top. Her shoulders were both badly bruised, with his finger marks showing clearly. She'd sworn to him last time that if he ever hurt her again, she'd do something about it.

He hadn't believed her.

Had she believed what she said herself? Did she really dare carry out her threat?

She stood staring at her reflection for a moment or two, then squared her shoulders. Yes, she could and would do it. She was at last going to take the two actions she'd often thought about and never dared perform. This time she really was.

Her heart fluttered in her chest and she found it hard to breathe steadily as she picked up the phone and began to tap out the number. She realised she'd hit a wrong digit and had to stop the call.

She put the phone down and stood staring at it. It took her a minute or two to summon up the courage to pick it up and start dialling again.

This time she wasn't going to chicken out. If Minnie could change and grow after all she'd suffered – also at the hands of the Fox men – then Dorothy could too. It was more than time.

Sally nodded to Sebastian across the table and arranged her papers in front of her. She might not need them, but it was best to be prepared. The mediator came in and smiled at them all.

Her smile in return was probably the most genuine in the room. Fox didn't even try.

She knew Jennifer Hilling slightly. The mediator was a shrewd woman and wouldn't let Sebastian Fox ride roughshod over her. Or Sally, either.

'We're here to see if we can settle the differences between you and come to some agreement before this case gets to court. Perhaps we could start by each of you giving a brief summary of your position? Mr Fox? I believe you drew up the will for your father.'

'I did. And it's entirely in accordance with his wishes, so my position hasn't changed in the slightest and I shan't waste anyone's time by restating the obvious.' He folded his arms.

Sally sighed. She'd expected this, but you could always hope for some slight shift in attitude.

'Ms Patel?'

'Could I speak last?'

The mediator looked round. Tressman nodded, Fox shrugged. 'Mr Tressman, then?'

'I've come to the conclusion that the will is unfair to Miranda Fox, who has been treated differently from her brother and sister. So I would be happy to come to an agreement about breaking the trust.'

'Ms Patel?'

Sally leant forward. 'I hold the same views as Mr Tressman. And in addition, I'd like to state that the will was made during the last year of James Fox's life, when the doctor had already started treating him for dementia.

I have a signed statement from his doctor to that effect.'

'Early dementia,' Sebastian said. 'He was still able to make his wishes known. And if we're talking of states of mind—'

Here it comes, thought Sally.

'—then I wish to put it on record that my sister had to be committed to a mental hospital when she was younger, and stayed there for nearly two years. This is the main reason my father left her money in trust.'

'My client was suffering from postnatal depression at the time,' Sally said. 'Nowadays there are drugs which help and doctors are more understanding. I think it was outrageous that she was not only hospitalised but kept on tranquillising drugs for what seems to me an unconscionable length of time. I'm not sure that she doesn't have a case against the system about that.'

The mediator looked at her narrowly. 'You're sure of your facts?'

'Very sure. I have the deposition of a nurse who was working there at the time.'

'My sister was admitted by a doctor, who must know far more than any nurse,' Sebastian said sharply.

'He was a GP, not a specialist in mental health. How he managed to stay in charge of the case, I'll never understand. But as he's dead and so is Miranda's father, we can't question them. Unfortunately.'

Sebastian breathed deeply.

The mediator waited a moment then changed the subject. They talked round in circles for nearly two hours, then the mediator held up one hand. 'I think enough has been said for today. I'll call another meeting for the same time next week; unless anyone is due to appear in court then?'

Sebastian made great play of pulling out his diary and leafing slowly through the pages. 'It's very inconvenient. I might not be due in court, but I shall have to reschedule several appointments that have been made for a long time. And I shall *not* change my mind, I promise you. This is a waste of my valuable time.'

'Thinking time is useful for everyone,' Ms Hilling said quietly. 'A week should help you all to put the problem in a better perspective.'

Sally walked slowly back to her rooms. Fox strode past her without a word. Mr Tressman fell into place beside her.

'He'll not change.'

She shrugged. 'Then we'll have to take the appeal to court.'

'It's such a waste of time,' he mourned. 'And money. And your services must be costing poor little Ms Fox a fortune.'

'I'm helping her pro bono, because I detest injustice.'

'Well . . .' he hesitated. 'I must admit that one of the reasons I've changed my mind is the way the trust is being administered. Mr Fox tried to cut off her income completely when she went to England recently. I refused to agree to that.'

Sally stopped walking. 'He did what?'

When they parted company, she knew she'd never let this case drop until justice was served. But how to break Sebastian Fox was more than she could at present work out.

But she would find a way. She usually did.

Katie picked up the phone, wondering who was calling so late at night.

'Mrs Parrish? I'm from the Joint Casualty and Compassionate Centre.'

She stiffened. The JCCC only called if a relative in the armed forces was seriously ill.

'Are you still there?'

'Yes. Sorry.'

'I'm afraid your husband has taken a turn for the worse and there may be important decisions to be made about his treatment. Can you come to him at once? If you can get to RAF Lyneham, we'll take you the rest of the way by helicopter.'

'I'll have to bring my son with me.'

'How old is he?'

'Five.'

'It'd be better if you found someone to care for him for a day or two.'

Her mind went blank, then she said, 'All right. I'll do that.'

'Let me give you the details. Darren is in Birmingham and . . .'

When she put the phone down, Katie didn't let herself

weep or weaken. What to do? Mum couldn't get here from Cornwall in time nor could the other military wives she was friendly with leave their children.

But her birth mother and father were here. Dare she ask them for help? Of course she did. She dare do anything for Darren. She picked up the phone again.

But there was no answer to Brody's phone. She left a message on his voicemail, outlining the situation, then rang her birth mother.

Miranda sounded sleepy, but her voice lost the blurred, sleepy tone when she heard what had happened. 'Of course I'll come and look after Ned.'

'Brody might want to come too. He does know Ned better than you do, but I'd really prefer you both to be there. I know you're not on the best of terms, but do you think—'

'I don't think either of us would let that stop us from helping you, Katie. I'll be there in half an hour at most.'

'Thank you.'

She went to wake Ned up and explain what was happening. He asked it again. 'Is Daddy going to die?'

'*No!* But he might lose his leg. It got badly damaged when he was shot.'

He stared at her in horror then looked down at his own feet. 'They might cut his leg off? Can they do that?'

'They put him to sleep first so that it doesn't hurt and afterwards they make artificial legs so that people can still walk.'

He clung to her suddenly. 'I don't want Daddy to lose his leg.'

'No. I don't, either. But the doctors are doing their best to save it. Only I need to be there too.'

'I want to come with you.'

'The army doesn't let children into hospitals when people are so . . . sick.'

He was too used to ultimatums that couldn't be changed to argue any more. Children like him learnt very young that the army wouldn't budge from certain rules.

'Oh.'

'Now, you'll be good for Miranda and Brody, won't you?'

'Yes.'

'Promise?'

'I promise.'

She forced herself to pull away from him, but took him into her bedroom to 'help' as she began packing, flinging clothes into a bag and scrabbling together her toiletries. Then they went downstairs and she gave Ned a biscuit and a drink before scribbling down instructions for looking after him. As an afterthought, she wrote a brief note authorising Miranda Fox and Brody Lanigan to take care of her son while she was with her injured husband.

By that time headlights had swept up to the house and there was the sound of a car door.

She let Miranda in, allowing her mother to hug her tightly for a moment, snatching at a few seconds of comfort. Then she sniffed away the tears that were threatening and grabbed her jacket. She had no time to weep.

'I'll phone as soon as I know anything. You have my mobile number.'

'Yes. Don't worry. If I can look after a ninety-four-year-old autocrat, I can cope with a five-year-old.' She smiled at the solemn-faced child. 'Ned and I will get on just fine, won't we?'

He looked at her thoughtfully then smiled. 'Yes.'

Katie was comforted by that smile.

Miranda and Ned went to the door and waved goodbye to his mother. He clung to her hand and when they went back inside, she knelt to give him a hug, feeling him hug her back convulsively.

'I know it's the middle of the night, but I think I'd like a drink of milk or hot chocolate, or whatever your mother has in her cupboard. Would you like something to drink?'

He nodded, brightening slightly. 'I don't have to go back to bed yet?'

'Not yet. Come and show me where everything is.'

There was drinking chocolate, so she made them both a mug and sat with him at the table.

'Are you an auntie?' he asked.

'Sort of,' was all she could think of to say.

'I've had lots of aunties. When we were living at the base, I called all Mum's friends "auntie". But then we came here and I didn't see them much, and there's no one to play with. Mum lived in this house when she was a little girl, you know.'

He sipped some more and she followed suit.

'Where do you live, Auntie Nanda?'

She didn't correct his pronunciation of her name, just tried to explain about coming from Australia and borrowing the cottage till she could find a house of her own. She saw his eyes beginning to look glazed. 'I think it's time we went to bed, don't you? I'm very tired.'

He nodded.

They walked up the stairs and he showed her his bedroom, his favourite toys and his photo of Daddy. Then he lay back against the pillows and fell straight asleep.

She envied him that. She felt far too uptight to sleep yet.

After waiting for a moment or two to make sure he really was asleep, she tiptoed out of the room. On the landing she hesitated, wondering where to sleep. It didn't seem right to use the master bedroom, so she made up the narrow bed in the third bedroom, a room only about two metres square with no other furniture, just several huge cardboard boxes. She hadn't brought any nightclothes with her and after some hesitation, went to search through Katie's clothes.

The nightwear was beautiful, silky and lace-trimmed in various colours. It was the sort of nightwear a woman would use to make herself beautiful for the man she loved. Miranda had never owned clothes like that and it was probably too late for her – except the man on the plane had seemed attracted and that had cheered her up a bit.

There was no law that said she couldn't wear pretty things. She was going to buy some for herself.

She stroked the soft fabrics and in the end chose a navy blue nightgown with a deep V-neck and an edging of matching navy lace. As she slipped it over her head, she marvelled at the feel of it. She'd buy another nightie for Katie to make up for borrowing this one.

Just at that moment the doorbell rang. Terrified that whoever it was would wake Ned, she flung on the dressing gown that went with the nightgown and ran down the stairs. There was a peephole and she used it before opening the door, which gave her a few seconds warning that it was Brody.

It wasn't nearly long enough.

When the phone rang in the middle of the night, Regina came awake instantly and snatched it up. 'Hallo?'

'Ms Fox? I'm calling from the hospital. Your daughter's condition has worsened. I'm afraid she's likely to lose the baby. You may like to be here with her.'

'Have you called Tim, the father of the baby?'

'You're listed as the contact person. It's up to you whether you tell anyone else.'

She replaced the handset and stared at it, tempted to go to the hospital on her own. No, that'd be unfair to Tim. She dialled his number and arranged to pick him up on the way there.

They got there to find the nursing station unattended and Nikki's room empty, which sent him into a panic.

'Calm down, Tim! We'll go and find someone to ask.'

He clutched her arm.

'Calm down,' she repeated more gently.

This time a nurse was just arriving back at the station.

'I'm Ms Fox. Someone called about my daughter.'

'Yes. I'm sorry, but she's lost the baby. They're checking things out at the moment. She'll be down from theatre in half an hour or so.'

So then there was more waiting, and the canteen wasn't open, only a machine that dispensed paper cups of what purported to be coffee and tasted more like dirty washing-up water. Regina set down her cup after one taste.

Tim sat beside her in the one lighted area of the big dark room, cradling his cup in his hands.

When she looked more closely she could see tears tracking down his cheeks. She didn't know how to comfort him, so settled for patting his arm.

He kept looking at his watch and when half an hour had passed, stood up. 'We should go back now.'

So they trudged along corridors that were lit only in a subdued way. It felt strange without other people around.

At the ward, the nurse looked up. 'She came back five minutes ago. She's very drowsy, probably won't make much sense.'

'She's all right?' Tim asked.

'Yes. She's fine. At her age, she'll soon get over it. Do you want to go and sit with her?'

He had turned towards Nikki's room before she even finished speaking.

'They're both very young for this,' the nurse said in a disapproving tone.

'Tell me about it. But I'm only the mother. What do I know?'

The nurse gave her a grudging smile. 'My daughter's fourteen. I'm already worrying.'

Regina walked slowly along to Nikki's room and stood in the doorway. Even a stranger would have seen how much Tim loved her daughter. Every line of his body seemed to show it. She doubted she'd ever felt that strongly about anyone in her whole life. Nikki came nearest, but somehow Regina had never been able to give herself fully to any relationship. She envied Tim that.

She moved forward just as Nikki opened her eyes and stared around as if having difficulty focusing. But it was Regina she looked at. 'Oh, Mum!' She began to cry.

Regina went to the other side of the bed from Tim and bent to hug her daughter. 'I'm sorry, darling.'

'It's my fault. I stopped wanting him and he died.'

'No, it's not your fault. These things happen and they're no one's fault.'

'We'll have other children,' Tim said, bending forward to kiss Nikki.

She flinched away from him. 'No. No, we won't. I'm never getting pregnant again, never!'

He turned to Regina for guidance and she shook her head slightly to tell him to back off.

When they looked down again, Nikki had dozed off. 'Not the time to talk about other children,' she said quietly to Tim.

He began to sob, trying to muffle the sound, and she had to get up and give him a hug. He was going to be a lot more hurt before this was finished, she was sure.

To her surprise, she found herself feeling sad that she was not to have a grandchild. She definitely hadn't expected to feel like that.

Chapter Nineteen

Miranda opened the door and stepped back. Brody walked in without a word. As he shut the door behind him, chill air swirled around them for a moment and she pulled the negligee more tightly around herself.

They stood in the hall staring at one another. The silence seemed so fragile she broke it quickly and neatly before he could hurl more hurtful words at her. 'You . . . um, got Katie's message?'

'Yes. What exactly happened?'

'Come into the kitchen. We might wake Ned if we talk here and he's only just got off to sleep.'

He followed her, not taking his jacket off, and leant against the sink, his face expressionless until she got to the part about Darren's leg. 'He may lose it.'

Brody closed his eyes for a moment, looking distressed. 'That's a bad one.'

'Yes.'

After a short silence, he said in a calm, controlled voice,

'Well, you can go home now. I'll take over here.'

She felt her mouth fall open in shock and closed it quickly. It took her a few moments to pull herself together and state her position. 'I'm staying.'

'There's no need. Ned knows me.'

'He's starting to know me, too. And I'm not leaving. Katie wants us both here, has made us jointly responsible for him.'

'*I* don't want you here,' he said loudly and slowly.

'Well, I'm staying. Get over it.'

There was a cry from upstairs and she was out of the kitchen before Brody, running up the stairs. By the landing light she could see Ned sitting up in bed looking terrified.

'Nanda!' he cried and began to sob.

She moved forward to one side of the bed, Brody to the other, and felt vindicated when Ned held out his arms to her.

'Nanda, I'm scared.'

'What about?'

'Daddy. I don't want them to cut off his leg.' He burrowed into her, sobbing.

She stroked his hair. 'The doctors will try to save it first. I think it'll help him to have your mummy there. She can talk to him, cheer him up.'

'I want her with me.'

'I know, and she will come back, but until then you've got me.' She looked across the bed and added, 'And Brody. He came to help, so you've got two of us.'

'Don't leave me, Nanda.'

'I won't. We'll all three stay here together till your mummy comes back.'

'She'll bring Daddy. We'll all look after him.'

Miranda closed her eyes briefly, praying to whatever gods might be watching that this soldier would come through his ordeal safely. So many died tragically young in wars. She shushed Ned gently and rocked him a little, murmuring endearments.

'I think he's asleep,' Brody whispered and left the room.

She thought about staying with the child then decided to go down and make sure Brody understood that she wasn't leaving till Katie got back. This, at least, she could do for her daughter. She'd been denied so much.

Katie was delivered to the hospital with the super-efficiency the army could produce on occasion. She was taken along empty, dimly lit corridors to the private room where Darren was lying.

He was unconscious but restless.

'You might like to sit beside him for a while,' the nurse said.

She replied very firmly. 'Let's get one thing straight. I'm not leaving his side again till he's a lot better than this.'

'It can help to have you here,' he admitted. 'We're doing everything possible, I promise you.'

No need for anyone to tell Katie that Darren was

feverish. There was hectic colour in his cheeks and his brow was hot. She sat down beside the bed and took his hand, telling him she was there, talking to him quietly.

Somehow her words seemed to penetrate and he became more peaceful, clutching her hand tightly as if he knew she was there, as if he needed her as desperately as she needed to be with him.

Some time later a voice said, 'Shall I bring you a cup of tea, Mrs Parrish?'

She turned, not having heard the nurse come back. 'Yes, please. That'd be wonderful. Goodness, it's starting to get light.'

She used the small en suite bathroom and went to sit beside her husband again. She'd read that it sometimes helped to talk to unconscious people, so began telling him about the thing that was on her mind: her birth parents, how she'd not been sure what to do, how tentative she'd been about meeting them. And how it was thanks to them that she had been able to get here so quickly.

She didn't rush her story, speaking slowly, stopping to ponder what had happened from time to time. It was a while before she realised that it was fully light, Darren's eyes were open and he was staring at her.

'It's not a dream,' he said. 'You *are* here.' Then he looked down at his leg which had a shelter over it. 'Have they amputated it?'

'No. There's a chance of saving it still. But whatever happens, I love you, Darren.'

'I love you, too.' He smiled drowsily. 'I'll get better now. I know I will. Don't let them cut it off.'

When Sebastian went home, he found the house empty and no signs of preparations for dinner. He was almost sure they weren't going out tonight but went to check the engagements diary, just in case something important had slipped his mind.

He found it in his home office, its pages torn out and scattered over his desk. Taped to the back of his chair was an envelope, addressed to him. Bewildered, not used to anything but perfect order, he stood there for a moment with the envelope in his hand. Then he put down his briefcase and looked for the letter opener. It was gone, but when he looked up he saw it sticking in his favourite painting, right in the heart of the hunting dog that had brought down a rabbit. Dorothy had always disliked that painting, but surely *she* hadn't done this?

Even more bewildered, he used the paperknife to open the envelope.

> *You've beaten me for the very last time, Sebastian.*
> *I've consulted a lawyer, seen a doctor to show him*
> *my latest bruises and I'm bringing assault charges*
> *against you.*
> *After that we can discuss our divorce.*
> *Dorothy*

The anger he found so hard to control surged up and he seemed to be seeing things through a mist. When it cleared he found he'd swept everything off his desk and smashed a valuable figurine against the wall. Panting, he sank into a chair, unable to believe this was happening.

It was a few moments before he realised the phone was ringing. He picked it up just as the voicemail kicked in and it was a moment before the recorded message faded and he could speak to the person at the other end.

'Hello?'

'Is that you, Dad?'

'Yes. John, it's good to hear from you, son. I'm afraid your mother isn't—'

'Is it true?'

'What?'

'That you've been beating Mother for years.'

Sebastian swallowed hard, not knowing what to say. He hadn't been *beating* her. Maybe he'd been a bit rough at times. It was his temper. He'd have to learn to control it better.

'Well? Have you?'

'Certainly not.'

'She's emailed me a photo of herself, with bruising and finger marks. She says you did it, not for the first time, and she's left you for good.'

'It's a temporary thing. We're going to sort it out.'

'Gerry and I thought you had sorted it out already. You told us years ago when we asked you that you were getting counselling. Clearly you didn't, so I'm glad Mum's come to her senses. You're a prize shit and, as far as I'm concerned, I never want to see you again.'

'I've been doing everything for you.'

John made a scornful noise. 'Rubbish. And as for stealing Auntie Minnie's money, forget about it. If ever anyone earned their inheritance, she did.'

'But she's mentally unstable.'

'It takes one to recognise one.'

The phone clicked off. Sebastian stared at it in outrage. He couldn't seem to think straight. He didn't know what to do.

He wished he was a drinking man, but he never had been able to take more than a glass or two.

Where could Dorothy have gone? He had to get her back. Had to. He couldn't manage without her.

Brody went into the kitchen and Miranda followed.

'Thank you for including me when you were talking to Ned. You could have easily used that to try to get rid of me.'

'I'd never use a child to get back at someone, and you can't have known me very well if you thought I would.'

'I came to the conclusion a long time ago that I didn't know you as well as I thought.'

'What did my father tell you?'

'As if you don't know.'

'I don't.'

He looked at her, frowning, clearly not believing her.

Just then her mobile phone rang. She went across to her handbag and fumbled for it, afraid it might be bad news.

'Miranda?'

'Regina. Is everything all right?'

'No, it isn't.'

Her sister started sobbing. 'It's Nikki. She's lost the baby. I thought I didn't care and I do, Miranda, I do!'

'I can't come to you, but you can come to me, if you like. I'm at Katie's, my daughter's house. Her husband's been injured and I'm looking after my grandson while she's at the hospital, so I can't leave here.'

Her voice was dull. 'You have a grandson. Mine just died.'

'I'm so sorry, more sorry than words can say.'

'Would you mind if I came to see you? I feel . . . lost.'

'Not at all.' She gave Regina the address and shut down the phone, staring at it for a moment before looking at Brody. 'Did you hear that?'

'Yes. Who's Nikki?'

'Regina's daughter. My niece. She's eighteen and she was pregnant. She wasn't well and had to go into hospital.'

'History repeating itself, like aunt, like niece.'

She couldn't believe he'd say anything so cruel but didn't say anything, just turned her back on him and busied herself putting the kettle on. Regina might want a hot drink.

'I'm sorry.'

She kept her back to him.

He moved to stand nearer to her. 'That was uncalled for. I really am sorry, Miranda.'

She turned, finding herself too close to him, especially with these clothes which seemed to offer no protection, no barrier, so flimsy were they.

He laid his right hand on her shoulder for a moment, then stepped back. 'I could do with a cup of coffee, if you're making some. I can't see us getting any sleep now. When she comes, I'll leave you and your sister to talk.'

She inclined her head. She didn't want to talk to him, didn't want to lay herself open to more sniping and insults. He might have apologised but he clearly had a very low opinion of her. Only . . . she'd always wondered what they'd told him. She'd ask him later. Her sister wouldn't be long, so there was no time to talk now.

Regina found the house easily. It was the only one in the street with lights on in several rooms. She got out of the car and hurried to the front door. Miranda opened it before she got there, holding her arms out. Regina walked into them and the two sisters hugged one another tightly.

Then Regina looked down the hall and saw a man standing watching them, a man who looked vaguely familiar. 'I didn't realise you weren't alone. I'm sorry if I've interrupted something.'

'You've not interrupted anything worth continuing,' Miranda said with a sharp edge to her voice. 'This is Brody, Katie's birth father.'

Regina gaped at him then looked back at Miranda. 'You two got together again?'

'Hardly, given the opinion he has of me. No. We have an armed truce while we look after our grandson. Shall you and I go into the sitting room?'

'I'll make you both some coffee if you like,' Brody offered.

'No, thank you.' Miranda walked past him into the front room.

Regina hesitated. 'I'd kill for a cup of coffee. Black. No sugar.'

'Miranda?' His voice was hesitant.

'I said no. If I want some, I'll get it myself. I don't intend to trouble you more than I have to.'

He vanished into the kitchen and Regina let out her breath in a faint whistle. Something was very wrong between these two. She followed her sister into the room and sat down on the couch. 'I'm sorry I interrupted you.'

'You only interrupted him insulting me.'

'Why would he do that?'

'If I knew exactly what Father and Sebastian had told him, I might be able to answer that question. But I don't know. And I'm not going to even try to find out. If Brody's mind is so closed, if he's so cynical, he can think what he likes about me.'

'My mind is *not* closed!' Brody came into the room, scowled at Miranda and dumped two cups of coffee on the low table. 'Drink it or not, as you please.' He walked out again.

Regina whistled softly again as she picked up the cup of coffee. 'You should tell him what happened from your point of view and find out what they said to him.'

'He'd not believe me if I did. And why bother? It's all in the past now, and I'm building a new life.'

'If you're going to continue seeing your daughter, it'd be a lot easier—' She broke off and held up one hand. 'All right. I'll mind my own business.'

'Tell me about Nikki.'

Dorothy looked out of the plane window as it came in to land in Sydney. She could see the huge old bridge and the Opera House quite clearly. It had been a while since she'd been here. Or anywhere. Sebastian didn't like going overseas, didn't even like touring in his own state, nor did he like her going away from him on her own.

Why had she put up with it for so long? Why had she let him even start treating her like that?

As she came out of the airport, she saw her older son waiting for her. John hurried towards her, his eyes searching her face anxiously as if she'd look different.

'Are you all right, Mother?'

'Yes.'

'Why didn't you tell us?'

'I was ashamed and embarrassed. That sort of thing doesn't happen to people like us, does it, just to uneducated people who don't know any better?'

'Gerry and I thought it had stopped.'

She was startled. 'You knew?'

'Of course we did. We could hardly help overhearing sometimes. But when I taxed him with it, he said he'd been stressed, but was getting help. I believed him. Well, I used to be as narrowly focused on my work as he was. It wasn't till I met Bron that I started learning how to relax, how to enjoy other things besides *getting on*, how to care for other people.'

'Does she mind me coming to stay?'

'No, of course not. I showed her the photo. She was as shocked about it as I was and she didn't hesitate.'

'I won't stay for long. I've been putting money aside for a while, and I still have skills that will earn me a living, even at my age. Your father doesn't know that I've been selling articles to journals for years, using a PO Box and keeping the money in a separate bank account.'

'You're being very brave.'

'No. I'm not. I'm scared witless. But if your Aunt Miranda can break free of Sebastian, after all he and their father did to her, then so can I.'

He frowned. 'What exactly did they do to her, apart from use her as a drudge?'

'I'll tell you about that another time. Let's go to your house. And if he calls . . . ?'

'I shan't tell him you're here. Actually, I rang him after I spoke to you and told him I want nothing to do with him or Aunt Minnie's money.'

She smiled. 'Good for you. She wants to be called Miranda now – and she's changed so much, the name suits her. Thank you for having me.'

She'd been touched by how quickly John had asked her to come and stay with him and his wife, how he'd offered to help her financially to set up a new life for herself. Tomorrow her lawyer would be delivering her ultimatum to Sebastian.

And Sally Patel would be reading the letter Dorothy had sent her.

She wasn't just going to set her own life in order. She'd stood by for years and let them treat poor Miranda badly. She felt ashamed of that now. But maybe she could make up for it a little.

Chapter Twenty

Miranda found Ned still sleeping peacefully when it was time to get him up for school. She heard a sound behind her and turned to see Brody standing in the doorway, looking at their grandson with a fond expression on his face.

She put one finger to her lips and moved towards him, indicating that they should move out of the room. 'I don't think we should wake him. He didn't get a lot of sleep.'

'I agree.' He hesitated. 'I really can look after him on my own if you have something to do.'

'I don't have anything I need to do for myself, but we ought to look at the food situation here and see if any shopping's needed.'

'Has Regina woken yet?'

'No. I peeped into Katie's bedroom and she's spark out too. I envy her. I always find it hard to sleep past my normal get-up time, even if I've had a disturbed night.'

'So do I.' As they entered the kitchen he stole a sideways glance at her, opened his mouth and closed it again.

'Did you want to ask something? As long as it's reasonably polite, go ahead.'

'I wondered what you'd been doing with yourself over the years. Did you ever finish your degree?'

'No. Father prevented that. He didn't trust me again.'

'Why the hell did you stay with him?'

'*Faute de mieux*. I had no money and nowhere else to go and . . . there were other threats.'

'You could have got a job. Other people support themselves.'

'There are things you don't know, things I don't want to talk about because they're too . . . painful.' And because most times when the subject of depression and mental hospitals came up, people began to look at her differently, as if she were less than human. She didn't think she could bear that sort of look from him on top of the insults.

She went to the fridge and peered inside, checking each shelf, then opened the freezer door and studied the contents, after which she investigated the pantry cupboard. 'I think she must have been due to go shopping because there's not a lot of fresh stuff here. And if you're still a hearty eater—' She remembered him having a big appetite and . . . better not go there.

'I am.'

'Then I'll have to visit the shops. I think I know my

way to the shopping centre in Wootton Bassett.'

'Bassett. Locals shorten it to just Bassett.'

'Oh. Right. What do you want for tea?'

'Whatever you like. Let me give you some money towards it.' He fumbled in his pocket.

'After I get back.' She went up to get her handbag and, after another peek at her sister, left.

Brody stayed in the kitchen, making another piece of toast and eating it slowly, thinking about Miranda. She didn't look her age. But she did look toned down, as if someone had taken all the vivid colour out of her.

He remembered suddenly that she used to start looking like that just before he took her home from university, and always insisted on being dropped some distance away from the house. What the hell had her family done to her?

'Good morning.'

He turned to see Regina come into the kitchen, her hair ruffled, her face creased where she must have lain on something with wrinkles in it. She headed straight for the kettle.

'I'm not human till I've had a cup of very strong coffee.'

'Help yourself.'

'Where's Miranda gone? It was her car engine starting up that woke me.'

'Shopping. The cupboard's almost bare.'

The phone rang and he hurried across to pick it

up. 'Katie! How is he . . . ? Oh, good. That sounds promising. Yes, we're fine. Ned's still asleep. He had a disturbed night so we didn't wake him or try to send him to school. I hope you don't mind . . . Miranda? She's gone out shopping for groceries . . . No, it doesn't matter. We'd have to eat anyway.'

He listened intently. 'Look, stay as long as you like, as long as you need. We'll be fine.'

Her next words annoyed him but he tried not to let that show in his voice. 'Yes, of course I'll give her a chance to explain. But she's refused to do that once already this morning, so don't hold your breath . . . OK then. I'll wait to hear from you.'

He put the phone down and saw Regina scowling at him. 'What?'

'Was it Miranda you were talking about just now? The one you'll kindly allow another chance to explain?'

'Yes.'

'She won't do it.'

'Why the hell not? Don't you think I'm owed an explanation?'

'Yes. So I'm going to do it for her.' Regina took a sip of coffee, hot as it was, then gestured to the dining room. 'Do you mind if we sit down? This might take a while.'

He followed her into the next room and sat at one end of the oval table, wondering what could be making her look so bleak. 'Well?'

She took another sip of coffee. 'I'm guessing you

haven't a clue what happened after Father found out about the baby?'

'Only that Miranda refused to see me.'

'She didn't refuse. They kept her prisoner.'

'What? In this day and age? Not possible.'

'She was so upset they insisted on calling in the doctor and Sebastian made sure she stayed at the house till he arrived. Sebastian has always enjoyed bullying and manhandling people.

'The doctor was quite elderly, old-fashioned about women. He gave her sedatives of some sort. I don't know what. I was fifteen, keeping out of their way, terrified by all the screaming and shouting. Sebastian held her down while the doctor gave her an injection. It must have been a strong one, because she slept for hours.'

He watched impatiently as she took another slurp of coffee.

'I don't think they let her surface properly till she was in the mental hospital,' Regina said at last.

Brody stared at her, feeling sick. '*Mental hospital?* Why the hell was she in a mental hospital?'

'Because the doctor put her there. And he continued to treat her, if you can call that treating. It was a private "home".' She waggled her fingers in the air to mock the word. 'After Miranda had the baby, they still kept her inside, still kept her tranquillised. From what I overheard, she wanted to keep the baby and refused to sign the adoption papers, so Sebastian forged her signature. I found a screwed-up piece of paper he'd been practising on. He was pretty good. It'd have fooled me.'

Regina waited again, head cocked on one side as if expecting some comment, but Brody couldn't speak for horror. In the end he managed to ask in a croaky voice he didn't recognise as his own, 'How did they get away with it?'

'Well, it was made easier because she really did have postnatal depression. Or was it just depression about what had happened? I don't know. They didn't let me visit her, but Father commented one day that she couldn't stop crying and she was in the best place. I think he'd persuaded himself by then that she really needed to be in there.'

Brody shook his head, near tears himself. 'It's hard to believe it was possible to do that.'

She raised one eyebrow. 'A respected judge like Father, a family doctor who hadn't a blemish on his record, the owner of a special home who liked extra payments? It wasn't all that hard to arrange. I've pieced together the details over the years from things they've let drop.

'There used to be a tradition of shoving people into mental hospitals when they did something socially inconvenient, you know. In the early seventies a Director of Social Services called Derrick Sheridan found several women in mental hospitals in the UK who'd been put inside and kept there merely for having illegitimate children.

'No one had done anything about them till he took

over, but because he had a background in mental health, he understood that area and its needs. Forty years some of them had been inside. And this was the seventies, not the Dark Ages.'

'I'm surprised they ever let Miranda out.'

'They didn't until she was thoroughly cowed, and they kept her on tranquillisers for years afterwards. In the end she found herself another doctor and since she didn't cause any trouble they let her come off the tablets. But by then they'd destroyed her self-esteem and confidence completely. Other people helped them unwittingly. Those who've been inside mental hospitals are often treated with suspicion afterwards, as if they can never truly recover.'

'But she stayed at home and looked after him until he died.'

'Yes. Amazing, isn't it? But remember she had no money, no history of employment either, because she'd never been employed. I got away from Australia, made sure they couldn't meddle with my life. I think Father set himself out to charm her after he'd had the stroke. He could be good company when he wanted, and he needed someone to look after him.

'After he died, she met a man called Lou Rayne, and he was the one who broke her out of her shell, the one who started to build up her confidence. He was dying and yet he took the time to look after her. That man must be in heaven, if anyone is.'

Brody tried to speak and couldn't. He found tears

welling in his eyes, tears of outrage at what had been done to her, tears of remorse at what he'd thought about her, accused her of.

How could he ever make that up to her? Would she even care now what he thought?

She was remarkably self-contained most of the time, like a walled citadel. He could see why. But now he wanted to break down the walls and find the old Miranda who'd been stolen from him. Surely she was still there?

Katie switched off her phone and slipped it into her handbag, smiling down at her husband. 'Ned's fine, still asleep. Brody said Miranda was out shopping and I'm not to worry. They can stay there and look after Ned as long as necessary.'

A new nurse came in, presumably the day shift. 'Good morning. I hear you're a little better today, Mr Parrish.' She took his obs and nodded. 'The doctor's coming soon so we need to unwrap your leg. Perhaps you could wait outside, Mrs Parrish? There isn't really room for everyone in here.'

'Go and get some breakfast, darling,' Darren said.

She smiled and nodded but waited outside the room. She wasn't going anywhere till she'd spoken to the doctor.

A man in a white coat with a stethoscope round his neck came along the corridor, attended by another nurse who had an air of authority about her.

Katie stepped forward. 'I'm Mrs Parrish, Doctor. I'd like to speak to you for a moment, after you've seen my husband.'

'Yes, of course.'

When he came out a few moments later, he said, 'Let's talk,' and led her into another little room with a few well-used seats, which made her feel even more apprehensive.

'How's his leg?'

'No worse. And his temperature is slightly better, which is a good sign. We're not out of the woods yet, but as long as he has a chance of keeping that leg, we'll hold off doing anything.'

She bent her head but the tears of relief wouldn't be held back. 'Thank goodness.'

'He might always have a limp, though, or walk stiffly. You can't expect joints and muscles which have been that badly damaged to function fully again.'

'I don't know how he'll cope with that.'

'One step at a time, eh? Let's save the leg first then worry about rehabilitation. I just wanted to warn you.'

'I appreciate that.' She watched him go, sitting on for a minute or two longer. Then she told herself not to be stupid. Darren was alive and had a chance of keeping the leg. That was the most important thing.

As Brody watched Regina drive away to go to the hospital and see Nikki, he heard sounds from upstairs. He listened. Yes, Ned had woken. He went upstairs to find the boy just coming out of the bathroom. 'Hello, sleepyhead.'

Ned looked at him for a moment as if wondering what he was doing there, then his lips made an O-shape as if he'd suddenly remembered and an anxious look came on his face.

'Your mummy just rang to say your daddy's a bit better this morning.'

Ned brightened a little. 'Can he walk again?'

'Not yet. He has to lie in bed till his leg's better. That takes longer than an appendix. Now, are you hungry?'

'Very hungry. Where's Nanda?'

'She's gone to the shops to buy some more food, because you've eaten it all up.' He ruffled the boy's hair slightly and grinned to show this was a joke. Such a solemn child.

'When Daddy's home, he eats a lot of food because he's a big man. Can I have my breakfast first then get dressed afterwards? I'm very hungry.'

'Of course.'

Chatting away, they went downstairs and Ned explained what he had for breakfast: a banana or apple then a plate of cereal with nuts sprinkled on the top. No coaxing this child to eat. He cleared his plate methodically then rinsed it carefully under the tap and put it in the dishwasher. He saw Brody looking and said, 'Daddy says I mustn't leave everything to Mummy, because he's not here to help her.'

'Well done you.'

The little boy beamed at him.

It was nearly noon by the time Miranda got back, by which time Brody was beginning to worry that she'd got lost. He went out to help her carry in the bags of groceries, but beyond a quick nod, she didn't speak to him.

As he was picking up the last bag he said quietly, 'Regina told me what happened to you.'

She stared at him in shock, then apprehension.

'We need to talk.'

'I don't want to talk about it.'

'Well, I do. You've not heard my side of the story.'

'I'm not mad and I never was.'

'I realise that. It's your father and brother who were crazy, if you ask me.'

'Even so, I still don't want to talk about it.' She walked inside and began chatting brightly to Ned.

Brody let the subject go for the moment but he intended to have that talk. If they could clear the air, perhaps they could become friends again. He didn't have a lot of friends – he wasn't good at social chit-chat, had spent too much of his life working alone.

And, heaven help him, he was still attracted to her. What was there about her that had coloured his view of women over so many years? He'd read of people hooking up with their childhood sweethearts in later life, but had never expected to meet his again, let alone want to get to know her again.

When Regina left Brody, she went straight to the hospital, not bothering to check up on visiting hours.

She found Nikki alone. 'Where's Tim?'

'He was driving me crazy fussing over me. I told him to go to school.'

Regina sat down by the bed. 'What do you want to do now? Tell me the truth.'

'You did say I could come home?'

'Yes, and I meant it, too. What about Tim?'

'I feel horribly guilty, but I don't want to live with him any more. He's so noisy and clumsy and . . . Well, if I ever marry, it'll be someone I've tried out for a year or two, someone who doesn't talk all the time when I'm trying to study.'

'You can't just leave Tim on his own with no family nearby.'

'I can't go back to him. Please don't make me, Mum.'

'No. I won't make you. But we'd better make sure he can afford the rent, with his family being up north.'

'I'd forgotten about that. Mum . . . am I terrible? I feel so relieved to be free again. I wasn't ready for a baby.'

'I know. I was older when I had you and I still didn't feel ready. But I think being that bit older made a big difference.' She stood up. 'Let me find the sister in charge and ask about taking you home.'

She came back a few minutes later, beaming. 'We have to wait for the doctor, but she's due shortly. If she says you're all right, you can go home and just get checked up by your own doctor in a day or two.'

Nikki promptly burst into tears and Regina had to comfort her as if she were a small child before she could settle down.

Hormone upheaval, she thought. *It's going to be hell.* She tried to distract her daughter. 'Has Tim gone to school?'

'Yes.'

'Then I'd better ring the school nurse and ask her to tell him you're out of hospital. Then when he comes round to see you this afternoon, you'll have to tell him what you've decided.'

'Can't you . . . ?'

'No, you have to do it. It'd be dreadfully unkind, and ungrateful too, to leave it to someone else to tell him.'

What a family they were for getting pregnant easily! She'd bet Nikki would be very careful about having sex from now on. As she had been. She didn't think Miranda had had any chance of getting to know other men, so had never needed to worry about taking precautions. Still, she'd worn well, so it mightn't be too late to remedy that. She'd need warning.

It wasn't going to be easy having Nikki back, though. Apart from the hormones settling down, her daughter had been changed by this experience; was more of an adult, not a child to be ordered around. There were bound to be clashes.

She was getting her daughter back, though, and her daughter was getting a chance to make a good life for herself. She couldn't help feeling happy about that.

Chapter Twenty-One

Sebastian had lunch sent into his office. He had to go to the damned mediation conference this afternoon and was feeling even more reluctant to cooperate than last time. He had enough on his plate managing at home without Dorothy to look after him and was thinking of hiring a private investigator to find out where she'd gone. He'd guess she was with one of their sons, but they were both refusing to answer his calls.

He'd get her back, whatever it took. He needed her. And he'd have something to say about his sons' disloyalty.

He'd have to hire a housekeeper, if this took much longer. He wasn't doing menial chores and he didn't know how to cook, nor did he want to learn. His father never had and he didn't intend to either.

The phone rang and his clerk said, 'Ms Patel to see you, sir.'

What was Sally doing here when they'd be meeting

later? Couldn't he have even an hour of peace? He was strongly tempted to refuse to see her, but his clerk had clearly given away the fact that he was here.

Besides, she was too well known to offend, however much she deserved it. He was quite sure she'd be a judge within a year or two. Women had such an unfair advantage over men these days. 'Send her in.'

He stood up as Sally entered the room, wondering what the hell this was about. 'Do take a seat. Have you come to withdraw your client's ridiculous appeal against her father's will?'

'Certainly not. I've come because your wife has contacted me and asked me to discuss something with you.'

He couldn't think what to say to that. Had Dorothy run mad? She knew he was in the opposing camp from Sally Patel and – then he realised. The bitch was trying to stab him in the back. He'd make sure she regretted that, too.

'I gather your wife has left you for a rather unpleasant reason.'

'I'd appreciate it if you'd keep the information about this to yourself. It's an unfortunate misunderstanding, that's all.'

'The fact that you've been beating her?'

'I don't beat her. It was just . . . a moment of weakness. I'd had a trying day.'

'That's not a good reason for thumping someone. And I gather it's not the first time. I will keep quiet about it, though, at her request, as long as certain conditions are met.'

'Which are?'

'That you agree to support revisions to your father's will, so that Miranda has the same benefits from her inheritance as you and your sister Regina. Your wife seems to think you brought unfair pressure to bear on your father to create that trust and she wants to set the matter right.'

Dark anger blurred his vision for a moment or two.

'Are you all right, Fox?'

He blinked at her. 'Sorry. I have a migraine starting. What exactly did my wife say to make you think there was unfair pressure?'

'She said the trust hadn't been your father's idea, and you'd boasted to her about persuading him to set it up. This happened while your sister was on holiday, I believe, which ties in with the date the will was signed.' She looked at him, head on one side, like a bird about to peck something off the ground.

'Hearsay. Won't hold up in court.'

'And she also told me what happened years ago when your sister was pregnant, how Miranda was unlawfully imprisoned, thanks to you and her father.'

'She was *not* imprisoned, she was kept in a very expensive private mental home until she recovered from a breakdown.'

'My first instinct was to lay that particular matter before the police and let them decide, but your wife says she has no desire to become a *cause célèbre*. My client holds similar views about becoming an object of public pity. All Miranda wants from you now is her financial independence.'

'I shall not change my mind about that.'

Sally gave him a pitying look – *pitying!* – and that was the final straw. His head was pounding with pain and she was making it worse. With a roar of fury he lunged for her, bumping into a corner of the desk as he moved round it. cursing as he stumbled.

Screaming for help at the top of her voice, she managed to get the door open before he reached her. The force of the blow made his hand sting and he paused as her screams cut off abruptly. She crashed into the wall and slid to the floor, not moving.

He took a step forward, hands outstretched to pull her to her feet. She was feigning unconsciousness, he knew it. The bitch! Making this look worse than it was, threatening to destroy his reputation. Well, he wasn't going to let her do that.

But as he reached out to get hold of her, someone grabbed his arm. He fought them off but others took hold and brought him down to the floor. He couldn't see, couldn't think, couldn't . . .

The group of lawyers stepped back and waited for Fox to stand up, sure he was faking unconsciousness because they hadn't hit him and he hadn't bumped his head on anything.

But he continued to lie there, not moving. They looked

at one another, not keen to touch him again.

One of the younger female lawyers bent over Ms Patel, who was beginning to stir, but no one attempted to touch Fox.

As the moments ticked past, the chief clerk said, 'Someone has to make sure he's all right.'

He bent down. Warily he felt for a pulse, clearly ready to jump out of the way if Fox let fly again.

That evening, even after Ned had gone to bed, Miranda refused point-blank to discuss anything with Brody.

'But we need to talk some more,' he protested.

'*You* need to talk. I don't. I've sorted out my life and am perfectly satisfied with what I'm doing. I refuse to discuss anything with you after the distrust you've shown in me. We can be civil when we meet, for Ned and Katie's sake, but that's as far as I'm prepared to go.'

He looked at her so sorrowfully she felt a shiver run through her. She didn't want him to touch her emotions in any way; didn't dare go down that path again. She'd escaped from Sebastian, moved on as much as she could, been reunited with her daughter, and that was it – unless Sally managed to get the will overthrown.

She was relieved when her mobile phone rang and fumbled in her handbag. 'Excuse me. This might be Katie. Hello?'

'Is that Miranda?'

'Yes.'

'It's Jonathon Tressman here, calling from Australia.'

'Oh. How can I help you?'

'I thought someone should let you know – your lawyer gave me your phone number and . . .'

His voice tailed off and she frowned in puzzlement. He was the last person she'd have expected to call, especially at this hour. 'Let me know what?' she prompted.

'Your brother Sebastian is dead. He had some sort of a seizure – well, apparently he ran mad and they had to restrain him. He attacked your lawyer and—'

'My brother's dead? But Sally's all right, isn't she?'

'She's in hospital for observation because he knocked her unconscious, but she's expected to make a full recovery. He was . . . very angry, beyond reason, they tell me.'

Miranda knew about that temper only too well. 'Why was he furious?'

'It's quite complicated. Apparently Dorothy has left Sebastian, who's been beating her for years.'

'*No!*' Miranda found it hard to believe the so-proper Sebastian could be a wife beater. The attack on Sally, in a fit of anger, was credible, but this . . . 'I can't believe it.'

'I too was surprised when I heard. If he had been beating her, I can't understand why she didn't get help sooner. Anyway, it seems he fell into a rage when Sally gave him a message from his wife and then he attacked poor Sally, out of the blue. The other lawyers had to restrain him and then he just . . . keeled over.'

His voice lowered and he cleared his throat. 'He died instantly, I'm afraid. They think it might have been a massive stroke. They won't know for certain until the autopsy.'

Sebastian dead! This time it really sank in what that meant. Relief flooded through Miranda like a flood tide. She couldn't help it, didn't care if it was wrong. She felt as if a huge burden had been lifted from her. 'I don't know what to say or do.'

'I don't think there's much you can do. As to your own situation, I'm sure we can get a judgement now to have the trust overthrown and your inheritance handed over to you, as your brother's and sister's were. In the meantime, I'll certainly pay the whole amount of income from the trust into your bank account and, if you wish, we can put that flat on the market. You'll receive considerably more money for it than before, about three times as much. It *was* a good investment. He was right about that, at least.'

'Oh. Well, thank you.' But it was the relief from Sebastian that she cared about most. Oh, the blessed relief!

'I'll . . . um, let you know what happens about your brother's funeral, in case you wish to attend.'

'I shan't.'

'I can understand that. Let me just say that if I'd had any idea of how badly they'd treated you, I'd not have been a party to this trust.'

'Thank you.'

'I gather Dorothy is returning to Perth with her elder son to deal with everything. And Sally says she'll be in touch with you when her head stops thumping.'

Would he never stop talking? Miranda wanted to think about the news, get used to true freedom. 'Thank you for letting me know, Mr Tressman. I won't keep you. You must have a lot to do.'

'Yes. I've only just come back from the hospital. There was no one else to deal with the situation, so, as I'm the family lawyer, they called me out.'

At last he finished the call and Miranda switched off the phone, her head spinning.

And suddenly she was weeping. She had no need to be brave any longer because Sebastian couldn't touch her now.

She was free! Really and truly free.

When Brody put his arms round her, she leant against him. When he guided her to the couch, she let him.

She'd still been afraid of Sebastian, even here in England. She hadn't realised how afraid till now.

Just think of all the years wasted because of him. So much of her life ruined.

It was a while before she could stop weeping and even then she didn't move away from the incredible comfort of Brody's warm body against hers.

'I don't think I've ever heard anyone weep like that,' he said gently. 'Do you want to tell me about it?'

Haltingly, she went through what had happened.

'I hadn't realised what a shadow he cast over you still.'

'Most of my life. He threatened sometimes to have

me locked away again. I didn't think he could do it, not really, but the fear of him even trying kept me quiet. And if that makes me a coward, then I don't care. You don't know what it was like to be locked up and drugged.'

The phone rang again.

She pulled away from him. 'I'd better answer that.'

'I'll do it.' He went across the room to pick the phone up. 'Regina? Yes, we just heard. Your sister is . . . upset by the circumstances, but relieved.'

He mouthed, '*Do you want to speak to her?*' but Miranda shook her head. 'Look, I'll get her to ring you tomorrow, when she's calmer . . . Yes, I promise I'll look after her.'

He put the phone down and came back to Miranda, who was huddled in a corner of the couch, clutching some damp, crumpled tissues. Kneeling down beside her, he took the tissues away then held her hands. 'What can I do to help you?'

She shook her head.

'Then let me just hold you. There's solace in that, don't you think?'

She looked at him warily, so he continued, 'I don't know where this is going to lead, but now that I know what happened I want to comfort you, and, I want to spend time with you and get to know you again.'

'Why did you leave Perth? I never understood why you left me; didn't come looking for me.'

'I couldn't find out where you were. I did try. But you can't do much without money and they made it impossible for me to get a job. Since you weren't answering my calls or letters, in the end I left.'

He raised one of her hands and absent-mindedly kissed it. 'I was angry with you afterwards because I still loved you. It never stopped hurting that you'd betrayed me and given away my child. My marriage failed because she wasn't you. I'm not proud of how I hurt her. She deserved better.'

Miranda didn't know what to say. Did she dare trust him now?

As the silence continued, he begged, 'Give me another chance, give *us* another chance.'

She made no move towards him because something had suddenly become clear to her. 'I can't talk about *us*, not in that way, until I've stopped grieving for Lou.'

'The man who helped you?'

'Yes. He was dying. He forbade me to fall in love with him, but I grew to love him anyway, not exactly a romantic love, but still, he was very special. I . . . can't just switch my feelings around like that.' She snapped her fingers to illustrate the point.

'No. I can understand that. I wish I'd met him. I'll never stop being grateful to him for rescuing you.'

'You'd have liked him. Everyone did.'

Brody nodded. 'I'm not going away, though. Not this time.'

'No. Don't. You and I can start by being friends again – can't we?'

'I'd like that, Miranda. We'll make a start and you

won't close the door to anything else happening later, will you? I think the magic could grow again between us, given time.' He put his arms round her and she leant against him with a sigh.

Brody held her close, feeling incredibly protective. They both needed time to get used to what had really happened in their lives, but he knew he'd never be satisfied with only friendship, not from Miranda.

When she fell asleep suddenly, he stayed seated, enjoying the feel of her in his arms. His hand and lower right arm were going numb and he was aching to move his body, but he didn't want to let go of her.

It was only half an hour before she woke, coming wide awake instantly, as she always had done, he remembered.

She looked sideways at him as if surprised to see him. 'Brody. It wasn't a dream, then. You're still here. And Sebastian really is dead.'

He eased himself away from her. 'Yes, and I'd like to keep hold of you, if only my arm wasn't going numb.' He winced as his hand flopped about, so numb he could feel nothing.

She helped him move it away carefully, smiling sympathetically as he winced again and shook his hand about as it started to regain sensation.

'You should have moved.'

'I didn't want to wake you.'

'You did that once before when I fell asleep on you. Do you remember?'

'Oh, yes. I didn't see you again after that night. There.

That's better.' He held out his hand to pull her to her feet and she took it. When he tried to keep hold of her, however, she moved away.

He didn't want her to go to bed. 'How about a glass of wine? A celebration.'

'Isn't it a bit late t—' she began then smiled and answered her own question. 'No, it isn't. Lou would tell me to enjoy life again, take a chance. He was a most unusual guardian angel.'

Brody led the way into the kitchen. 'He sounds to have been a great guy.'

'He was.' She raised her glass. 'To Lou, who set my feet on the right track again.'

They clinked and sipped, then Brody held out his glass again. 'To life.'

Miranda felt breathless suddenly, younger and lighter, as she touched her glass against his. 'To a full and happy life.'

Somehow she was sure she'd find happiness now, with or without Brody. Lou had taught her to value and enjoy life, given her confidence in herself. He would probably have told her to seize the moment with Brody, but this was her choice, her life, and she didn't want to rush into anything.

Maybe she'd find happiness with Brody again. She hoped so. Oh, she definitely did!

When the phone rang, she was nearest, so picked it up. 'Katie . . . Oh, I'm delighted to hear that Darren is improving . . . No, Ned is fine. Take as long as you like, but try to ring when Ned's awake next time. I'm sure that'll comfort him . . . All right. Bye.'

She held the phone out to Brody. 'She wants to speak to you.'

He listened, nodding once or twice. 'Yes, we've talked, really talked . . . I'm glad too . . . All right. Look after yourself. Bye.'

He put the phone down and smiled at Miranda. 'I think we have our daughter back in our lives.'

'And a grandson. Isn't that marvellous?' She couldn't help returning his smile, unable to stay aloof because he seemed to have shed years and become the old Brody, the one she'd fallen in love with.

He held out his glass to her and said, 'One final toast . . . To second chances!'

Without hesitation, she clinked hers against it. 'To second chances!'

She could have sworn she heard Lou's voice echoing behind theirs.

ANNA JACOBS is the author of over ninety novels and is addicted to storytelling. She grew up in Lancashire, emigrated to Australia in the 1970s and writes stories set in both countries. She loves to return to England regularly to visit her family and soak up the history. She has two grown-up daughters and a grandson, and lives with her husband in a spacious home near the Swan Valley, the earliest wine-growing area in Western Australia. Her house is crammed with thousands of books.

annajacobs.com

If you enjoyed *Winds of Change*, look out for more
books by Anna Jacobs . . .

To discover more great fiction and to place an order
visit our website
www.allisonandbusby.com
or call us on
02039507834